THE TRUTH
ABOUT JULIA

THE TRUTH ABOUT JULIA

ANNA SCHAFFNER

ALLEN&UNWIN

Published in trade paperback in Great Britain in 2016 by Allen & Unwin

Allen & Unwin
c/o Atlantic Books
Ormond House
26–27 Boswell Street
London WC1N 3JZ

Phone: 020 7269 1610
Fax: 020 7430 0916
Email: UK@allenandunwin.com
Web: www.allenandunwin.co.uk

A CIP catalogue record for this book is available from the British Library.

Trade paperback ISBN 978 1 76029 011 5
Ebook ISBN 978 1 92526 753 2

Printed in Great Britain by Ashford Colour Press Ltd, Gosport, Hants

10 9 8 7 6 5 4 3 2 1

For Shane and Helena

'In the beginning was the Word.'
The Gospel According to St John

'In the beginning was the deed.'
Goethe, *Faust, Part One*

PREFACE

London, 21 November 2014

Dear George,

I'm afraid this letter contains bad news: I failed. I'm sorry. I let you down. There is no manuscript. My advance (why not confess it all at once) is used up, too – it ran through my fingers like sand. Right now, I'm not in a position to return the sum to you, and it's likely to be some time before I will be able to do so.

You will have heard by now where I am. The story was all over the news. This place is the natural home of the fog that has taken dominion in my mind and that casts everything in grey. Here it has company and a name and no longer hovers in solitude. It's as though this place has been summoning me all along. It's strangely liberating that I can now finally succumb to the thoughts that have been weighing on me like a mud-soaked cloak for months; that I can stop pretending, and finally face the fact that I can no longer tell right from wrong.

Let me address the professional dimension of the situation first (I need to start somewhere). You know that what happened is utterly out of character and unprecedented in the long history of our working relationship. I always deliver; I always meet my deadlines; you could always count on me. Until catastrophe struck. The first one, I mean. I haven't been myself for years – you knew that, of course, and in spite of everything I am immensely grateful for the fact that you never lost faith in me.

It is so strange, being here, George – I wonder what you would make of this place. I still catch myself thinking this is a bad dream from which I will awake any minute now, back at home, cuddled up in my bed, with Aisha purring on the duvet beside me. But I know that this, here, is real. The sharp white lights and the sulphurous walls that look like they have been rubbed in rancid butter; the muffled groans emerging from neighbouring rooms; the helpless despondency in my sister's eyes; her agitated conversations with the doctors in the corridors which she thinks I can't hear, but the meaning of which I understand all too well.

I have never let you down before, and I owe you not only an apology but also a full explanation. You are not just my editor but my dearest, oldest friend. I need you to understand what happened to me, and to tell me why. I hold you in the highest regard, and I know that this feeling is not entirely unreciprocated – regardless of everything that has happened between us. Our minds work in similar ways, we see eye to eye on so many things. I need your sharp, clear intellect; I need you to tell me who the villains are in this drama, and who the heroes. I need you to help me differentiate between right and wrong. I'm so lost, George, tormented by doubt and guilt. And the image of those eyes – those big, clear, innocent eyes that haunt me so.

I cannot trust Amanda with this task. She's a wonderful sister, and I love her, and she takes such good care of me, but she simply cannot help me with this. I keep returning to the scene that brought me here, and to the fateful events that preceded it, and to all these loose ends in my and Julia's narratives that wriggle and slide and glisten maliciously in garish colours, like snake tails, and which I simply cannot master.

It is 2.41 in the morning. I managed to convince the cleaner to supply me with a pen and paper – my sister and the doctors wouldn't hear of letting me write. She is a big woman with a big smile and a deep velvet chuckle. In spite of her size, she moves as gracefully as a dancer when she swings her mop through the corridors. We struck a deal: in return for her help I gave her the latest boxes of chocolates I received. Why does everyone send me chocolates? I never liked sweet things.

All is quiet on the ward, except for the soft hum of the lights and the periodic sound of the night nurse's tired feet flapping across the green linoleum floors. I so desperately want to talk to you – I cannot bear the company of my thoughts. As I write to you, I keep imagining your responses, your smile and the way you nod your head when you are listening intently. I imagine you folding me into your arms, pressing my head against your chest. I imagine your cinnamon scent, and the feel of your warm hand on the back of my head, stroking my hair.

I need to begin, but where? How far back do I have to go so that all of this makes sense? I don't have much time – the daily programme here starts so brutally early. The nurses wake and wash us at 5.30 – can you believe it? As though the days in a place like this were not endless enough as it is – time here is like treacle. So anywhere will have to do, anywhere I can think of now.

Was there a definitive turning point? Probably not. I always felt that epiphanies are the stuff of fiction. Real life doesn't work that way; in reality, we change gradually, sliding ever deeper into the muddy waters of our psyches, little by little, until we go under. The timing of my fateful encounter with Julia was certainly not lacking in tragic irony. The day before, I had just returned from a seven-day spell in the cottage, to which I had fled, and I was ready to face the consequences of my failure to produce the manuscript. I *was* – I had steeled myself to face your wrath, and had switched my phone back on with the firm intention of calling you right there and then, to confess it all, but then I found Julia's lawyer's message instead, urging me to call her back at once.

Have I ever told you about the cottage? I can't remember – it used to belong to my parents and is situated in an isolated spot in the Kentish countryside. Its bulbous walls look like a sunken cake with dirty icing. Its thatched roof hangs so low that it almost touches the ground. Amanda and I were born there, and although neither of us ever visits the cottage we could never bring ourselves to sell it or even to rent it out. It's a place filled with memories, and with countless cobwebs, and an intricate network of fine fissures and cracks. I hadn't been there for years.

It was there that I must have suffered something like a nervous breakdown. After my meeting with Grace, and my argument with Laura, I asked my neighbour to take care of Aisha for a while, packed my bags and drove out of London, away from my computer and all my files, away from my email, away from everything. And it was at my parents' cottage that I ended up. It wasn't planned. It must have been a primal instinct that directed me there, like those frogs that always return to the ponds that smell of their childhood to spawn and to die, regardless of how long the journey takes them. The road map is hardwired into their brains – you could take them all the way up Ben Nevis and they would still know how to get back to the waters in which they were born.

I didn't have the energy to clean the place when I arrived, and besides, I felt quite at home amidst the dirt, the dust and the debris. On the first day, I drove to a superstore about an hour away and bought provisions (tinned soup and whisky), firewood, a large supply of candles and a small gas cooker (there's neither gas nor electricity there, and no hot water). On the second day, I tried to have lunch in a pub in the nearby village, but I couldn't swallow my food and felt uneasy, sitting on my own among the regular guests who all seemed troubled by the business of this strange woman in their midst. That was my last outing. In the days that followed, I didn't see a soul.

On the third day, I switched off my phone. I couldn't bear its angry vibrations – I knew you and Amanda were trying to reach me, both of you furious, and I couldn't face talking to either of you. Eventually my anxiety lessened, giving way to apathy and weariness. I grew weaker by the day. I felt a terrible tiredness, as though my very soul had become a thing of lead. I thought I had lost everything – my career, you, even Laura and Amanda. My old familiar sadness about the paths not taken returned with such force that it almost strangled me from the inside. Late on the sixth day, however, something changed. As always, I was sitting in my pyjamas in a brown armchair by the fireplace, a large drink in my hand, wrapped in a threadbare dressing gown and a coarse woollen blanket, both of which used to belong to my father (I could no longer muster the energy to get dressed). My hair was unwashed and my skin felt like ancient papyrus, parched and cracked. You would barely have recognized me, George. Although I was sitting so close to the flames that I feared my skin might catch fire, their warmth didn't reach me. I was so cold. I had been unable to stop shivering for weeks, and it was getting worse each day. No matter how high I put the thermostat in my flat in London, no matter how big a fire I built in the cottage – no amount of blankets, drinks and cups of tea could thaw the frozen sea inside me.

Then something compelled me to detach my gaze from the flames, and I looked up. I saw the pictures of my family on the mantelpiece; three faded sepia portraits of my parents and grandparents – upright, proud people, good people, anchored and strong. Did I ever tell you that my maternal grandmother walked to this country all the way from Germany? My mother was just four years old when, one evening, while the family was having supper, my grandfather was arrested. Five men in slick black uniforms kicked in the front door, dragged him from his chair and into the street. Nobody spoke a word; nobody made a sound. The incident lasted less than a minute. When the men had left, my grandmother found she was still clutching her spoon. On the very same evening, she decided to escape – she had no intention of acquiescing to a similarly sinister fate. First, she dyed her and my mother's hair light blonde. Then she ripped the yellow stars from their overcoats and gathered together all the valuables she could carry. She also took a small revolver, which my mother later bequeathed to me in her will and which has been lying in my closet in a box containing jewellery and other family heirlooms ever since.

They left in the dark of a starless night. The two of them travelled on foot, through woods, moors and marshland, for twenty-four days. They sheltered in sheds and stables and hunters' huts. The year was 1943, and their old coats were no match for the furious November winds. My grandmother never lost the cough she picked up on that journey. They walked all the way from Lüneburg in Lower Saxony to Denmark, and then managed to trade their portable family heirlooms for two much-coveted stowaway places on a boat that stopped in Norway before heading towards the safe shores of Grimsby.

It was my grandmother's picture that caught my eye that night. After her arrival in England, she cut off her long blonde hair, burned it and henceforth wore it dark and clipped like a man. At that moment, I felt as though she was staring down at me, judging me for my weakness and my cowardice. I could hear her harsh cough, impeaching and accusatory; her hazel eyes burned holes into my paper skin. I knew then that I had to make a choice. I had grown so very weak during my time in the cottage. I had been unable to eat; my stock of tinned soup remained almost untouched. I could have faded away peacefully there. How I wish I had. I could have spared so many people so much suffering. But instead I decided to face the consequences of my failure to complete the manuscript, and all the other conflicts from which I had been hiding – your wrath, Amanda's reproaches, Laura's disappointment. I forced myself to eat some soup. The next morning – it was 6 November – I drove back to London. At home, I immediately switched my phone on to call you and confess, ready to do penance. But then I found Julia's lawyer's message, offering a glimmer of hope. The following morning, I visited Julia, and later that day... well, you know the rest of the story, although I will tell you my own version of it in due course.

Yesterday evening, while Amanda was talking to the doctors, I asked Laura to go into my flat to find my diary and all the materials and documents I had gathered on Julia's case, and to bring them here: the folder with the interview transcriptions, my notebooks, my laptop, paper and my favourite fountain pen, the black one. She knows where it all is. Unlike my sister, I can always rely on Laura. Even now, in spite of everything, she still has faith in my judgement. How I regret the hurt I must have caused her.

I owe you an explanation, George – and, in due course, Laura and Amanda, too. I can't bear the thought that you should think ill of me. And I need to make sense of it all, to find some way of holding at bay the dreadful guilt that is tearing me apart. I will write it down. Everything. How it all happened. How it got to this.

I have to stop now, as day is breaking and my back hurts and the nurses will be here soon. Please don't be angry with me, George. I really did try my best – it simply wasn't good enough.

Don't visit or contact me until I get in touch. I need to commit my story to paper before I am ready to see you in person. There is so much you need to know first. I will send you the document when my tale is told. I don't know how long it will take. In any case, I will have a lot of time on my hands while awaiting the trial – and who knows how much time thereafter. Years? Decades? I don't think they will keep me here for that much longer. I will no doubt soon be moved to lodgings patrolled by guards rather than nurses. But that suits me fine, since I will be able to write my story better in a cell than in a bed.

With much love,
    Clare

EDITORIAL NOTE

Clare Hardenberg is the most talented non-fiction writer I know, and we have been working together for more than sixteen years. She first caught my attention when she was writing for the *Guardian*; I much admired her clear, strong voice, her wit, her verbal precision, and her courage. I liked one of her articles so much that I contacted her to ask whether she would be interested in writing a book on the topic. She was, and her first as well as all her subsequent books proved to be so successful that, ten years ago, she was able to give up her day job and work as a freelance writer. Clare has published thirteen books, four under her own name, the others ghost-written; five have been bestsellers and three have been honoured with awards. *Why Your Sneakers Kill* (2006) won the Samuel Johnson Prize.

Yet Clare's life was marked by two tragedies, and I am convinced that the second wouldn't have taken place without the first. I feel responsible for both, as they resulted directly from the books I commissioned her to write. The reader will no doubt recall the scandalous revelations concerning the investment banker Adrian Temple, whose reckless actions brought ruin and misery to legions of small-time investors.

It was Clare who meticulously collected the distasteful evidence, which was published in what is arguably her most important book, *The Deal* (2009). Alas, in spite of what seemed to be a clear-cut case, Temple was never convicted of his crimes. Instead it was Clare who was tried and charged with libel, for a trivial detail that had nothing to do with the main thrust of the case. We couldn't protect her, as the charges related to statements she made in interviews that followed the publication of her book. After the trial, Clare was ordered to pay damages and the court costs. She kept her head above water by ghosting biographies, but I knew that she was bitterly disillusioned.

Over the past four years, I didn't see her very much; she had become ever more reclusive. I thought of her often, and I felt guilty. Once in a blue moon I managed to convince her to let me take her out for dinner, and it hurt me to see her so dejected, her sharp wit dulled, her spirit broken. I owed her. When she approached me to ask if she could write Julia White's biography I thought it a brilliant idea. It was the first time since the Temple trial that she had expressed a desire to work on a serious topic again. And Clare, I felt, was just the right person to tackle this important and complex task. I strongly believed that the biography would give her the opportunity to demonstrate her true worth as a writer. Yet, sadly, the project morphed into a poison much more dangerous than the wound it was supposed to heal.

At first, all seemed to be going well. Clare sent me regular updates that sounded promising, but then they became rarer and finally dried up. I had grown apprehensive about three months into the project, as she was ignoring my messages. This was very unlike her. We had agreed on the submission of the manuscript within fourteen weeks. Five days before the submission date, I waited all night outside her flat to confront her, but she must already have been at her cottage in Kent. I had a bad feeling, but there wasn't anything I could do. I didn't have her sister's contact details – psychoanalysts are notorious for keeping their phone numbers private – and none of our mutual friends had heard from Clare for a long time.

Then, on 8 November, the day after the deadline, I bought the papers and there she was on every front page: emaciated, a wild look in her eyes, her auburn bob dirty and dishevelled, her hands handcuffed behind her back. I couldn't believe what I was reading. In the first instance, and quite likely as a result of her sister's lobbying, she had been placed in the secure unit of a psychiatric hospital, where she was to await her trial. I tried to see her straight away, but she refused to receive any visitors apart from her sister and niece.

Then, seven days after her arrest, I received Clare's letter, in which she promised me an explanation. Eleven weeks later, Laura came to see me in my office and brought me Clare's long confessional letter, which I had been awaiting anxiously and devoured in one sitting.

At the earliest opportunity, I visited Clare in the grim all-female prison to which she had been transferred a fortnight after her arrest. When I first saw her in the visitors' room I found, to my great relief, a woman who more or less resembled the Clare I had known before her breakdown: she still looked terribly thin and pale, but otherwise appeared fine. Her eyes were alert and had regained their luminosity. She neither looked nor acted like a mad person. She smiled her usual warm smile. We hugged. It took us a long time to recover our composure and even longer before we managed to speak.

I have visited her on every single one of her visiting days since; we had and have so much to talk about – both personal and professional. I think she found our conversations helpful, but whether I was able to provide the answers she so desperately needed from me I don't know. I sincerely doubt it. I did, however, gradually manage to convince her to allow me to publish her text. I felt very strongly that Clare's story, as well as the interviews she had collected, and especially the one with Julia, needed to be published. I believe that, taken as a whole; the different narratives about Julia that Clare managed to assemble do indeed answer some of the questions with which we have all been wrestling in the aftermath of the terror. Clare's own story, moreover, has of course become a matter of public interest in its own right. Clare's act polarized the country: there are some who openly admire her – she showed me the bags of fan mail she receives every week, and I couldn't believe my eyes – but also many who strongly condemn her action. The book you are about to read is as much Clare's story as it is Julia's. It was, for her, no longer possible to disentangle the two.

George Cohen (Cohen & Green Publishing)
London, May 2015

I

Where to begin, George? Time is not the problem – the heap of shapeless moments I am facing, demanding to be structured and filled, is growing more menacing every day. Three nights in a row now I've dreamed I was trying to cross a stretch of marshland, but I couldn't move, the mud gluing my feet to the ground and then, slowly, dragging me under. Four days ago I was declared sane and stable (in spite of Amanda's protests) and was transferred to my new abode. I've been spared the horror of having to share my cell, for which I am immensely grateful. I have always cherished my privacy, and I couldn't bear it if what little of it remains here were to be taken from me. But most importantly, I can now write whenever I feel like it – at night, at noon, at four in the morning when I snap awake. My cell contains a narrow single bed with a squeaking plastic mattress and coarse covers; the walls are painted a shade of ochre that makes me feel nauseous whenever I look at it for too long. I also have a small TV set, some wobbly shelves and a small plywood wardrobe. But the most essential items are a little wooden desk, into which numerous previous occupants have carved an intricate pattern of initials and expletives, and a small red metal chair.

I dread the encounters with the other inmates, those moments in the day when I have to leave my cell and when small talk is required: in the showers, at mealtimes and during the mandatory daily courtyard outings. I have entirely lost the ability to think of normal things to say, to anyone, and I constantly wonder whether the women here know what I did and why I am among them. I feel as though they are watching me, waiting for the right moment to pounce. I don't think I have either the strength or the willpower to defend myself. In fact, a part of me wishes they would just get on with it and put an end to all this.

Curiously, it is not the creature comforts I miss most – such as food that is actually edible (what they serve here sinks like wet cement to the bottom of our stomachs and renders its victims simultaneously overweight and undernourished). Neither, to my own surprise, do I miss alcohol (my cravings for the state of comfortable numbness that I had sought so regularly in the past few years have disappeared completely), and nor do I miss my soft green velvet sofa, my books, my film collection, and my comfortable bed.

But I do miss company. Although Amanda and Laura faithfully visit twice a week, and call every day, I feel as lonely as never before in my life. The gaps, both old and new, are looming so ominously. I cherish my visiting day more than anything, even if I can barely summon the courage to look Amanda and Laura in the eye. And I miss Aisha. Badly. Every time I wake up, during those few seconds it takes the mind to re-orientate itself in space and time, I turn to touch her, my hand expecting in vain to find her curled up into a furry ball on the duvet right next to me. But what I miss most is having a project. Aims. Something to do. The human animal is lost without tasks. They are what keep us functioning; without desires, without something on which to concentrate our energies, we have nothing to distract us from the abyss.

I need to choose a starting point. I will begin with the day of the attack. It was 23 July, a sweltering Wednesday, the heat having held the city in a tight, sweaty embrace for four long days. I woke up early, feeling sticky and lethargic. Aisha had fallen ill that night – small pools of vomit were scattered all over the flat, as though my wooden floorboards had developed a weeping skin disease. When I found her lying under the sofa she looked even more listless than I felt. Her moon-coloured eyes were clouded, her normally lustrous silver fur looked tarnished and knotted.

I was in my vet's waiting room in Mayfair when the news broke. There were six other women, each nervously attending to a small ailing animal on their lap, plus the receptionist. The woman next to me (who had been preoccupied with whispering soothing words into the ear of a coughing terrier) suddenly cried: 'Good God!' Her mouth fell open as she stared at the television screen mounted on the wall behind the receptionist's desk, showing the news without sound. Alarmed by the woman's outburst, we collectively raised our eyes to the screen. 'Christ!' another woman shouted; 'Holy shit!' wailed the receptionist, who had jumped up and turned around. The vet, startled by the commotion, had joined us. Disbelief slackened our features; something bad had happened right in our midst, in central London. We had risen from our seats and put down our animals (some had been dropped rather unceremoniously), staring wide-eyed at the screen. The receptionist had turned up the sound. Thus we stood united for a few moments, a small community of the frightened. The woman next to me grabbed my hand and squeezed it so tightly that her rings left marks in my flesh.

Not much was known at that point, only that a bomb had exploded in a Café Olé branch on Paternoster Square, right next to the London Stock Exchange. There was carnage; there were casualties. I remember that the face of the young BBC correspondent, who happened to be at the scene by chance and reported live from the square, looked as ravaged as the remains of the scorched storefront, from which thin plumes of smoke were still rising, like translucent ribbons of mourning. Forensic experts in white overalls rushed in and out. They carried a seemingly endless number of black body bags past the reporter, who, stunned by the gruesome procession, kept repeating 'They're dead, they're all dead, they're all dead in there', until a colleague took the microphone from her white hand and led her out of the picture.

Only a few minutes had gone by while we were taking in the facts, and none of us had moved or spoken. Then, as though a spell had been lifted, we began to search for our phones and tried to reach our loved ones. Suddenly there was chaos in the room – everyone was shouting to make themselves understood. I called Amanda, who had not yet heard about the attack, and who was so shocked that she was unable to say anything at all. When she finally recovered her speech, she just whispered 'Laura', and I let her off the line so that she could call her daughter. I wanted nothing more than to call Laura myself – I was sick with worry – but the first call was Amanda's prerogative. The vet tried to reach her husband, but was unable to get through to him and grew ever more panicky – he worked in a bank just around the corner from the scene of the bombing, and often ate lunch in one of the restaurants on the square. After a few failed attempts she told us the practice was closed for the day and to return tomorrow. Only then did we remember our animals, who had begun to wail pitifully: dumbstruck, afraid, feeling the terror but unable either to articulate or to make sense of it, they appeared to me an apt image of our traumatized nation. Aisha, who is usually the gentlest of souls and whose grotesquely raised hair made her look like a woollen blowfish, scratched me when I tried to put her back in the carrier.

I drove straight to Amanda's house in Golders Green. She had just seen her last patient of the day. We hugged hard and long. She and I spent the rest of the day glued to the television screen, making and taking phone calls, and waiting anxiously for news from Laura. Most networks were down – there was too much traffic in the air. Late in the afternoon, Laura finally joined us. When the attack happened, she had been busy selling salads, sandwiches and cakes in the Blue Nile, an organic fair-trade café in Bloomsbury that she had set up with her friend Moira two years before. It took her almost five hours to get home, as numerous stations had been shut down for security reasons and the entire Tube system was so overcrowded that she had to wait for an hour before she could get on a train, and another hour to get on one of the replacement buses to continue her journey. All of London seemed to be out swarming on the streets, like frenzied bees whose hive had been violated.

Laura was visibly shaken by the apocalyptic scenes she had witnessed on her way home. When things go wrong, the thin veneer of civilized behaviour that we think of as natural wears off as quickly as make-up in the rain. People, Laura said, got into ugly fights to secure places on the overcrowded buses; an old man brutally pushed a girl out of the bus to make room for his wife. The girl fell on her face and didn't move, and nobody got off to help her (Laura was pressed tightly against a window on the upper deck, from where she could see but not intervene). When the bus was full to breaking point the driver was too scared to stop at the designated stops, where angry mobs were waiting to get on, prepared to use violence to fight for their right to get home.

The three of us sat closely huddled together on the sofa all evening and stayed up until the early hours. We kept pressing each other's hands and stared at the TV in disbelief. Around midnight, when the identity of the attacker was revealed, the shock was almost worse than the one I had experienced in the vet's waiting room when the story first broke. Nobody was prepared for this. I suppose we all assumed that a group of fanatical Islamists, angry alienated jihadists with nothing to lose, were responsible. When the bomber's picture first flickered across our screens, I (and I am sure the rest of the nation, too) thought that this had to be a mistake. I found myself incapable of establishing a connection between the image of the beautiful, earnest-looking young woman and the other pictures we had seen – the twenty-two body bags lined up in a grim, neat row on Paternoster Square, and the footage of the victims who had survived, and of the relatives of the dead howling in pain, burying their faces in their hands, and of the terrible scene of devastation that gaped like a raw, deep wound right in the heart of our city.

Something struck me about Julia White's face, from the moment I first saw it. I couldn't quite articulate it then. I thought it at once utterly alien and at the same time uncannily familiar. Above all I was fascinated by the serenity of her gaze: her still, slightly slanted green eyes in that finely chiselled, delicately pale face suggested an old-souled wisdom, someone who has seen more than their fair share of sadness and suffering, and yet there was something else in those eyes that I couldn't quite fathom. Julia was looking straight into the camera, her full lips unsmiling, her expression strangely unreadable. There was an unsettling contrast between her disconcerting gaze and her soft, milky-white skin. In that first picture to enter the public domain (many others were to follow) her long chestnut-brown hair was tied back into a bun, and she was wearing a crisp white man's shirt and a grey sleeveless pullover. Like an Oxford student from the seventies; perhaps with a hint of Marlene Dietrich. As I learned later, this picture was taken four years before the attacks, one month before Julia dropped out of university and went travelling.

I think the seeds for what happened later were sown the very moment I saw that picture (and that particular image was to remain the one that haunted me – it still does): I simply couldn't imagine what might have led a beautiful, highly intelligent young woman, privileged in all sorts of ways, to perpetrate the most ruthless terrorist act that had been committed in Britain since the Lockerbie bombing and the 7/7 attacks. I think the most disturbing thing was that she appeared to be so very much *like us* – twenty-seven, just two years older than Laura, and similar in so many ways. I could picture the two of them chatting away in Laura's café and becoming friends. Julia could have been my daughter. She reminded me of my younger self – confident and idealistic, driven by an unshakeable trust in the idea that it is possible to shape the future. From the very start, Julia's face touched something in me, bringing back the memory of things I had lost and for which I must have been mourning – much more strongly than I was aware. In that picture in particular, she looked so proud and safe and at home in her skin and her beliefs. I found myself vacillating between fascination and disgust – after all, this woman had blood, so much blood, on her hands.

On the day following the terror attack, Julia's 'manifesto' was published on the front page of every newspaper in the country. The number of her victims had risen to twenty-three, and one woman, still in a critical condition, would later succumb to her injuries, bringing the total to two dozen. Apart from the manifesto, Julia, who had turned herself in to the police straight after the attack, remained silent. She refused to see anyone but her lawyer. She refused all contact with her family. She refused to receive friends and members of the various political groups to which she had belonged. She refused to speak to journalists. Even during her trial, she never uttered a word. It was almost as though her silence was her second, perhaps even crueller attack: she simply refused to grace us with an explanation.

Her manifesto rehearsed some standard anti-capitalist slogans and a few anti-globalization catchphrases. She denounced the unethical exploitation of workers in the so-called Third World; she decried the apolitical consumerism that dominates our age and the shocking lack of public interest in the suffering of the oppressed in countries other than our own; and she called for a radical rethinking of neo-liberal economic policies that pursue growth at all costs. But the manifesto's rhetoric was strangely unimaginative and lacklustre. I couldn't help feeling that she was mocking the idea of manifesto-writing, or perhaps even political activism as such. I feared it was nothing but a teaser, a deliberate slap in the face for those in search of answers.

Unsurprisingly, as Julia remained shtum, others began to speak in her stead – both about her and (unauthorized, of course) on her behalf. A chorus of overexcited voices populated the airwaves and flooded the print media, trying to drown out Julia's uncanny silence. Anecdotes, half-truths, legends and myths soon began to circulate and multiply at an astounding speed. People from all professions were anxious to categorize and analyse Julia and her acts, to explain and thus somehow to master them. Predictably, psychologists and psychiatrists were the most sought-after talk-show guests – psychology, after all, is still the most apolitical and reconciliatory master narrative out there, as everything can safely be explained with recourse to Mummy's or Daddy's lack of unconditional love for their offspring (I feel like Amanda just kicked me hard in the shin from afar). But there were also politicians, historians, sociologists, economists, teachers, theologians – the line-up of so-called terrorism experts eager to share their views on the matter was endless. Was Julia ill or evil, pathological or a sinner? A victim of false ideology or a dangerously deluded radical? A disturbed maverick or an alarmingly symptomatic product of our perverse age? Should the professed political justification of her deed be debated seriously, or was she simply a nihilistic sadist? How did she fit in with her terrorist cousins – Latin American guerrilla fighters, IRA activists, the German Red Army Faction, Islamist suicide bombers, militant animal-rights campaigners? What did the anti-globalization movement, the causes of which she had seemingly embraced in her manifesto, make of her? Had she acted alone or were there others who had supported her? And who were the parents who had produced this spawn of the devil?

Julia's life-story became the stuff of endless speculation, and the fact that she was beautiful and silent only fuelled the public's interest further. I admit that I, too, was spellbound from the very start – my fascination consisted mainly of repulsion and horror, but also awe. I don't mean that I was in any way condoning or admiring her horrendous act – of course not; I have seen the human cost of her ugly work. I think what I felt was a general kind of admiration for radical mindsets, for people who are not prepared to compromise, who have visions so strong they defend them with their lives, and who courageously dedicate their entire existence to ideas, regardless of the consequences. In our exhausted political landscape this species is almost extinct. Think about it: what forms of serious political activism are left today? Our streets are populated by swarms of twee retro-fetishists and bearded hipsters with ironic spectacles, who appear to believe that drinking flat whites in cafés that play ukulele music and buying chia seeds and black quinoa in wholefood shops are worthwhile political statements in their own right.

I devoured every single article about Julia, and I had numerous discussions with Amanda about her that usually resulted in heated disagreements. Although I don't deny the attraction of psychoanalytical explanatory models, I simply don't believe that they can account for *everything*, as Amanda does. You, too, George, confessed to me once that you found Amanda's views curiously limited, blind to all political and historical considerations. In addition, Amanda soon made it clear that she felt I had become unhealthily obsessed with Julia White – of course she had many a theory up her sleeve to explain *why* Julia appealed to me so, and *what* she appealed to in me, but I refused to listen. Maybe, with hindsight, I should have.

Then I decided to transform my obsession into something productive. It made complete sense: I would write Julia White's biography. I would try to unravel the mystery of her strange allure and at the same time turn my research into a much-needed new book. For the first time since the trial, I felt strong enough to tackle a serious project. I didn't even need to convince you. This was the first project since the accursed trial that wasn't just a bread-and-butter job, which you had kindly pushed my way and that came with an acceptable cheque that would go towards paying off my debts. The biography was my chance to shake off my sense of failure, the conviction that I was a sell-out. I had been producing nothing but shallow entertainment porn since 2010, and you can't imagine how much that hurt. I used to live and breathe for my work – it meant *everything* to me. It was all I had. I'm sorry, George – I am of course infinitely grateful for every job you sent my way, and I am acutely aware that you reserved the most lucrative commissions for me, but they did inevitably also tend to be the most facile ones. I had been living like a ghost for the past four years; I felt so hollow.

The generous advance you negotiated for me was of course also more than welcome – my finances were (and still are) a mess so horrific to behold that I had left the task to a trusted financial adviser, who fed me only manageable nuggets of information when she felt I was able to cope. The last I had heard from her was that it would take me at least fifteen years to clear my debt – provided the commercial commissions kept coming in regularly.

I admit that I was also attracted by the challenge. It was clear that I had to research and write the book as quickly as possible, as other publishers would want to cash in on the Julia hype, too. It was a race both against time and against the competition – whoever got their book out first would win the lion's share of the potentially vast number of readers interested in Julia's story. I had set myself the ambitious task of delivering the complete manuscript in only fourteen weeks.

But time wasn't the only problem: since it was clear from the start that the subject of my book wouldn't grant me an interview, I would instead have to gather all my materials from the people who knew her best. That, too, would be far from easy, but I was used to dealing with difficulties of that kind. I had written three unauthorized celebrity biographies under extreme time pressure before (of a young pop star who had taken too many horse tranquillizers and lost her mind, a suicidal TV chef, and a firmly facelifted politician with a penchant for parading through our numerous reality TV shows in outfits that are too tight and too bright). I was confident I would be able to master this one, too. I used to win people's trust easily. I could get almost anyone to reveal their secrets to me.

A part of me was also secretly hoping that Julia would make an exception and agree to speak to me after all (I cannot tell you how much I wish she hadn't now). Right at the beginning, I contacted the lawyer who was representing

Julia, asking her to pass my request for an interview on to her client, and I sent her two follow-up messages a few weeks later when I didn't receive a response. In any case, in the first instance my plan was to contact Julia's family and friends. I knew there would also be university acquaintances, teachers, neighbours, distant relatives, old playmates and political activists who would no doubt be eager to share with me their version of events. Normally, all kinds of people crawl out of the woodwork when they sniff the elusive fragrance of fame, even if it is just by association.

As soon as I had signed the hastily drawn-up contract in your office, I threw myself heart and soul into the project. All of a sudden, the weariness that had been oppressing me for four long years lifted and I felt almost like my old self again. Besides, Aisha had thankfully recovered from her illness (it turned out to be a harmless stomach bug), and there were exciting developments in Laura's life. In spite of the fact that the Blue Nile is a non-fussy, down-to-earth affair that consistently privileges quality over hipness, hidden away in one of the less busy side-streets in Bloomsbury, it had received enthusiastic reviews in various papers. Even more thrilling was the fact that Laura and Moira had just found out that they had been nominated for the *Time Out* Best Newcomer of the Year award (in the organic/wholefood category). Amanda and I were incredibly proud of Laura, and, to be honest, enormously relieved that things had turned out so well for her.

I miss going to the Blue Nile – I used to drop in once or twice a week, to sample their ever-changing repertoire of delicious grain, rice and pulse salads, and when Laura wasn't too busy, we caught up over a cup of tea. Laura is a very special person – she always knew exactly what she wanted in life, and also how to get it. She has loved cooking from a very early age (although, as you well know, neither Amanda nor I has any talent at all in that domain), and trained as a chef when all her friends went to university, before pairing up with Moira to realize her dream of running an organic café. Moira had the necessary funds and business connections, while Laura supplied the concept, the creative energy and her sure-footed food intelligence. You must visit the Blue Nile for me when you find the time, George – I always felt very much at home there, and would be really grateful if you could occasionally check on Laura to see how she is doing. I worry so much about how all of this is affecting her. She is a sensitive soul, underneath it all.

II

I sleep badly. Each night, I snap awake countless times and, sitting up, contemplate the darkness of my cell, too agitated to read or write. I can't see the night sky; my shoebox-sized window exposes a view only of the depressing facade of the adjacent building. And when I do sleep, my dreams are so disturbing that I am grateful for waking up again. I keep seeing Julia. In my dreams, I drown in her eyes, which are the colour of ponds, the grey-green surfaces of her irises surrounded by a dark-blue outer ring and scattered with tiny splashes of amber and gold, like flecks of sunlight. Sometimes she stands with her arms folded and her head up high, looking down on me, a cruel smile playing on her lips, and sometimes she beckons me to follow her, and I do, in spite of myself, driven by forces over which I have no control. I also see his wide-open eyes, and how they cycle through disbelief, terror and abhorrence, and then, just before they close, succumb to a leaden weariness. And of course I see the little girl. Over and over again. I see her tiny white face, eerie as the moon, and her caterpillar eyebrows, and her sand-coloured plaits that stopped bouncing so abruptly and then hung on her unmoving. I still see her standing still as a statue in her festive pink satin dress. I see her small candy-coloured mouth with her lips pressed tightly together. I see the movement of her large grey eyes as they travelled, very slowly, from her father to her mother and back again, and then to me, and it was on me that they came to rest. I couldn't bear that gaze. She alone remained silent, standing so perfectly still, even when all hell broke loose around us. Her eyes were still on me when they dragged me away.

None of the other inmates has threatened me yet, but the peace seems precarious. They stare at me, but I stare right back at them. I can't let them see my fear. A few days ago, a frightened-looking new girl arrived, mushroom-pale, her eyes always wet and her hands shaking so badly that she barely manages to cut her food with the frail plastic knives they give us here. Her name is Sarah and she sits next to me whenever she can, but she has barely spoken a word as yet. I am grateful for her company; with her around, I feel a little less alone. And there is a black woman, about my age, with the most expressionless face I have ever seen. She always carries a book and keeps to herself. She has looked at me a few times, not unkindly. I wonder why she is here.

Yesterday, my lawyer told me that my trial will commence sometime in March – a date that seems centuries away. Unsurprisingly, her second attempt to get me out on bail was rejected, too. I didn't expect otherwise. But what does surprise me, George, is the bags of fan mail I receive every week – large numbers of the most outlandish letters. I'm genuinely horrified that I appear to have inspired the kind of people who write these letters, and that they have turned me into some twisted heroine. I read every single one of them, but they all evoke the same feeling in me: shame.

But I should get on with my story. In early August, Amy White was the first to respond to the carefully phrased letter I had sent to all members of Julia's family, in which I explained the nature of my project and asked whether it would be possible to meet for an informal conversation. I didn't expect a reaction from anybody at that stage, but Amy emailed me just two days later. She suggested we meet in an Italian café in Soho. An odd choice, I thought, a place into which tired tourists stumble when they find there are no seats in the more appealing alternatives in the vicinity. Amy is twenty-three, four years younger than her sister, holds a BA and an MA with distinction from Corpus Christi College, Cambridge, and is currently studying for a PhD in English Literature at UCL. She has been working on her research project (provisionally entitled 'Representations of Sisterhood in Early Victorian Women's Fiction') for about a year.

I arrived early, but Amy was already waiting for me. Apart from her, there were only an elderly German couple clad in eminently practical travelling outfits, and a big, dreadlocked man with a Labrador, with whom he appeared to be sharing his pizza. A listless waiter followed a soundless football match on a small TV, which contrasted oddly with the faded pictures of Tuscan landscapes that hung either side of it on the limoncello-coloured walls. I was able to identify Amy without difficulty. She had chosen a table in the corner that was as far away as possible from the window and the waiter, and sat uneasily on the edge of her green plastic chair. Christ, she was thin. Skeletal, George. It pained me just to look at her. The big wound-like eyes in her small sunken face made her look like a terminally ill cancer patient. Although she wore a shapeless, oversized pullover and baggy corduroy trousers, her spiky shoulders and knees looked as though they were about to cut right through the fabric. Her light-brown hair was dull and brittle, and tied together in a ponytail. She didn't resemble her sister in any way.

We shook hands and I tried to engage her in small talk to make her relax a little, since she seemed terribly tense. She kept scratching a patch of skin at the back of her head, and repeatedly glanced at the other customers in the café, as though she needed to reassure herself that they didn't pose a threat. Nevertheless, it became clear almost immediately that Amy was desperate to talk about her sister – to anyone who would listen. Although she disclosed private and no doubt very painful memories, our encounter remained curiously impersonal: once she got started she just couldn't seem to stop talking. There was so much pent up inside her that she needed to relieve herself with the utmost urgency, to heave it all out as quickly as possible while someone was listening, anyone, making the most of the time she had before they abandoned her. Her account was a rapid, almost uninterrupted torrent, mingling memories, impressions and anecdotes, which were (surprisingly for a PhD student, I thought) only very rarely supported by any attempts at analysis. Amy's story sounded very much like the report of someone who was still too shell-shocked to be able to make any sense of their traumatic experiences. I barely said anything myself. Apart from the odd short question, I just let her talk.

We sat together in the café for four and a half hours, until we were thrown out by the exasperated waiter, and we met again the next day for another long session at a very similar place. I felt as though I was listening to the anguished song of an impossibly frail bird that had fallen out of its nest and broken all its bones. Even Amy's voice was bird-like – feeble but piercing. I had the disturbing impression that I was the first human being to whom Amy had talked for a very long time. (Had she not spoken to her family about this at all? I wondered. As a family, you can't just ignore a catastrophe of this magnitude – or can you? What of the parents – where were they, and why didn't they take this sad little creature back under their wings?)

Unsurprisingly, Amy rejected my offer of lunch, and I felt uncomfortable as I consumed a salad and a sandwich on my own during the course of our two interview marathons. She didn't mind me recording our conversations. It was very much my impression that she didn't care at all about the afterlife of her story; she just needed to tell it, to deposit it somewhere. What follows is Amy's story in her own words, based on the two interviews I conducted on 10 and 11 August 2014. Here and there, I imposed chronological coherence and eliminated the repetitiveness that marked her original narrative, but otherwise this report is faithful to Amy's original account.

| | |

I was the kind of younger sister who always tags along. I followed my sister everywhere, a bit like a slightly annoying puppy, you know? And Julia was the kind of older sister who didn't mind, who was just nice and generous about it. Or at least she never let me feel it if I did get on her nerves. Until she came back from her gap year, that is – after that, everything changed. Or maybe I just didn't get the message before then. I don't know. I must have misunderstood *something* along the way. I often do that, misread people. I'm really not very good at picking up on the finer nuances of interpersonal exchanges. Everybody else in my family seems to be able to do that just fine. They're all confident and functional and socially at ease, and all that.

Julia has always been fiercely protective of me, from the very start, really. There are more pictures of *her* holding me when I was a baby than there are of my mother. Actually, thinking about it, there are barely any photographs in our family album in which we aren't together: usually I'm holding her hand and we're dressed in matching outfits. Or at least that was the idea – I was a bit of a copy-cat. I always wanted to wear exactly what Julia was wearing. But my outfits kind of ended up being not just pale but comic and weird-looking imitations of hers – I just didn't have Julia's sense of style, and of course I didn't have the aura and personality that one needs to get away with more risky choices, either. Even on those days when Julia was super-nice to me and chose every single item of my outfit, and put together a really beautiful combination that would have looked amazing on anyone, it didn't work. The other day, I flipped through one of our old photo albums again, and almost every picture of me made me cringe.

When Julia went through a brief Goth phase – I think she was about fourteen or fifteen – I also insisted on wearing only black and on painting my eyes dark with kohl, trying never to smile and all that. But while Julia looked like a beautiful Victorian vampire in her velvet capes and long lace dresses, I just looked like a soot-covered chimney sweep. When Julia and her friends hung out in someone's house to smoke and read world-weary poetry and listen to The Cure, and when they went to gigs, I trailed along. I don't know how the others saw me – they probably thought of me as a peculiar little mascot or something like that. I'm pretty sure I did real damage to the group's otherwise impeccable cool-factor.

I really don't know whether Julia thought of me that way, back then. I hope not. She never said so. But who knows? Maybe she was just being nice, and it cost her a superhuman effort not to lose her temper around me. Or maybe she just felt sorry for me. I don't know how she did it, putting up with me like that, day after day, for years on end. How annoying must it be when someone copies everything pretty you do, and makes it all look totally ridiculous in the process, like a caricature or something? Not that I would know, of course – nobody would ever want to copy *my* style.

Back then, Julia was always lovely and supportive and nice to me – really, I can't remember a single occasion when I didn't feel safe and protected in her company. She was simply amazing. She was the only person I ever felt at ease with, like I could just be myself and it was OK, you know? She still is, although she doesn't speak to me anymore, of course.

In any case, none of her friends ever dared to question why I was always with her – she could be pretty scary and forbidding when she felt that people were criticizing her decisions. When I was with Julia nobody ever had the nerve to treat me with anything but respect. And being with her meant that I could be in a group of people who would normally not even have looked at me – her friends were always by far the coolest types around. But without Julia by my side, I was nothing – the weird, sickly freak-sister, whom no one would ever speak to.

I've always been frail – I have asthma and was born with a little hole in my heart, and other things I won't bore you with. I needed a lot of medical attention when I was little. For some reason, it was always Julia and not my mother – although, ironically, she's actually a surgeon – who made sure I took my medication and who came with me to every one of the hundreds of medical appointments I had to endure. Julia always insisted on sleeping in a bed next to me when I had to stay in hospital overnight. She really was that kind of person, you know? Just nice and caring. She was always there for me. I don't know exactly why Julia took on that mother role – perhaps she really did love me as much as she always told me she did, back then. But sometimes, in my darker moments, I wonder whether I was just her guinea-pig, her first 'case' – a downtrodden creature in need of a strong helper. This obviously came to be her thing, later on. All of a sudden, she cared for all the other wretched of this earth, the far-away ones, and dropped me like a hot potato. But who knows what her real motives were. That kind of stuff is impossible to tell, isn't it?

Our parents weren't at all 'bad' parents – I'm sure that's what everyone thinks. They were supportive in many ways, and massively proud of Julia, of course. The worst I can say about them really is that they weren't at home much, because they both had pretty demanding jobs. Everyone but me in my family is some kind of high flyer. I think my mother was incredibly grateful that Julia looked out for me – it took a big weight off her shoulders. My parents always thought the world of Julia – my dad even more so than my mother; he totally idolized her. She was the bright star in our family, the angel, the super-clever one. They trusted her completely, and so did I, of course. They never questioned a single one of Julia's choices. In their view, she simply couldn't put a foot wrong. I think Jonathan found that a little difficult at times, like he was second-rate or something, but the truth is, we both *were* second-rate compared to her.

When I finished primary school Julia fought like a lion to get me into her own school, a fee-paying one. I think originally my parents didn't believe I was worth it – they'd already paid through the nose for Jonathan's and Julia's private education, and probably felt that I wasn't academically minded enough, or something like that, to justify another massive financial investment of that kind. Obviously they didn't really put it that way – they claimed that Julia's school was much further away than the local comprehensive, and that the daily commute would exhaust me. They said they'd prefer me not to be subjected to a too-demanding physical and intellectual regime like the one Julia's school was famous for, since I didn't have the strength to cope well with stress. And they argued that I'd be able to explore my 'creative inclinations' better in the local school, which had a fantastic drama and art society. And so on – I'm sure you can imagine it.

It's true that I didn't exactly shine in primary school, but that was also because of my shyness. I was so timid and frightened as a child that I rarely spoke a word without Julia by my side. On my first day at school, for example, I desperately needed to go to the loo, but was too scared to ask for permission. After a few hours, I just couldn't hold it in any longer and simultaneously started to cry and to pee in my seat, right in front of everyone. Of course the other kids never let me forget that scene – I was 'Amy-the-Pant-Pisser' for four years.

Anyway. I can remember really clearly the evening when Julia convinced my parents to change their mind about my schooling. I was eleven years old – I had started school a year later than normal because of my health – and Julia had just turned sixteen. Jonathan had recently left home for university, which was kind of a relief, to be honest. Julia and I found his pedantic and self-important attitude and his constant outbursts of jealousy a bit annoying. I think ultimately he was resentful about the fact that Julia was better than him at everything, and also that she and I got on so well. After supper that day Julia told me to go to my room because she had to talk to our parents about something important. Obviously, I was incredibly curious about her secret business, and hid behind the half-closed dining-room door. I couldn't see the three of them, but I could hear everything they said. It was the first time I heard Julia use her rhetorical skills for a specific aim. I can tell you one thing – not many people are able to stand up to her when she's set on achieving something. Actually, I've never met anyone who could. She's an incredibly persuasive speaker – she can argue the case for almost anything, and she does it with wit and charm besides, if she feels like it. She can also get a little intense when things don't go her way, but that didn't happen very often.

She started by asking my parents on what grounds they could justify two of their children being worthy of an expensive education, and the third not. Then she proceeded to make a powerful argument for my as yet underdeveloped but clearly highly promising academic aptitude. She painted a gruesome picture of the rough and dangerous social environment that awaited me at the comprehensive, and of the cruel bullying that vulnerable girls like me tend to suffer in such places. She said she needed to be near me to look after me at all times, and especially at school – did my parents even have the slightest inkling what a jungle it was out there? What monstrosities schoolchildren were capable of inflicting upon their weaker peers? She illustrated this point with a few well-chosen examples that included locked cupboards and toilet bowls and that made my mother gasp. She said that of all three of us it was me they should have sent to private school, as it was clearly I who was the most fragile and in need of extra care and attention, much more so than she and Jonathan ever had been. She said she really couldn't follow my parents' logic. At all.

And then Julia made my parents feel even more ashamed of themselves than they no doubt already did: she must have stood up – I heard a chair moving. She lowered her voice rather than raising it, and spoke very quietly and intently – that's a method I've seen her use on many later occasions, too. She probably also used her hands – Julia gestures a lot when she speaks, and the movements of her hands are fluid and calm, and very effective. They can hypnotize you if you're not careful.

'I need to protect Amy, *especially* at school, can't you see that?' she said. 'And I won't even mention the double standards behind your decision not to pay for a proper education for your youngest daughter, who is already so cruelly disadvantaged by nature. Amy will have to struggle with health problems *for the rest of her life,*' Julia said, very quietly and clearly. 'I'm sure you never hesitated for a second when deciding whether or not Jonathan was worth the investment. Did you? Jonathan isn't one bit more intelligent than Amy. In fact, I'm pretty sure the opposite is the case. And neither is he more talented than her – he's just louder and more confident. The key difference is quite simply that he is a *man*. Are you seriously telling me that you're not prepared to pay the tuition fees for your youngest, sickest child simply because she's a *girl*? Or,' and here Julia paused as though she couldn't quite bring herself to say what she felt she had to next, 'are your motivations even more sinister? Is it *precisely* because Amy is sick that you think it's pointless to invest your money in the education of this child? Is it because you think she will die sooner than us, and that paying for proper schooling would therefore not be worth it?'

My mother was so upset she couldn't respond at all. I felt pretty bad about it, to be honest – although I appreciated Julia's campaign, I thought she'd gone a bit too far. Dad tried to refute her points: 'Of course not, of course not, sweetheart; how can you think that of us, Julia, *darling*!' he kept saying, and he, too, sounded shocked and shaken by her accusations. But Julia said nothing more and simply left the room. Of course she found me eavesdropping behind the door, but rather than being angry with me she just took my hand and led me upstairs to her room. That night, she let me sleep in her bed – she used to do that on special occasions. Just before I fell asleep she whispered: 'All will be OK tomorrow, my pet, you'll see. Trust me.'

And she was right, of course. My parents never mentioned the comprehensive again. The very next day they enrolled me at Julia's school. I couldn't help but be impressed with her manoeuvre, but I found out later that two months before Julia's intervention, my father had lost a big sum on the stock market. Jonathan told me. Apparently it was such a large amount that my parents were afraid of having to declare bankruptcy for a while. But somehow they managed to pay my fees in any case – how exactly they did it I don't know. And a few years later, their finances had recovered, and all was well again on that front.

The only time I ever saw Julia use violence was at a party she took me to when I was twelve. By then she'd shed her black costumes and her flirtation with Weltschmerz. She's always been pretty extreme in her tastes and interests – it's all or nothing for her. Quite abruptly, she'd moved on from death to politics and economics, and had raided our mother's wardrobe and all the charity shops in town in search of seventies clothes. Of course, as always, I followed suit. On the evening of the party, she was wearing flared brown corduroys, red leather cowboy boots and a flowery purple blouse. Her long brown hair, parted in the centre, glistened like wet chestnuts. Her hair has always been glossy and full – not like mine, which is catastrophically brittle. You wouldn't think we had the same genes, would you? She'd also put on lots of Indian bracelets with little silver bells that chimed whenever she moved her hands.

Julia is the kind of person who inspires trends and attracts followers wherever she goes. Not just me, I mean: at least half of her year were trying to emulate her style. When we arrived at her friend's house, The Doors were playing, and everyone was giggling and smoking bongs and sitting cross-legged on the carpet – you can imagine the scene. All of Julia's friends were boys – girls didn't really interest her. Of those male friends, almost all were in love with her, and I could totally see why – I mean, how couldn't they be? My sister was so incredibly beautiful and smart and brave. Julia was used to being adored, but generally didn't pay much attention to her admirers. But there was one boy in her group of friends who didn't give the impression of being particularly enamoured with her – he was called Josh, and the party was at his house. Josh's seeming lack of interest had awoken Julia's own. The night before, she had initiated me in her plan to seduce Josh at his party. Not because she was in love with him, or anything like that. He was a very ordinary person – I can't even really remember his face. I think she did it simply because she considered it a challenge. I always kind of suspected that because she was so much more intelligent than everyone around her and because everything came to her so easily and quickly, she was actually pretty bored most of the time. I think she needed little challenges like that just to keep herself entertained, you know? But in any case, we'd sat up in her bed the night before and plotted seduction strategies: what she would wear, what she would say and in which tone of voice, how she would look at him and when she would touch his hand – that kind of stuff. Ultimately, I ended up being much more nervous and excited about the whole thing than she was. At that point, sexuality and all that hadn't really featured much in our lives.

Unsurprisingly, Julia's seduction strategy worked completely according to plan. Josh, who'd probably just been shy about expressing his affection, or else was a little slow or something, was massively flattered by Julia's perceived interest in him, and he chitchatted animatedly with her. He was totally ridiculous, and I remember that it really annoyed me, the way he kept casting proud glances around the room to check that everyone was taking notice that the coolest girl in the school was gracing him with her attention. As always on these occasions, I sat next to Julia and observed her every move. I've studied her very carefully over the years. When we were still close, I mean. Sometimes, she'd throw me a conspiratorial little smile. I was terribly thrilled and quite agitated. I knew that the next step would be for her to casually put her hand on Josh's knee, whisper something in his ear, and then she'd lead him to his parents' bedroom, and... you can imagine it. She'd even bought some condoms, because she didn't think Josh was the type who would have any himself.

And again, everything went just as we'd imagined it would. Before Julia left the room with Josh, she kissed me on the forehead and said: 'You'll be all right on your own for a bit, Amy, won't you? I won't be long – I promise.' I'd never really been alone with her friends before, and didn't know what to do with myself. I guess I must have looked lost and even sadder than usual because one of them, Tobias, took pity and sat down on the floor next to me. He was quite cute, and I actually really liked him. But almost immediately he began quizzing me about my sister – everybody only ever wants to talk about Julia with me. Even you, right? Anyway, Tobias asked all sorts of questions about her – what she was reading, what bands she liked, what perfume she wore, that kind of stuff. He jokingly offered me a bottle of beer, and looked terribly uneasy when I accepted it. I'd never drunk alcohol before, and it affected me immediately. Somehow, I allowed myself to believe that Tobias was actually interested in *me* rather than in Julia, and that she was simply the only shared topic of conversation we had at that point. Somehow, I even managed to convince myself that Tobias wasn't just interested in me in a general kind of way, but interested in me sexually. I told you I was really bad at reading people. I blame it on the beer.

Anyway. There I was sitting on the floor drinking beer with Tobias, in a little makeshift hippy outfit that Julia had put together for me. I was wearing this knee-length flower-patterned blouse of hers with a thin leather belt – it was supposed to be a dress – a few of Julia's necklaces, and even some lipstick and mascara. No doubt I looked grotesque, like a little girl who'd just raided her mother's wardrobe and played around with her make-up, or a prostitute child bride or something like that. But after having drunk half of my beer, I decided to seduce Tobias: I wanted him to kiss me. For once, I, too, would have something exciting I could tell Julia. I started to look at Tobias in the way I'd seen Julia look at Josh – a look that she'd practised on me the night before. I think he must have found that really amusing, and he started to be playfully flirtatious back. Very gently though, I should add. He wasn't a bad person, and I still feel pretty guilty about what happened later. I was feeling increasingly dizzy. I kept swaying towards him half-deliberately and half-drunkenly, and I began to slur my words. Some of his friends were watching us. No doubt they were all laughing at me.

'Kiss me,' I said finally. 'I want you to kiss me.'

'Kiss you?' Tobias laughed. 'Amy, with all due respect, you're a bit young for me.'

'Just kiss me,' I insisted. I was speaking louder than I had intended.

'Come on, Tobe, be a gentleman,' one of his friends sitting on the other side of the room shouted.

'Just do it, you coward,' another one cried. Everyone was laughing and firing Tobias on.

Tobias looked totally embarrassed for a while, but then shrugged and finally said, in a resigned voice, 'OK, just one quick kiss to make you happy then.'

Just as he bent over to plant a quick kiss on my lips, cheered on by the entire room, Julia came back down. Everybody fell silent at once. For a split second, she just stood there and looked at us. Her skin was alabaster-white, her eyes were narrow green slits and her lips pressed together so tightly that they'd turned white, too. She looked like an angry goddess about to wreak havoc, but who didn't really know where to begin. She let her gaze travel slowly across the room. She looked at Tobias, and at the half-empty beer bottle in my hand, and then she looked at Tobias again.

Tobias got up immediately and said, 'Look, Julia, don't get angry, it's not what it looks like. We were just having fun. Amy asked me to... '

But Julia interrupted him. 'How *dare* you,' she said very quietly. Her voice cut through the room like a whiplash. What followed happened very quickly. She walked over to where Tobias and I were sitting. She stood right up against Tobias and looked at him for a few seconds that felt like an eternity. Everyone was holding their breath. Then she took the half-empty beer bottle from my hand, and smashed it down on Tobias's head. He howled, and sank to his knees, holding his forehead in his hands. Blood was beginning to trickle from a small wound on his left temple.

'For fuck's sake. Damn you,' he shouted. 'You're totally mad, Julia. It was a bloody *game* – your sister *asked* me to kiss her.'

But Julia wasn't interested in his story. 'That'll teach you, you piece of shit,' she hissed. Then she grabbed me by the hand and dragged me outside. We walked home in silence. I was crying, and Julia was still pulling my hand and going far too quickly for me to keep up. I wanted to tell her that it was true and that I'd asked Tobias to kiss me, but I didn't dare. Eventually, she stopped her frantic walking and took me in her arms. She, too, was crying at that point.

'I'm so sorry, Amy. I'm so sorry, forgive me, forgive me,' she kept saying. 'I'll never leave you alone again like that in a room full of hormonal drunken arseholes, I promise.'

Again I wanted to tell her what had really happened, but she stopped me: 'Hush, hush, now, it's fine, let's not talk about it anymore.'

Julia never spoke to anyone who was at that party again. I know I should have told her what had really happened, but

I was too ashamed, and too scared to provoke her anger and lose her affection. It was all I had and cared for, you know? I'm not proud of it. Much later, I was to lose her affection anyway, but for a totally different reason.

When Julia was seventeen she started to do volunteer work at a homeless shelter, where she helped in the soup kitchen one evening a week. She also worked at an Oxfam shop on Saturday afternoons. And she founded a debating society at school, and led a weekly discussion group on current political issues. The debates quickly became super-popular, and a huge crowd regularly flocked to the school library on Thursday afternoons to listen to Julia and her provocative speeches.

I still followed Julia like a shadow at the beginning of that year, and tried to help with all her initiatives. At the homeless shelter, for example, Julia chatted away to the shelter's visitors while they had their meals in the dining room, and in the meantime I'd collect their empty plates and put them in the dishwasher, clean up the kitchen and serve seconds, and things like that. Unlike Julia, I'm hopeless at small talk. But Julia was really interested in the stories of the homeless – she wanted to know everything about them: where they came from, what they'd done in the past, how they had ended up on the street, how they were spending their days, what they thought of government policies on tackling homelessness, and so on. The shelter crowd adored Julia – they called her 'angel' and felt incredibly flattered by her interest in them. They had a glow in their eyes when they spoke to her, and some even cried when she touched them – she often took their hands in hers, rubbed their backs, and removed leaves from their hair.

During the weekly school debates, I'd usually sit right by my sister's side, and fetch things like water, crackers and pens when needed, and otherwise just listened to her rhetorical artistry, completely spellbound like the rest of the audience. Julia set specific topics for each session, such as 'Should Rapists be Castrated?'; 'The Psycho-Politics of Charity: Altruism or Narcissism?'; and 'Redistribution: Ethical Obligation or Economic Suicide?' Usually two or three kids agreed to debate with her each week, which was pretty brave considering that Julia always won any argument, no matter whether she really believed in the side she had adopted for the purposes of the discussion. No one ever even got close to posing a semi-serious intellectual challenge to her. I think she saw these debates as practice, like a boxer who lets laughably unworthy opponents into the ring just to keep himself fit for a real fight in the future. In any case, the rest of us just enjoyed the show. But after a few months Julia got bored with the society, appointed a new president and debate leader and moved on. The society withered away soon after her departure.

Her waning interest in the debating society was also directly related to her growing interest in someone she'd recently met at the Oxfam shop. He was twenty-three years old, tall, and had floppy blond hair that kept tumbling into his face. He used to flip it back with a jerk of his head that made him look like a camp horse attempting to get rid of a bothersome fly. He always wore green corduroys, white shirts with cuffs, cravats and a tweed jacket – a bit *Brideshead Revisited*, you know? That ridiculously arch lord-of-the-manor style? Five Saturdays in a row, he lingered for hours in the shop during Julia's shifts, pretending to study the record and book collection. Behind his back we giggled because he was just so totally obvious – we couldn't believe the amount of time and energy he invested in keeping up this farce. It was clear what he was really interested in. Julia would always politely ask him whether she could help him with anything, and he'd blush, shake his head, tug at his ridiculous cravat and pull out a random book, which he'd then stare at for half an hour.

Eventually – I think it took him about six or seven weeks – he mustered up the courage to ask Julia out for a coffee. He was called Jeremy and was studying for an MA in Politics at King's. Obviously I trailed along to their first date. We went to some boho café in town after Julia's shift, where the two of them hotly debated until closing time whether or not communism was compatible with human nature, or whether the accumulation of private property and personal privileges was a necessary driving force for economic and creative productivity. I got bored with their discussion, and I can't remember what they agreed on in the end. I was also disturbed by some changes I perceived in Julia that day. All evening, she didn't make any effort to include me in the discussion, not even once. Usually, she'd do that, and make sure that her friends spoke to me, too, so that I wouldn't feel left out. But that evening, she didn't even look at me – her gaze remained fixed on Jeremy. They agreed to meet again the next day.

On our way home Julia was silent. I was kind of hoping she'd mock Jeremy's absurdly posh accent, or his vain hair-tossing, or that she'd dismiss his preposterous political positions, but she didn't. I asked whether I could sleep in her bed that night, but she said she was tired and needed to rest. The next day – it was a bright autumn afternoon that contrasted starkly with my darkening mood – we all went to the zoo together. Julia and Jeremy were outraged by the perversity of taking animals out of their natural habitat and imprisoning them in cages so that they could satisfy the voyeuristic desires of bored bourgeois families. They hatched plans to liberate a black panther that had attracted their sympathy because of his sad eyes and psychotic pacing in his little cage. They made all kinds of other ridiculous plans like that. Again, they didn't pay any attention to me at all. I fell behind at some point, and from a distance I saw that Jeremy took Julia's hand and that she didn't pull it away. It really turned my stomach, that moment.

After the zoo, Jeremy took us to a vegetarian restaurant for supper. They talked non-stop, really intensely, again until closing time. I hadn't eaten my meal because I had kind of lost my appetite, but nobody noticed and nobody asked whether I wanted anything else. When Julia and Jeremy shared a dessert they didn't offer me any of it. It really was as though I had ceased to exist, all of a sudden. At some point later in the evening I went to the loo because I just couldn't repress any longer the sobs that were threatening to break out. I didn't want to cry in front of Jeremy – I'd started to massively dislike the guy. I stayed there for at least twenty minutes, and expected Julia to come and look for me, but she never did. When I finally returned to the table, I saw that Jeremy's hand was on her arm. I stood behind them for a while, just looking, and trying to control my agitation. They hadn't noticed that I'd come back.

'Can I see you again tomorrow?' Jeremy asked.

'Sure,' Julia said. 'We could go and see a film together – actually, Amy and I really wanted to see *Psycho* again. I think it's showing tomorrow afternoon at the Curzon.'

'Look, Julia, what I meant was can I see *you*, not you and your sister. I find it a little creepy, the way she follows you around. No offence, but it just doesn't seem quite right at her age – doesn't she have any friends of her own? And what about you – don't you ever get tired of having to drag her along?'

And then he looked at her, from below, in that slimy, puppy-dog kind of way, you know? My heart started pounding like mad when I heard that. Surely Julia would throw her drink into Jeremy's face, get up and never see him again. Surely she wouldn't let that go unpunished. She'd smashed someone on the head with a bottle once for having kissed me, after all. What would she do to Jeremy? Spit in his face? Stick her fork into his arm? I held my breath. But Julia did nothing of the kind. Instead, she laughed. Then she pressed his hand and said:

'OK, I suppose Amy can go and watch *Psycho* on her own tomorrow.'

I slipped away and then returned to the table a few minutes later, white and shaking. Not that anyone noticed. The next day, Julia went off after school to meet Jeremy without me. For the first time ever, I had to take the bus home on my own. The house felt cold and empty – our parents always used to come home late. I did my homework in the kitchen. When I had finished I just didn't know what to do with myself. I went up to my room and sat on the bed all evening, waiting for Julia to return. I refused to come down to eat with my parents. I was kind of hoping that Julia's date was going horribly wrong, that she'd burst into my room outraged and tell me what an atrocious kisser Jeremy was, that he had mackerel breath, and that he was a clownish toff. That she was sorry for having neglected me so horribly the other day. Then we would both cry and embrace and she'd let me sleep in her bed that night and confess everything that had happened between her and Jeremy. We'd laugh about it and all would be as before. But that wasn't what happened. Julia didn't come home before two in the morning. When she checked in on me, I pretended to be asleep. I had cried so much that night I'd run out of tears.

From that day, the rift between her and me grew wider and wider. She spent all her days and most of her evenings with Jeremy, and when I saw her in the mornings and sometimes on the school bus – the only occasions when we still spent time together – she seemed totally preoccupied.

She didn't share her thoughts with me anymore. She never said a single negative word about Jeremy and only ever told me how fantastic and beautiful and intelligent he was, you know? Most of our conversations revolved around what Jeremy thought about this and what Jeremy thought about that. It was tedious, and I began to really hate the guy, more than I'd ever hated anyone in my life. He had taken the only thing I ever really cared for away from me. He had changed my sister beyond recognition.

I think it must have been around that time that my health began to deteriorate. I mean, I obviously didn't plan this or anything, I just felt really down and lost my appetite and grew more and more listless. I spent a lot of time lying on my bed. I just didn't know what to do with my life without Julia in it. Mum tried to speak to me about Julia a couple of times, but in a fairly half-hearted way. She must have noticed that she couldn't really rely on Julia to care for my wellbeing anymore, and considered it her duty to at least pretend to care. One evening, when I had again refused to leave my bedroom and have supper with my parents, she came upstairs and sat with me on my bed. She took my hand and talked about first experiences of love, and explained they can be intense and all-consuming and all that. She said she was sure that Julia loved me just as much as before but that I had to give her some space for a while and allow her to explore her feelings. She said that Julia had been the most selfless and caring sister imaginable, and that I had to accept that there were parts of her life now in which I could no longer participate. She reminded me that I wasn't a child anymore, and that Julia had grown into a young woman. She suggested I get out more, find some friends, play sports, and so on. What any half-decent mother would say. I'm sure you can imagine it.

I lost a lot of weight in the first few weeks after Jeremy had destroyed the only close bond I ever had. I missed school a couple of times because I just felt too ill to face the outside world. On a Sunday afternoon, about two months after Jeremy had first asked her out, Julia returned home earlier than usual. She said she wanted to spend some time with me. She said she was worried about me and that she felt we'd lost touch. Those were exactly the words I'd been dying to hear for weeks, but when I finally did hear them I just couldn't believe that she really meant what she was saying. It had taken her too long, you know? Far too long. I kept thinking that our mother must have asked Julia to talk to me, that she'd much rather be with Jeremy and that I'd become nothing but a nuisance and a chore, a limp, sick albatross around her neck. But she still managed to coax me into getting dressed, and to go out and have coffee with her.

'What's wrong with you, Amy?' she asked when we were seated at a small table in the very same café where she and Jeremy had met for their first date, which I thought was a rather unfortunate choice, to be honest. 'Why have you stopped eating? Why do you spend all your time locked up in your room? I so wish you could be happy for me – I'm in love, you know? It's wonderful, and it'll happen to you soon, too, I'm sure. This should be a special time for me, but I feel like you're punishing me for something. I haven't abandoned you, you know? You're still my lovely little sister, and I care so much for you. Can't you see that? But I have to start living my own life, and you need to start living yours.'

I began to cry. I couldn't speak. This wasn't at all what I'd expected. A part of me had still been hoping that I'd become her confidante once again, like in the old days, that she'd finally admit that Jeremy wasn't that great after all, that he was terrible in bed and really boring company. But Julia wasn't impressed with my tears. Instead of hugging me, she sighed, rolled her eyes and ordered cake. It was pretty cold, I thought, to be honest.

'You really need to start eating again, Amy. Mum and Dad are terribly worried about you, and so am I. But I also feel that your little hunger strike is a bit passive-aggressive, as though you're trying to make me feel guilty. Don't do that to me, OK? Come on, let's be friends again. These cakes look delicious, don't they?'

It was a totally unfair accusation, and really infantilizing, too, and I didn't like it one bit. Then she started to talk about how wonderfully clever Jeremy and his friends were, what an exciting time she was having, how the two of them went to all kinds of political gatherings, and that their entire group of friends would travel to Cuba over the winter holidays for two weeks. She had long finished her cake – a large slice of Black Forest gateau – and I could tell that she was watching me and expecting me to eat mine, too, but I just couldn't swallow. I couldn't. I pushed bits of cake around my plate to give the impression I was engaging with my food, but every time I lifted my fork I felt like my throat was constricting and my mouth was going dry.

The next morning, Mum came up to my room and sat down on my bed again. She took my hand and suggested I see a therapist because she and Dad were extremely concerned about my weight loss – it was totally obvious to me that Julia had instructed her to do so. She was clearly trying to pass on responsibility to someone else once again, so that she could stop worrying about me. Someone who'd get paid for it, like a nanny or something. It was humiliating. But once a week for three years to come – until I, too, left home for university – I visited the consultancy of a woman called Molly Unsworth-Todd, who tried to help me to come to terms with what she called my 'issues with nurture'. But our sessions didn't help at all, as you can probably tell. I didn't like that woman, and I don't think she liked me much, either. Often, we sat in silence for almost the entire fifty minutes. It was pretty uncomfortable, actually. Most of the time, I just didn't feel like sharing anything with her. She wore this weirdly shaped small golden medallion on a chain around her neck, and I kept thinking that she'd somehow convince me to join some strange cult if I opened up to her. I also didn't like the way she folded her plump white little hands in her lap, like she was secretly praying to some obscure divinity. She was getting paid to listen to me, that was her job, and I just never believed her for a second when she said she cared, you know? I mean, obviously she didn't. She just did it for the money.

Julia did travel to Cuba, and apparently had an amazing time there, and she stayed together with Jeremy for another two months. But shortly before she finished school, she broke up with him – she'd decided quite suddenly that he was a total hypocrite, all words and no action. She seemed to get over the end of her relationship very quickly, in spite of what Mum had told me about the 'intensity' and 'all-consuming nature' of first love. She delivered a highly politicized speech at our school's end-of-year ceremony, which enraged some of the parents so much that they hissed and heckled. It was pretty amazing, really. Virtually all the school kids, in contrast, supported her, and we broke into loud 'Julia' chants that completely drowned out the parental sounds of discontent. Lots of parents got up and left the hall in protest. When she'd finished, Julia raised her right fist and smiled triumphantly – she looked stunning at that moment. Her long hair shone in the limelight, she had put on mauve lipstick that emphasized her pale, delicate skin, and she wore a simple black shift dress with old Doc Marten boots. Everyone who was still in the hall stood up and cheered. It was a totally memorable event, and even the local newspaper ran an article about the 'beautiful communist graduate' who had 'transformed a traditionally dull and peaceful ceremony into a generational battlefield'.

Just a couple of weeks later, Julia packed the super-light green backpack that my parents had given her together with a plane ticket as a reward for her amazing A-level results, and left for India. Before she departed for her gap year, we made a deal: Julia promised to email me as often as possible, and in return, I had to promise her to eat. In the few weeks between her breakup with Jeremy and her departure for India, we had grown a bit closer again. For the very last time, I felt like I was an important part of her life. She told me some pretty hilarious stories about Jeremy and his phony champagne-socialist friends – I think they all ended up really annoying her in the end. But otherwise, she focused all her energies on planning her trip. We'd sit cross-legged on the floor in her room, looking at maps together, deciding on routes and marking up her *Lonely Planet* guidebook. Her plan was to travel the country for three months and then join a volunteer organization based in Punjab that fought for fairer trade rules and economic justice for the agricultural labourers of the region. We ended up deciding that she'd spend three weeks in Mumbai, then travel south to Goa, where she was planning to visit some alternative communities and two yogis whom some friends had recommended to her. After about two months, she'd travel north, along the coast by bus and train, passing through Maharashtra, Gujarat and Rajasthan until she reached her volunteer post in a small village on the border with Pakistan.

I accompanied her on numerous shopping trips to buy her travel equipment: together, we chose heavy watertight walking boots and a pair of strong sandals; two sets of khaki-coloured cargo pants and white linen shirts; one fleece pullover; a good-quality rain-jacket; a pocket knife; pepper spray; a sleeping bag and a sleeping mat; a lightweight one-person tent and a tiny gas cooker. We'd often lie on her bed and she would read aloud to me the texts she was studying in preparation: histories of India and various books about economics, globalization and the fair-trade movement. She also started to read Salman Rushdie, but gave up on him almost immediately. She never really liked fiction.

My parents and Julia clashed over something a few weeks before she left. I heard their raised voices in the kitchen one night, long after supper, and I think I also heard Julia crying, but I never found out what it was all about. The door was firmly shut and I couldn't hear the details, no matter how hard I tried. She seemed strange and distant after that for a few days, wandering around dazed, like a sleepwalker, but then she gradually switched back to her normal lovely self.

We all accompanied her to Heathrow on the day of her departure. Even Jonathan had joined us to say goodbye. I'm pretty sure he was secretly relieved that she was leaving the country for a year. But I just couldn't stop crying. I simply couldn't believe that I wouldn't see her for twelve months. I had no idea how I'd even begin to get through the year without her. I was kind of hoping that she would hate it in India and miss me so badly that she'd come back early. I even secretly hoped that she'd get malaria or cholera or some other hideous disease, so that she'd be forced to come home and I could nurse her back to health. I still remember the moment she walked through passport control: straight and bright-eyed and full of anticipation, wearing the cargo pants we chose together and a white pullover, her hair braided into a long, thick plait. She turned back three times to wave at us all, blew me a final kiss, and then disappeared.

I checked my inbox almost hourly in the first days after she'd left – I was so desperate to hear from her, and to learn that she was safe, and find out what she was doing, you know? But her first email arrived only after two long weeks, and it was a lengthy and pretty angry report on the appalling scenes of poverty she'd witnessed in Mumbai. She wrote about beggar children whose parents had mutilated them in horrific ways so that they would elicit more generous donations from tourists. She wrote about the thousands of people who slept under bridges and on sidewalks and who didn't even own enough to cover their emaciated bodies with clothes or blankets. She wrote about the perverse contrast between the rich and the poor, and said it made her sick. She wrote that wherever she went she was pursued by a flock of ravenous, disease-ridden children who tore at her clothes and backpack, begging her for food and money. She wrote about the appalling attitudes to women she'd witnessed and the primitive sense of sexual entitlement of Indian men. There was nothing personal at all in her message, and my heart sank when I realized that it wasn't even addressed to me directly but to a long list of friends and family to whom she had promised updates from her travels. Almost all of her subsequent emails from India were similar. I sent her long, regular emails about my own admittedly pretty uneventful and empty days, but only very rarely received a personal message in response. Usually, she told me that she hoped I was eating well and that she thought of me and that we were all terribly fortunate and owed the world some compensation for our privileges.

She ended up not following our carefully developed travel plan at all, and left Goa after just one week. She wrote that she had no interest in the drug and clubbing culture she encountered there, and that in fact she utterly despised it. Yoga, meditation and various other spiritual practices and doctrines people down there were interested in didn't strike her as valid preoccupations either – she thought that the yogis and their mainly Western followers she visited were hypocrites, privileging the pseudo-enlightenment of a chosen few over the much more urgent task of redistributing wealth and establishing fairer economic conditions for the many. Or something like that. Her emails had become quite ranty in tone. She travelled through hundreds of small villages and visited numerous factories and farms on her way up north. She'd also inspected some sweatshops, and described in extremely graphic detail the conditions she saw there. Then she forbade everyone on her mailing list from buying textiles produced by a long catalogue of Western companies which she said mercilessly exploited Indian women and children. Every single one of my favourite brands was on that list. We could all tell that she'd become restless, and increasingly impatient to do something about all the horrors she was witnessing on her travels. In the end, she took up her work placement one month earlier than originally planned.

Once she was installed in Punjab, her messages to us became less and less frequent. The organization she was working for was helping local wheat and palm-oil farmers to secure fair-trade deals: I think they provided practical, financial and legal support, that kind of stuff. Julia wrote a few articles about the initiative that were published in various British newspapers. She spent a lot of time interviewing the villagers in the Pakistani border area about their daily plight and she uncovered some totally scandalous practices for which two very well-known Western companies were responsible.

After five months, her very infrequent personal messages to me dried up completely. It's probably fair to say that she broke her part of our deal. I think that compared to the sufferings she encountered in India on a daily basis, my own issues must have paled into insignificance. I can't really blame her, I guess. I know that my problems are boring. But it still hurt really badly that she just completely ripped me out of her life, like a weed or something.

When she returned after twelve months I felt she'd changed. She talked mainly about economics and political stuff. She reacted quite badly to the fact that I was still battling with my weight, and told me really brutally that I needed to get a grip and snap out of that phase. She said it made her incredibly sad that I, who had everything and all kinds of privileges, wasn't able to appreciate my gifts, and that I should travel to India sometime to see what children who aren't starving for fun but for real look like. It was a pretty horrible thing to say. I felt like she wasn't really interested in hearing about how I was. When I tried to talk to her, she seemed distracted and impatient.

Shortly after her return, she left home to study PPE at St John's College, Oxford. And then I just didn't see her very often anymore. Only at big family gatherings, really. She sent me birthday cards, but that was it. Even when I was hospitalized for five weeks – I was being force-fed against my will – Julia didn't come to visit. Not once. I mean, that's pretty extreme, isn't it?

She graduated, with a sky-high First, of course, and then went to Edinburgh to take up a scholarship to study for an MA. You probably know the rest of the story. About halfway through her programme, she dropped out and went travelling again, with someone she'd met up in Scotland, I think. We didn't hear much from her during that period, apart from the odd postcard. Mum and Dad worried a lot about her, and so did I. After about two years, she came back to London. Again I only really saw her at family gatherings, and even then very rarely. I don't know what she did all day here. She had weird friends – people in radical political groups, activist types. The one person who was still in regular contact with her was Dad, and he was under the impression that she went to a lot of demonstrations and occupations and anti-globalization gatherings, and that kind of thing. The last two times we saw her, on Christmas Day last year and on Dad's sixtieth birthday, were strained. She was pretty caustic and seemed on the war path with everyone. During Dad's birthday dinner she made a long, passionate speech against the consumption of meat that just about spoiled everyone's appetite. I guess she thought we were all hypocrites or something.

I don't know what to say about the attack. I really don't. I haven't seen Julia since it happened. I still can't believe that my sister is supposed to have murdered all those people. She must have been corrupted by someone. I don't think she's well. The person who came back from those trips wasn't the Julia I knew and loved. Something must have happened to her abroad. Someone must have radicalized her. Perhaps it even started as far back as with that Jeremy guy. One bad friend after another, you know? I wish she'd stayed with me; I wish I'd never lost her. Together, we could have done anything. She only ever wanted to make the world a better place. I really don't know what to say about the attack. She totally broke my parents' hearts. And mine.

IV

Amy seemed so starved of human contact, and so awfully thin, and so terribly fragile both physically and mentally, that I decided to contact her parents and her supervisor at UCL to alert them to her condition straight after our second meeting. Her supervisor emailed back right away and thanked me for my concern, but explained there was nothing they could do since Amy had been battling with anorexia for many years and was refusing treatment. Amy's parents didn't get back to me until later.

Amy's story troubled me, on various levels. Although I *did* find her account utterly heart-wrenching (and there is no doubt that she really was and still is suffering), I couldn't help but feel that there was also a passive-aggressive impulse that was driving her to starve herself to death. Anorexia is one of those conditions that is masochistic only on the surface. After all, while Amy is getting some (admittedly very sad and twisted) form of pleasure from her physical vanishing act, she is forcing those who love her to watch helplessly from the sidelines. Most acts of self-destruction are ultimately fuelled by reproach. You observed something similar once about Lailah: sometimes, you told me, you could catch fleeting glimpses of the furious hatred behind your wife's limp and lifeless facade – and it made your blood freeze.

Although Julia's manner of dealing with Amy's pain seemed hard, I could at least partly understand her reaction: her refusal to play the role that Amy wanted her to play in her psychodrama was also a refusal to be coerced into feeling guilty when, in fact, she had done nothing wrong. After all, what seems to have triggered Amy's rapid physical decline is simply the fact that Julia had fallen in love with someone and subsequently loosened her sister's dependency on her, which had, in any case, become decidedly odd. Perhaps she severed these strings too abruptly. But then again, being in love *can* be overpowering. I had to fight very hard not to lose focus when we got together for the first time, George – it cost me all my energy and willpower. I could have succumbed so easily to the impulse to let our relationship transform all my priorities and everything I ever cared for, in that radical, fairy-tale metamorphosis kind of way. But something in me resisted it. Whether it was genuinely my love of work, as I thought back then, or perhaps fear, I don't know. And I still believe that you never forgave me for that.

In any case, it was strange that Julia responded to her sister's psychological problems so strongly, almost with aversion, and that her affection for Amy, which appeared deep and genuine, could have been stifled so abruptly. But even that reaction, I am ashamed to admit, wasn't one that was completely unfamiliar to me. Amy's story reminded me of a scene when Amanda and I were teenagers. I think I might have told you about it, during that phase when we told each other (almost) everything about ourselves, when we, with a mixture of anxiety and shy pride, spread out the darker details of our past lives before each other, hoping that they, too, would be met with approval. When I was young, I was driven by an insatiable curiosity. My mind was always busy – I read everything I could lay my hands on, indiscriminately, sucking up all kinds of information like a starved sponge; I wrote; I loved to argue; I liked to be among people; I was always pursuing projects. I wished the days had a hundred hours, and I simply didn't have time for teenage angst, skipping that phase completely. But Amanda didn't, and when she was fourteen and I was sixteen, it began to affect our relationship. I think in some strange way it still does.

Even you admitted once that Amanda is much more beautiful than me. I have always thought that she looks like a skilfully Photoshopped and more feminine version of me: she is taller and her figure is fuller, her skin is purer and smoother, her hair longer and glossier. Her hair colour, too, is much more striking than mine, a richer, deeper shade of the dark burgundy that both of us inherited from our mother. Hers always made me think of moist Tuscan clay sizzling in the sun. Amanda would never be seen without mascara and her signature stardust-coloured eye-shadow, both of which further enhance the beauty of her eyes, which are ice-blue just like mine, only bigger and better – like everything else about her. Even her voice is smooth and sweet, while mine has more than once been compared to a scratchy jazz record, and, not very flatteringly, to that of a chain-smoking nightclub singer. Yet, in spite of all this, it was Amanda and not I who became obsessed with her appearance when she crossed the thorny threshold into adulthood, and she found it sorely wanting: her weight, her skin, her hair, her style – she began to dislike *everything* about herself. Soon, all her energy was consumed internally, used up in the perpetuation of self-flagellating thoughts. I hated seeing her doing that to herself; it pained me and I just couldn't understand where it was coming from.

It is such a sad female speciality, self-hatred – I see it everywhere, even here, even among the most intimidating and seemingly confident-looking women: they over- or else under-eat, they cut themselves, they drink, they smoke, they take drugs, they fall for people they can't have or who treat them like shit, they cover their skins with crude tattoos that, like marks of Cain, loudly announce to all and sundry that they have broken the law, and not one of them uses her time to enhance her prospects for post-prison life. Instead, they turn on each other just to pass the time. Every day, the guards have to intervene in the many scuffles that keep breaking out. But so far, they all leave me be – even the most belligerent ones. I don't know why. Perhaps word has got round about my crime. Perhaps that knowledge scares them as much as it scares me. I try not to think about it.

Amanda had always been shy, but in her teens her timidity became so extreme that she would barely speak a word unless she was among family. She didn't go out much and passed entire days alone in her bedroom, doing nothing; she struggled at school and grew ever more reclusive and lifeless, as though she was wilting on the inside. I realized just how much she had changed one Saturday in August. It was our great-aunt Myrtle's birthday. As every year, Myrtle held a grand garden party in her Hampstead home. All our relatives and many of my parents' friends came; attendance was a family obligation. Some cousins and nieces travelled all the way from France and Germany to be there.

'She says she's not coming,' my father said in a low voice. My mother wrung her hands. Dressed up and ready to go, they were standing at the bottom of the stairs, looking uneasily at the closed door of my sister's room on the first floor, as though something bad they couldn't quite grasp was happening behind it. Although they didn't speak about it, they had been worrying about Amanda in their quiet way for months. I found their silent sadness unbearable, and decided to go up and shake Amanda out of her stupor.

'Amanda, I'm coming in,' I called before opening her bedroom door. The air in her room was heavy with sweat and misery – it was a sweltering day, but her windows were closed and the curtains drawn, and my sister was lying fully clothed on her bed.

'God, it's stuffy in here!' I said before drawing the curtain and opening her window.

Amanda moaned and covered her face with her hands, as though the sunlight was hurting her eyes.

'Dad said you're not coming. We always go – Aunt Myrtle will be heartbroken if she doesn't get to pinch your cheeks this year. Honestly, Amanda, get your act together. You know that Mum and Dad are too nice to force you, but they'll be terribly disappointed if you don't come. And why wouldn't you? Look, it's such a lovely day!'

'I can't,' Amanda said.

'What do you mean, you can't? It's not like you've lined up an exciting alternative programme for the day, is it? A bit of sunlight will do you good.'

'I can't,' she repeated.

'Why not?'

'Can't face it.'

'Can't face *what*? It's our family – it's not like you'd be walking into a place filled with hostile strangers. They all love you and would be really sad not to see you.' I was genuinely puzzled.

Amanda sat up and glared at me. 'I know you don't understand, but I just can't. Everything always seems so easy to you. I never know what to say to anyone. I freeze up; I get flustered and stiff. People don't feel comfortable around me. I'm so awkward it's infectious. I embarrass them.'

I didn't know what to say. I had been aware that Amanda had confidence issues, but I had never realized just how crippling and deep-seated they were. Besides, she had said these things sharply, almost aggressively, as though the whole matter was somehow my fault.

'But sweetie,' I said eventually. 'This is *crazy*. You're clever and interesting and original, and lovely besides, and totally gorgeous. I don't understand what you're talking about. Everyone loves you – I think people like you much more than they like me, in fact. *I'm* the one who annoys people. I talk too much and too loudly and I'm terribly opinionated and I laugh like a drunken hyena at my own jokes. I'd always prefer your company to mine.'

Amanda started to cry, and I tried to take her hand, but she pulled it away. 'Bullshit,' she sobbed. 'That's bullshit. You just don't get it. You just can't understand what it feels like to have no skin, to be constantly afraid of what others might think or say. It's hell; I don't want to go out ever again. I hate talking to others.'

'But sis, I really can't follow you,' I said. 'That's all in your head. Nobody thinks that of you. Nobody. Really. Everyone thinks you're lovely – perhaps a little shy, but that's a good thing. Shy people are much nicer and better listeners. I'd say everyone actually prefers the company of a shy person to that of annoying blabbering extroverts. Like me. Really. I mean it.'

Amanda didn't respond.

'Come on,' I said after a while. 'I'll stay at your side, OK? I can always just step in if you can't think of anything to say. I'll just make some stupid offensive jokes as usual.'

But Amanda turned her back to me and pulled her duvet over her head.

'Seriously?' I said. 'You really aren't coming? But you won't even have to worry about small talk! I mean it. I'll do it for you, OK? Come on – let's go. Mum and Dad are waiting downstairs.'

But Amanda remained silent, ignoring all my further attempts to change her mind. Eventually I gave up and left the room, and we went to the party without her. Somehow, her refusal to attend the party felt like a watershed moment. It was from that day on that we understood that what we had thought was a phase went deeper, but we couldn't really grasp what it was. Worse, we had no idea how to help her.

What is more – and I am not proud of this, George – at some point Amanda's causeless sadness and her passivity began to infuriate me. I wasn't sympathetic to her state of mind – the self-pity and the dull darkness of it all. Somehow, it smelled bad, like a forgotten sock rotting in the washing machine. I wanted the old Amanda back, but I didn't know where to find her. Most of the time I just wanted to shake her and to tell her to snap out of it. Once I really did shake her, and she was flapping to and fro, like a sack of flour, with no tension or resistance. Yet there was also something about her weakness that must quite simply have terrified me – I can see that now.

In any case, I left home and then so did she, and at university she slowly got better, discovered her ersatz religion, and found men who – for a while at least – managed to make her happy, before they abandoned her and tore open her old wounds and she had to start all over again. What really helped her permanently was Laura – even though the two of them don't always have an easy relationship.

Sometimes I suspect that deep down Amanda blames *me* for what has happened, that it is somehow payback for my life choices. Sometimes I even wonder whether she doesn't secretly feel just a little bit vindicated, behind all her caring and worrying. Think about it: I rejected everything that has shaped her own life and that she values: motherhood, marriage, career sacrifice. For a long time it looked as though everything I did was blessed somehow. I was always the more successful one of the two of us. Until it all dissolved into thin air. But, of course, Amanda's own happiness-plan has not worked out quite so well, either – just like me, she is alone now, but *after* having dedicated the best years of her life to two worthless exploiter types, *after* two cripplingly expensive and time-consuming divorces, and *after* so much heartache. And I still think she is wasting her talents on all those people with too much time and money on their hands, who lie on her couch day after day (sometimes for years), complaining about the fact that their mothers were cold and their fathers absent. But then again, who am I to cast judgement, on anyone? After all, I am the one who's in prison now, and whose life is in ruins.

I'm digressing. But I have been thinking about my relationship with Amanda a lot, lately. I'm sad about all those barriers between us, and I don't mean the literal one. I miss her, I feel more than ever the distance between us, which, in some strange way, started to emerge on the day of Myrtle's garden party, and my inability to coax her out of her dark hole and to properly understand and connect with her pain.

What I couldn't help thinking after my encounter with Amy was that Julia's abrupt abandonment of her sister seemed caused not only by the refusal to be made to feel guilty and the subliminal fear of contagion that witnessing weakness can provoke – we sometimes turn to anger in order better to defend ourselves against it. In Julia's case, the decision to turn her back on her sister seemed driven by a *moral* judgement: it almost sounded as though she considered Amy's illness an insult, a slap in the face of those who were struggling with 'real' problems – poverty, illness, political disenfranchisement. But is it legitimate to privilege one form of suffering over another, and to arrange it into neat hierarchies in such a simplistic manner? Is mental anguish really less worthy or serious than socio-political or physical forms of distress? What of the sufferings of the soul? After all, they can be fatal, too.

V

Nothing much is happening here; time hangs heavily and the minutes crawl past. The other day, after lunch, someone else entered the small library, which I had discovered on my second day and have had all to myself so far. It was the black woman with the expressionless face. She nodded briskly, but then ignored me. I watched her while pretending to continue reading the paper. I would love to speak to her – I'm so starved of decent conversation – but I didn't dare say anything.

I have consented to taking sleeping pills – I just can't cope with the images that haunt me so, especially at night. I had a medical check-up the other day and the doctor wasn't happy with my weight, which continues to hover on the low side. Neither did he like my drawn, tired look, nor my low blood pressure. He asked whether I felt depressed. I didn't even know how to begin to answer that question. Who doesn't feel depressed here? And how could one not, all things considered? I have no idea yet if and how I will be able to live with what I've done. Amanda and Laura try very hard to keep up my spirits – they send me books and clothes, and pictures and plants and other such things from the world I have lost. To fill the silences during their visits and phone calls, they tell me droll little stories, about trying patients and impertinent customers and mad food critics and so on. But I just don't have much to say to them right now. What I really want to talk about I can't, not yet.

Jonathan White, Julia's older brother, neither responded to my first letter nor agreed to take any of my follow-up phone calls. But I am used to people refusing to speak to me when I first approach them. My next strategy was to confront him directly. Once I get a chance to speak to people face to face, I usually succeed in convincing them to open up to me.

Jonathan works as a Senior Asset Manager at J.P. Morgan. I called his PA under a false pretext and managed to find out that he usually leaves his office around 7.30 in the evening. I had, after all, done research in the City before (although I sincerely wish I'd never set a foot in that world). At 7.15 p.m. on 15 August, an airless, oppressive Wednesday, I took up my position next to the revolving doors of the high-rise glass and steel building on Canary Wharf that houses the J.P. Morgan offices, and carefully observed every man in his early thirties who passed through them. I had been able to find an old picture of Jonathan online, and hoped I would be able to identify him on that basis. At 7.32 p.m., a strongly built, pale-looking man in an expensively tailored suit exited the building. He wore his light-brown hair slicked back. His hairline was receding – but methodically, as though following a plan, like a well-trained army retreating in perfect synchrony, leaving two sharp triangular recesses on each side of his forehead. He looked nothing like Julia, but I knew he was my man.

'Jonathan White?' I asked him. He flinched when he heard his name, and quickened his pace. He was heading towards the Tube station entry on the other side of the square.

'I don't talk to journalists,' he barked at me. His tone was an odd combination of hectic and fierce, as though he was undecided whether to suffer a nervous breakdown or to erupt into violence. 'Make an appointment with my PA if your query concerns Morgan business, and get lost if it doesn't.'

'My name is Clare Hardenberg,' I said, trying to keep up with him. 'I sent you a letter. I'm writing a book about your sister. I've already spoken to Amy and... '

'Get lost,' Jonathan shouted, 'I won't talk to you. And leave my family alone! Don't you people have any respect? Can't you imagine how traumatic this is for us? What on earth makes you think we'd want to discuss this tragedy with a random stranger who has come to spread lies and gossip about us?' Red patches had appeared on his neck and began to spread across his cheeks and forehead. I noticed this with interest. Anger can provide a way in. If one plays one's cards right.

'You're wrong. It's precisely out of respect for your family that I'm trying to speak to you,' I responded. I, too, had raised my voice. I'd expected him to use that argument. 'I want to hear *your* side of the story. And for your information, I'm not writing the kind of sensationalist, gossip-mongering book that you imagine. But believe me, these books *will* be written, and not just one of them – very soon, there'll be a flood of unauthorized biographies of your sister in every bookshop in the country, and you and your family will feature prominently in every one of them, whether you like it or not. That's the reality of the situation. You're a clever man – you know that there are thousands of people out there who'll want to cash in on the drama. That *is* going to happen – it's beyond your control to stop it.'

Jonathan glanced at me and narrowed his eyes.

'What you *can* control,' I continued, 'is the narrative in the very first study of Julia that will come out – mine. I'm fast, I'm good, and I'll win the race. The first book that'll come out will determine what comes after it. That's how it works. I'm offering you and your family the opportunity to shape your own story *with* me. Otherwise, the public perception of you and your parents will be shaped *for* you, by whatever comes after my book, and trust me, you don't want that to happen.'

Jonathan was still marching along in fast, long strides, and we'd already crossed about two-thirds of the square. He didn't respond to my speech. I could see that he was clenching his jaw. Then, by chance, while I was desperately trying to keep up with him, I caught a glimpse of his wedding ring on the hand that was carrying his briefcase. It was wider and shinier than your average ring – a purposeful statement. I decided to try another approach. I didn't have much time. Once he reached the Tube station entrance, I would lose him for good.

'Jonathan, do you know what the public's gut response to people like your sister is? It's to blame their parents. You can thank Freud for that, but it's a statistical fact that 98 per cent of the British public believes that those who commit violent crimes come from broken homes and must have been subjected to severe physical or psychological abuse themselves.' (I confess I made up that statistic on the spur of the moment. I have no idea what the actual numbers are.) 'Most people believe that violence is bred by violence. Do you want the public to think that about your family? I've spoken to Amy at length, and it wasn't at all my impression that you were brought up in an atmosphere of abuse and neglect. But that's what everyone – and I'm telling you, *everyone* – will think.'

Jonathan still didn't respond, and I had to deliver my final lines fast.

'And let me tell you something else: the vast majority of Julia's biographers will pursue *precisely* this line of enquiry. Cod-psychologizing is the oldest and cheapest trick in the biographer's handbook, and some of my colleagues are unimaginative and ruthless bastards. They'll mercilessly shine the light on your family; they'll exaggerate small details and blow things completely out of proportion; they'll twist the facts or make them up; they'll speak to "friends of the family" who'll be more than happy to report all kinds of fantasy horror stories, particularly about your mother. Mothers tend to attract most of the hostility. It's sad but true. Society nowadays likes to blame the mother. That's why I need *you* to play an active part in my investigation.

We need to pre-empt this default response. I think we can do it if you decide to work with me. If you care just a tiny little bit for your parents, you'll help me to prevent this from happening. I don't know how your parents are doing right now, but things will get so much worse for them if you don't act.'

I decided to take a risk and to stop walking at that point. Besides, I was completely out of breath. My heart was pounding hard. I also had to be careful not to seem too desperate; I needed to make it clear that if we were to collaborate I was doing him a favour just as much as he was doing me one. I had to signal that I could easily write my book without him. And I had just played my last and most powerful card. Would he press on or would he turn around? I was standing at the edge of Reuter Square, trying to steady my breathing. Out of the corner of my eye, on the big outdoor screen towering above the plaza, I could see the stock market information flashing past in red numerals, like a column of frenzied fire ants. We were perilously close to the escalators that led down into the crowded belly of the Tube station. If he reached them, that would be it. But after a moment that seemed like an eternity, Jonathan did slow down, and then he stopped, and then he turned around. I'd guessed right – he was a family man. He was standing about ten metres away from me, and he looked at me properly for the first time. I'd dressed up for the occasion, and was wearing a sharp white satin shirt, a black leather pencil skirt and mauve suede heels. After having looked me up and down, he rubbed his eyes with his fists, like a tired child unwilling to wake up. For a moment, he looked terribly vulnerable. But then he pulled his shoulders back, pushed his chin forward, and walked towards me.

'What are your credentials,' he barked when he was standing right in front of me. 'Who are you working for and what else have you written.' He was one of those people who didn't change the intonation at the end of their sentences when they asked questions.

I told him.

He hesitated for another few seconds, but then he pulled a card from his wallet and handed it to me. 'Call my secretary and make an appointment.' And then he turned round and disappeared down the escalator.

I arranged a meeting with him three days later, on Saturday morning at his home. Unlike Amy, he didn't want to speak to me in a public place. Jonathan lives in a neat white Georgian townhouse in Chelsea, on a neat white little square not far from the King's Road. Inside, the house was stylish in a fashion-catalogue kind of way, with polished hardwood floors, numerous orchids in white ceramic pots, an assembly of modern vases, and decorative artworks on the walls, the colours of which matched carefully selected items of designer furniture. The only signs of life were a few kids' toys scattered in the hallway and the living room. Jonathan asked me to sit on a black leather chaise longue in the drawing room, and offered coffee. He seemed nervous, much less confident than on the square. His wife and two kids were in Surrey for the weekend, he told me, to visit family.

'How old are your kids?' I asked him when he returned with an expertly brewed espresso that had no doubt come from a shiny Italian designer coffee machine.

That got him talking a little. I learned that he had two girls, Eleanor and Elsa, who were five and two, and whom he clearly loved to bits. His wife, Susanna, designed vases. She had a little pottery workshop in the backyard, and sold some of her designs to boutiques in Islington and at craft markets in the Cotswolds.

Then Jonathan asked a number of legal questions concerning the book (he had done his research), and demanded the right to see and edit his interview before it was printed. I was happy to grant him this request, and, having settled these formalities, he started to tell me his side of the story.

Below I include the version Jonathan finally approved. As in Amy's case, I slightly reordered and shaped his account, while trying to remain faithful to his voice. I should also mention that Jonathan did make use of the editorial rights he negotiated – he sent back the original transcript of our conversation heavily marked up; there were various things on which he decided to elaborate further in writing and quite a few he decided to cut (including most of the expletives, of which he used surprisingly many during our meeting, particularly towards the end). We had to exchange numerous drafts until he was fully happy with the result. The following text is based on an interview conducted on 18 August 2014, and was revised and amended six times between 21 August and 6 September 2014.

VI

We are decent people. My childhood was a happy one. I love my parents and I care deeply for Amy. Contrary to what the media have insinuated, we used to be a perfectly normal and, all things considered, a happy family. I always hoped for nothing more than to live life just like my parents did. Timothy White, my father, is a highly successful corporate lawyer who specializes in international mergers and acquisitions. He is one of the very best in the country. He became a partner at his firm when he was just twenty-six. He was a genuine hot-shot, and his career has gone from strength to strength ever since. My mother, Rose, is a senior cardiologist at the Wellington Hospital. She saves lives on a daily basis. She, too, has thrived in her profession, and is highly respected in her field. They are decent, hard-working people. I am very proud of both of them. My father is a truly inspirational figure. I still look up to him, in spite of the difficulties we have faced as a result of my sister. My parents didn't deserve this. None of it.

Both love their professions, but they also very much love their children. All of them, even my sister. Especially my sister, I should say. Until the bombing, of course. But even now they probably still love her. They sent all of us to the best schools money could buy, even when they had temporarily fallen on hard times because of an unfortunate stock-market deal. It was the only imprudent financial decision Dad ever made. Usually, his instincts are spot-on. In fact, it is from him that I have learned my own humble investment skills.

Although both my parents worked in very demanding professions, they always made a point of being home in time for supper with us. No matter how busy they were. Our family suppers were sacred. You could only be excused in exceptional circumstances. Every evening, we would sit together for hours, even long after the meal had finished. There was a lot of talk and laughter. Dad is a fantastic storyteller. He always made us giggle. At weekends, he would do the cooking. On top of all his other talents, he is also fantastic in the kitchen. He cooked all our favourite dishes: pizza, lasagne, and sausages and mash. Often, my sister and I would help him in the kitchen. He happily delegated even complicated tasks to us. He strongly believed that children should be challenged. I agree with him. It is vital for character formation and confidence building. I am trying to pass these values on to my own children, too.

At the age of eleven, Julia decided to become a vegetarian. She had watched a documentary on TV about the plight of chickens and other farm animals, and declared it unethical to torture and kill sentient creatures for our culinary pleasures. As far as I know, she never touched a piece of meat thereafter. She could be very determined that way. Or fanatical. However you want to describe it. My parents still cooked meat for the rest of us, but always prepared her a little extra vegetarian option. Mushroom pizza, aubergine-tomato lasagne, that kind of thing. Dad used to stick a little green paper flag in my sister's dishes, to highlight their meat-free status. She loved that, of course. It made her feel special. And righteous. She has always had an I-am-holier-than-thou attitude, a moral superiority complex. Even as a child. Unfortunately, my parents always took my sister's whims seriously. No matter how absurd they were.

When I was ten we went on a long summer holiday to Spain. Dad had rented a big camper, and we drove all the way from Madrid through Castilla-La Mancha to Andalucía. We had an incredible time. I don't know how my parents managed. Julia was seven and Amy just three. Amy cried a lot as a child. She was quite poorly from birth and my mother worried about her constantly. But generally they were laid back about everything. Each morning, we just headed off into the unknown. Dad used to let me sit right next to him while he was driving. He would tell me all about the advantages and disadvantages of the various makes of cars that passed, and stories about how the Moors used to rule in that land and how their empire had fallen. On a few occasions, all camping sites in the area were full and we parked our camper in a wild meadow for the night instead.

In the evenings, we always built a fire. My sister and I would go and gather the firewood. We would conscientiously arrange it exactly in the way Dad had shown us: putting small pieces of bark and kindling in the centre and arranging the bigger logs in a tepee structure above them. Dad plays the guitar. Very well, actually. He used to be in a folk band and they even produced an album before I was born. After supper, when we were all gathered around the fire, he and my mother would sing old English ballads together. My sister and I took turns holding Amy on these occasions, so that my mother could focus on the singing. She has a beautiful voice.

Dad and I used to have a special relationship. He can chat away to anyone – cleaners, janitors, CEOs, politicians. He is a great small-talker and makes people immediately feel at ease. When I was young he would sometimes take me hiking with his male friends in the Lake District. Later, when I was a teenager, he would talk to me at length after work about some of his cases and explain to me in detail the complex financial and legal decisions his clients were facing. I learned so much from him. My interest in finance and business was definitely stimulated by my dad. It was only because of my sister that there were tensions between us.

When I was eleven I developed an interest in British military history. I started to collect little tin soldiers, the kind you had to paint yourself. The tin soldiers were another thing over which Dad and I bonded. We would spend many evenings after supper in the games room, painting different types of more or less historically accurate uniforms onto the blank figurines. While we were painting, Dad would tell me about heroic British military achievements in the Napoleonic Wars and during the Normandy landings. I never wanted to hear about losses and defeats. We would re-create famous battles on a big wooden board with our painted mini-troops. One evening we were about to set up our armies for the Battle of Waterloo. Both of us had been looking forward to it for days. But then we noticed something appalling when we opened the box in which our soldiers were kept: every single one of the figurines had either an arm or a leg missing. Sometimes both. With painstaking precision and iron determination, someone had broken off the limbs of about two hundred tiny tin soldiers. A few of them even had their heads removed, probably with a small metal saw or pliers.

Dad and I had no doubts about who the author of the tin soldier massacre was. My sister, who was about eight years old at the time, must have dedicated an entire day to her dark task. I was terribly upset about my mutilated toys, and started to cry. I demanded she be punished for what she had done. Dad took me in his arms and tried to calm me down. We sat there for a long time. He murmured soothing words into my ears and stroked my hair. Later, we went up to Julia's room, hand in hand, to confront her. Julia and Amy were lying on the carpet. I think they were looking at an illustrated fairy-tale book together.

'Julia,' Dad said gently but firmly, 'why did you destroy Jonathan's toys? Look how upset he is!'

'I'm sorry, Daddy; I didn't mean to upset Jonathan. But that's what happens in wars: people lose their arms and legs and sometimes much more than that, and many people die all the time. I saw it on TV. War is not something fun, you know. It's not a game.'

I was far from satisfied with that explanation. I still believe that she did what she did purely out of jealousy and spite rather than to educate me, as she claimed. But Dad could, as so often, see her point. Julia can be very convincing. She is an expert manipulator of people. Unfortunately, Dad wasn't immune to her powers of persuasion. I fear he still isn't, even now, after everything she did. He gave Julia a little half-hearted sermon on the value of other people's property and their right to explore things in their own way, even if she had different opinions on the matter. But he didn't mean it. Even then I could see that secretly he was enormously proud of his daughter, who was so intelligent and articulate and original and mature beyond her years. He tried to hide it then and there. He probably felt he owed it to me to be stern with her and to take my anguish seriously. But just two hours later, when I went back into the games room to take another look at the calamity that had befallen my troops, I saw Julia sitting on his lap. Dad's eyes were shining with pride. He spoke with an animation that I never noticed when he was talking to me.

The first thing I ever openly disagreed about with Dad was my sister's perverse relationship with Amy. Just look at her now: she is a physical and psychological wreck, and she has been in that state for years. I firmly believe that Amy was my sister's first true victim. Julia played a sick game with the poor girl. To the outside world it looked as though she was a saintly super-sister, who had altruistically taken it upon herself to care for her poorly younger sibling. In reality, however, she had fucked Amy up from the very start. Moreover, I am convinced she did it on purpose. Now more so than ever.

Julia always needed followers. She enjoyed having a little groupie-admirer kid-sister trailing behind her throughout her teens. It made her look good. She loved power games and manipulating others. And she first honed her dark art on Amy. Amy was her creature: a star-struck and utterly defenceless devotee. And when Julia got bored with Amy she just dropped her overnight, without warning. The cruel rejection she suffered at the hands of her adored sister broke Amy completely. She has never recovered from it.

I tried to reason with my parents about that issue many times, but they were too in awe of Julia. They thought the sun shone out of her arse. In their view, she was perfection incarnate: beautiful, good, clever, brave and oh-so-caring. They just couldn't see the psychotic hatred beneath her pretty exterior. We had numerous arguments about Julia's corruption of Amy. Especially about all the age-inappropriate activities to which she dragged her along. No sane person would like it if their ten-year-old sister were taken to violent political protests, or to the local cemetery where all the junkies hung out, or to all kinds of dubious parties. But my sister had wrapped everyone in my family so tightly around her finger that they always sided with her. I, on the other hand, got a reputation for being an uncool conservative killjoy as a result of my attempts to protect Amy. Even Amy never thanked me for it. On the contrary, I think she felt I was her enemy. Julia had corrupted her so deeply that she never fully trusted me. She still doesn't. We are not very close.

My parents were strangely blind with regard to my sister's true nature. They just wouldn't listen to me. Their persistent misjudgement of her character really is the only thing for which I blame them. But then again, it was intricately bound up with the qualities I cherish most: their tolerance, their family loyalty and their generosity. They simply never really believed in the existence of evil in people, least of all in their beloved daughter.

There were numerous incidents that should have made my parents' alarm bells ring. One occurred when Julia was fifteen and I was eighteen, in my final year at school. It was early summer, a few weeks before the end of term. There was a heatwave and everyone was tense. All of a sudden, stories began to circulate about a PE teacher at our school, Johnny Harris. He was rumoured to have touched girls inappropriately. Personally, I never believed these stories. Mr Harris had taught me for two years and I had never seen him touch anyone in an improper manner. He was simply a tactile teacher, an old-fashioned sports instructor. He would put his hands on both girls and boys when showing them how to mount and dismount the pommel horse. There was nothing dubious about that, in my view. But there is so much paranoia about sexual abuse around these days that he probably did make himself vulnerable to criticism by doing things the way he did.

In any case, a growing number of girls grew hysterical about him. My sister was aware of the stories that were circulating. I could see her having hushed discussions with a small group of older girls after school. I suspected they were up to something. My sister wasn't even in any of Mr Harris's classes, but had nevertheless decided to fight the cause of the other girls who were complaining about him. In my view, the whole affair was a witch-hunt.

Back then already, Julia was entirely devoid of scruples when it came to achieving her aims. One day she drugged Mr Harris's coffee during lunch. How exactly she did that I never found out. Perhaps she used some of my mother's sleeping pills. When he was fast asleep in a soft chair in the gym, she sneaked in and with pink superglue wrote 'PERV' on his forehead. I will never forget the hurt and bewildered look on the man's face when he rushed past us in the corridor a few hours later, after someone had found and woken him. The defamatory word was clearly legible for all to see.

Julia was caught entering and leaving the gym on CCTV. She was summoned by the headmaster that very afternoon. Our parents were called in, too. But my sister must once again have delivered one of her manipulative speeches, since she was never punished for what she did. Instead, Mr Harris was forced to accept a package and to resign. There was never any solid evidence against him apart from the hyped-up stories of a few pubescent girls. Four years ago, by pure chance, I read in the papers that he had been killed by a train on a small level-crossing in Sussex. It didn't sound like an accident to me.

I think Julia has always hated me. When she was younger, she treated me with open hostility, and later with cold contempt and mockery. I suppose in her twisted view of the world I stood for everything she despised most. In her eyes, I was the epitome of self-satisfied bourgeois normality. I never had a teenage rebellious phase; I never wallowed in angst; I have never felt guilty about my privileges, just blessed. I always believed that a good work ethic, self-discipline and intelligence can get you anywhere, regardless of your background. I always had concrete aims and realizable dreams, and I worked bloody hard to achieve them. I am not ashamed of anything I have done.

When I was seventeen I told my family that I had decided to study for a business degree. Julia just laughed out loud, in that scornful way that she masters so well. Then she said: 'Of course you have, Jonathan. What else would you study?' When I announced to my family a few years later that Susanna and I had decided to get married she rolled her eyes and once again laughed out loud.

'How cuuuuute,' she said. 'Congratulations!'

There was so much loathing in her voice that Susanna, who was present, was really taken aback. She just couldn't understand where Julia's contempt was coming from. She found it really upsetting. But as we were to find out, that incident was nothing compared to what my sister did on our wedding day.

Susanna and I got married on a Saturday in August 2008. Julia was studying at Oxford at the time. I think it was her last year. She had very reluctantly agreed to come down and celebrate the big day with us. I think my parents must have more or less forced her. We got married in a beautiful thirteenth-century church in a little village in Surrey, close to where Susanna was born. Her parents still own a large country house there. After the ceremony, we celebrated in their beautiful gardens. We had erected a white marquee for the occasion. It was a stunning day and everyone was in great spirits. There were about 150 guests, many of whom had brought along their children. They were chasing around between the tables and the trees. There was laughter and birdsong, and the sun was shining. Susanna was six months pregnant, and looked dazzling in her white lace dress. We just couldn't stop smiling at each other. It looked like it really would be the perfect day of which we had dreamed.

My sister missed the church ceremony in the morning, which really upset Susanna, who is more religious than I am. She turned up late in the afternoon. She was wearing ripped jeans and a washed-out oversized T-shirt that kept slipping down her shoulder. It was a slap in the face, that outfit.

Susanna and I had carefully planned every detail of our big day. We had debated at great length different wedding menu options. In the end we opted for a Middle Eastern finger-food buffet. A little unconventional, but we wanted something that wasn't too formal, so that people wouldn't get stuck at one table and with one group all evening. It worked out perfectly. Our guests kept drifting to the buffet table and mingled freely in the marquee. During the wedding supper, friends and family delivered various speeches. My best man gave a wonderful speech, and the atmosphere was fantastic. But then, to our horror, Julia signalled that she wished to give a speech, too. And speak she did. I will never forget it and I will never forgive her.

'Congratulations to the artfully made-up bride and her solid groom!' she began, in a mockingly sweet tone. 'To the charming setting, the expensive pink champagne that is bubbling away so cheerfully in our glasses, and to the tasteful finger-food buffet! Jonathan, my brother: may your wealth and happiness increase in equal measure. I wish you the best. May all your dreams of shiny SUVs and Bentleys, of two-point-four kids, and of a chic townhouse in Chelsea, come true. Now, with a ring on your finger that fully confirms your traditionalist credentials, will you finally follow the siren call of duty and accept a nomination as Conservative candidate on the local council? After all, the Tories have had their eyes on you since you reached the age of three.'

At this point, people were still laughing, but Susanna and I had grown tense. I didn't like where this was going one bit.

'You are their man, Jonathan. You were born to fight for the petty little rights of petty little citizens, such as wider parking spaces so that people in oversized cars don't suffer discrimination. You could launch a petition to paint all kittens white so that we can see them in the night. You could start a campaign to ban the competition-stifling caps on bonuses for bankers – isn't it outrageous that some deluded continental Europeans think that 500 per cent of one's annual salary should be enough? You could fight for a special policeman to watch over the playground your two-point-four children will be frequenting, to make sure that no poor people and no black people ever set foot in it. Hurrah for the family values of middle England!'

Most people, except for a few very drunk ones, had stopped laughing. There was an uncomfortable silence in the marquee when Julia continued.

'Oh, but hang on... What do I see in my hand-blown crystal champagne flute? Dark clouds are gathering in the future. I see a midlife crisis in your early thirties – no surprises there, either: you've always acted twenty years older than your age. But the horror! Your once-so-pretty housewife has grown bored with the kids and her little creative pottery projects. She's started to comfort-eat and – I hate to break this to you, Susanna, I know how much your looks matter to you – she's grown fat. She has begun to hate herself and her out-of-control body that never quite got back into shape after the second pregnancy, and she resents you because you're always working. She's nagging you. The nagging is benevolent at first, but over the years her attacks grow ever more vicious; she hates the way you chew, the way you swallow your food with an audible gulp, the way you button up your shirts to the very top; she hates the too-pungent scent of your aftershave. She also resents the hell out of you for having a life outside the family, and for having a successful career. You now regularly stay out late and go to strip-clubs with your banker-friends to avoid the spiteful spouse who's waiting for you at home, ready to attack you as soon as she hears your keys in the lock. You no longer touch each other; you stopped having sex after the second child. Instead, to satisfy your still active cravings, you fuck your average-looking but willing secretary on your desk twice a week after everyone else has left the building.'

'Stop it, Julia, that's quite enough now,' my mother, who had stood up, said sharply. 'I think it's time for more music, don't you all agree?'

'Sorry, Mum,' Julia said. 'I'm almost done, I promise. I hate to break it to you, Jonathan – after all, this is a festive occasion, isn't it? – but things are getting even worse. Oh dear! Your once gorgeous girl-children, who've grown up in an atmosphere of barely repressed hostility and poisonous resentment that has done horrible damage to their psycho-sexual development, are troubled. Seriously troubled. One of them is firmly in the clutches of a classic middle-class eating disorder. The other daughter is more aggressive; she's angry as hell. She feels she's never been properly loved; she feels that her mother has never forgiven her for ruining her pre-pregnancy figure. She marries young, just like you and Susanna, she gives birth to two-point-four gorgeous girl-children, but she can't really bring herself to love them, and she soon begins to resent the hell out of her husband, who is always away, and she repeats the whole pointless story all over again. So, once again, my warmest congratulations to you two! Hurrah! To Jonathan and Susanna!'

Nobody clapped, nobody laughed. Everyone had stopped eating and drinking. My parents looked pale and sombre, and Amy had started to cry. It was blatantly obvious to everyone that this wasn't just a drunken, ill-judged attempt to deliver a funny speech. In fact, Julia was completely sober.

She never drinks. It was an aggressive, malicious affront, deeply insulting to both Susanna and me, and designed to spoil our wedding day.

'What, no applause?' my sister said, staring mock-angrily at the wedding guests. 'That's SO disappointing. I've thought about this speech for months, and I've worked on it day and night!' Then she got up from the table and left the party.

We never spoke again after that. I occasionally heard about her from Dad and my mother and Amy, of course. About her dropping out of university and all her mad travelling. But I saw Julia only very rarely, at a few big family celebrations, at which we avoided each other's company. I wasn't at all surprised when she finally acted out and went on her murderous rampage. I always thought she had the capacity for ruthless violence written all over her in big, bright neon letters. I always thought the psychotic bitch should be sectioned. Unfortunately, nobody ever listened to me.

I am sure you expect me to provide an analysis now and to explain how an intelligent, privileged middle-class girl who was very much loved by her parents could have turned into a mass murderer. There is only one thing I can say, and I have said it before: my parents are decent people. We are all decent people, our entire family, with one very extreme exception. We have done absolutely nothing wrong. None of us deserve any of this. We would have lived happily ever after had it not been for my monstrous sister, that incubus that must have crawled straight from hell. And for no good reason and right from the start, the bitch set her sick mind on destroying us and everything we stand for.

The bombing wasn't political. That manifesto is bullshit. It's a farce staged for the media to make her look interesting. The bombing was deeply personal. Julia could just as well have placed the bomb in my parents' house, last Christmas when we were all there, and annihilated our entire family with a single stroke. But I suppose she thought that her alternative plan would be so much worse. And she was absolutely right about that. She probably weighed up the options carefully in that revolting brain of hers, and decided that keeping us alive would be more fun. Death would have been too merciful an option. Mercy, as I am sure you will agree, is not one of Julia's attributes.

The bombing was nothing but the inevitable climax of a pernicious campaign to throw dirt on everything cherished by decent people like us. Julia was always already a hate-filled psychopath, even as a young girl. A stranger in our midst, a different species. But she managed to deceive my parents about her true nature until the very end. They were simply too kind and too naive to face the bitter truth: their angelic-looking, oh-so-talented favourite child was a malicious murderess in the making, intent on causing maximum damage and distress.

Why did she hate us so much? What have we ever done to her to deserve this? I don't believe any of the bullshit psychologizing, the finger-pointing and the traumamongering that are so fashionable these days. In my view, Julia was simply born evil. Wickedness had been indelibly imprinted on her soul from the start. My sister is malice incarnate.

VII

Ah, evil – this gloriously lazy theological catch-all. I don't believe in it. I don't believe that some people just happen to be born demonic. I don't believe that nature can remain unaffected by nurture (but neither do I believe that nurture can explain everything, as Amanda does). Julia, sadistic spawn of Satan, who visited this pure, good, innocent family like an evil spirit in a horror movie – no, I thought, there had to be more to her than that. Jonathan's assumption of an Iago-like motiveless malignancy seemed far too simplistic, and also morally dubious.

Besides, I thought it very obvious that Jonathan's portrait of his sister was distorted by a hefty dose of sibling rivalry. In his view, Julia had destroyed the bond he cherished most in this world: his special relationship with his father. Sibling rivalry can be such a powerful force in shaping our actions and aspirations. I'm not just thinking of the obvious meaning of the concept – the irreparable damage to our narcissistic bubbles when we have to acknowledge that we are no longer the only sun shining in our parents' universe. Sibling rivalry can be an ongoing way of defining one's identity against somebody else's – somebody who is simultaneously both like us and not like us.

Consider Amanda and me, for example: we couldn't be more different, character-wise, and we used to operate in completely dissimilar spheres, professionally and socially, and yet we could never quite free ourselves from the urge to compare our lives to each other's. Especially recently, of course. Although purely professionally speaking, I used to be the more successful one (which I am sure must have irked Amanda), I often secretly wondered whether somewhere down the line I had not made some fatally bad choices in other areas of my life.

While I have no doubt that our parents loved us equally, they always appeared much prouder of my achievements than hers, something of which Amanda reminds me frequently, and I concede the point. I wish they had been slightly more diplomatic, since this issue has contributed significantly to the tensions between my sister and me. For example, there were seven pictures of me receiving various awards on the walls in my parents' house, and three of Laura (as a shiny plump newborn, as a feisty pigtailed primary-school girl, and as a tanned backpacker admiring the wares of a street-food vendor in Thailand). But there was only one of Amanda and her first husband, Peter, in which she was slightly out of focus, her face and body in Peter's shadow. (My parents never warmed to her second husband, and stayed in touch with Peter long after the acrimonious divorce, much to Amanda's distress.)

When we emptied their house, a few months after they died, we found a series of eleven heavy, leather-bound albums in one of the cupboards: they revealed that my father had diligently cut out and collected every article I had ever published, starting with the first hot-headed piece I wrote for a student paper in the eighties, and ending with a feature story printed in the *New Statesman* just three days before a distracted driver ended my parents' lives (and his) on the M5. In another album (golden) my father had collected all the positive reviews of my books; a much smaller red one contained the (thankfully not very many) critical responses my works had attracted. My books, in pristine condition, were proudly displayed on a single book shelf in the centre of the drawing room, which also held some prize paraphernalia (Amanda used to refer to it as my 'shrine'). In my father's study, we also found used second copies of each one of my books that had evidently been read carefully, and which contained many underlinings. When Amanda and I discovered the albums, she burst into tears and I didn't know how to console her.

'I feel like I'm the little girl who just got an orange for Christmas, while her sister got a bicycle,' she sobbed.

But at some point, things shifted and the scales tipped the other way – gradually at first, and then ever faster. When Laura was born and when I first held her, I marvelled at her tiny hands and her seductively sweet milkshake scent, and I felt a short, sharp pang of regret and envy. This feeling disappeared for a few years while Laura was little and hard work and screamed a lot. But it resurfaced even more strongly when she was beginning to talk and to articulate her view of the world, which has fascinated me ever since. I love Laura, I love her deeply, and although

I see her frequently, I often wish she were properly mine.

Then there were Peter and Frank, Amanda's husbands. While I found neither of them particularly attractive or interesting, I felt it again in their presence, that strange mixture of regret and envy. For example, when I happened to observe little gestures or looks they exchanged with my sister – betraying an intimacy that I had never known myself. Peter had this way of gently tugging a stubborn strand of hair that kept falling into Amanda's face back behind her ear; Frank would fold his arms around her from behind and plant a kiss on the nape of her neck (always exactly in the same place – a place that made Amanda shiver with pleasure).

I have observed that unspoken, affectionate familiarity between you and Lailah, too, George (in the beginning, at least). The way you always helped her into her coat, and then tenderly rearranged her scarves and collars, or her hair; the way she always saved some of her pudding at dinner parties and discreetly passed it over to you, because she knows just how much you love sweet things. I have noted many times how you steered conversations away from topics that you knew might upset her: ignorant opinions on Middle Eastern politics; crudely Western-centric views on veil-wearing Arab women; anything that reeked of unreconstructed orientalism. In the early days of your marriage, I saw Lailah quietly but firmly insisting that Sundays should be kept free for her and your daughter, regardless of how prestigious and important the invitation was that you had to decline to follow her bidding. And you never let the two of them down.

Very soon, the family Sunday became law in your world. Once, I saw you all in St James's Park (from afar) watching the ducks, and you two, with proud smiles, marvelling at the miracle that is your daughter. I couldn't breathe, as though something was choking me from the inside. Sometimes, the regret I feel about never having had a child of my own is so strong that the pain overwhelms me.

When my world fell to pieces after the trial, Amanda was there for me, as were you, of course. But sometimes I couldn't help but wonder whether she didn't (perhaps only a tiny bit) get some secret satisfaction from my failure. After all, the high flyer to whom everything had come so easily had suddenly crashed down to earth. Now I was the one languishing in a dirty pool of debts and shattered dreams, while Amanda still had her work, her patients, and, above all, Laura. Now, it looked as though I was finally paying for my past choices, and that hers had somehow been retrospectively valorized.

I remember that, while working on the transcription of the interview, I was struck by Jonathan's repeated emphasis on decency – a moral term. Why was he so keen to emphasize the family's decency? I wondered. Was that simply to counter as strongly as possible the potentially negative public perception of himself and his parents? Or might it be driven by a secret fear that decency was precisely the quality his family was lacking? Sometimes, we protest most forcefully against what, deep down, we fear to be true. Even now I can't shake the feeling that some form of censorship, or even whitewashing, has shaped his account.

I understand the impulse, though; after all, the only reason he spoke to me in the first place was to clear his family's name.

I wonder, now, whether I didn't judge Jonathan too harshly back then, all things considered. I admit I didn't like him much, but perhaps that had less to do with him as a person and more with his line of work and what it has come to represent for me. After all, my experiences with City traders haven't exactly been pleasant. I had come to associate the entire world of investment banking with one figure only – Adrian Temple, my glib nemesis.

Since the day of my trial – 21 May 2010, I still remember every little detail of it as though it were yesterday – I had fantasized so often about taking matters into my own hands, bringing about the kind of justice that the judicial system had denied me, like some heroic vigilante in an American movie. (Have you ever noticed that virtually all Hollywood action films celebrate the solitary ethical outsider, who courageously stands up to corrupt institutions and seeks justice on their own terms?) But I did no such thing. Instead, I just reacted allergically to people such as Jonathan, which is hardly a heroic act, and nor is it fair. I know, of course, that not all of them are criminals. Not all of them are ruthless confidence tricksters, responsible for the ruin of thousands of small-scale investors and the cause of numerous suicides in its aftermath. But one of them is. And they allowed him to get away with it. I still can't believe they let him walk that day – not just unpunished but victorious, free to continue with his ruthless gambling. Which is of course precisely what he did. His triumphant glare after the sentence was read still burns on my skin, even today.

But I tried very hard to follow Amanda's advice in the early stages of the project. For the first time since that fateful May day, I actually felt hopeful and excited about my future. I knew that I needed to let go of the past, I needed to bury it and move on with my life, and that was what I was doing. During the first few weeks of my research I felt fine. In fact, more than that: I felt exalted – I was, after all, working once more on something meaningful. After all those years – who would have guessed?

VIII

I'm not just a prisoner because my movements are restricted – I don't mind that part so much. Right now, I wouldn't know where to go even if I were free. What's worse is being subjected to the drab sameness, the soul-destroying routine of strictly monitored and rigidly timed activities. It's the imposition of external rhythms that gets to me most, the knowledge that someone else is the master of my time. Every day, at 6.30, we are driven to the shower rooms, like a flock of sluggish sheep. There, we are at our most vulnerable – you would blush scarlet if I told you the demeaningly obscene things women are capable of saying about one another's bodies. The faint trickle of water is lukewarm at best, and the scratchy towels we are given smell of vinegar.

At 7.30, we have to assemble in the dining hall, a place I have come to loathe. Even though it gets scrubbed three times a day, its lime-green lino floor is eternally greasy (on my first day I slipped on it like a novice skater on ice, making an embarrassing spectacle of myself). Sixteen long, beige plastic tables stand neatly aligned in the centre, like the bars of a zebra crossing. The seating politics are complex – I have yet to figure them out. For the moment, I sit on the table frequented by other newcomers and the long-term loners; often, the seats around me remain empty. There's a counter connected with the kitchen, behind which two big women with bare arms and hairnets ladle things onto our plates that would make Laura fume with indignation. The smell of frying oil stains the air, and it has permeated our skin and hair. No matter how rigorously we scrub ourselves with the little scentless soap bars we are handed every morning, it just won't come off.

After breakfast, we are allowed to spend time in the common room or return to our cells. Some go off to their jobs – they produce things in workshops, or work in the kitchen or the laundry room. From ten to eleven, we have to take some exercise in the courtyard. Most do so in groups of two, three or four; but quite a few walk around on their own. Some defy the request to be physically active completely and just lean against the brick wall, smoking and watching. A few women run and do push-ups. At twelve thirty, we are summoned once again to the hall of horrors for lunch. It's the two hours after lunch that I cherish most: then, we are allowed to explore freely the few leisure activities available here. There's a gym, a games room, a TV room, and, thank God, the library. It's a small, quiet room with a few sparsely filled shelves. It's a peaceful space, a refuge of sorts; there are a few armchairs and two small, round tables, and they even have a selection of daily newspapers. I sit in the same armchair every day reading the papers. Hardly anyone else comes in, and I think of the room as my little sanctum.

Visiting hours tend to be between four and six. In addition to consultations with my lawyer, I'm allowed two one-hour visits a week in the heavily guarded visitors' room, where we sit for an hour at one of the twenty or so small tables with our loved ones, whom we are not allowed to touch. So far, Amanda and Laura haven't missed a single opportunity to see me. But Amanda seemed strained and tense during our most recent encounter. The other day, she reprimanded me rather too sharply for the fact that I'm still not eating properly. I try, but I find the idea of chewing and swallowing nauseating, and it's not even because of what they serve us here.

Anyway. Jonathan must have urged his parents to speak to me, having convinced them that it was in the interest of the family's reputation, because at the beginning of September, only a few days after my interview with him, I received a phone call from Timothy White. In a pleasant, gentle voice he asked whether I would be able to meet him and his wife the following day, and suggested 8 p.m. at his company's offices. Timothy's law firm is situated in an imperial Georgian building on a quiet side-street off the Strand. When I entered the marble-panelled lobby a porter asked me to sign the visitors' book and take a seat. I had just sat down on one of a group of hard, black leather armchairs when Timothy came down the stairs. I was immediately struck by his appearance: a tall and naturally elegant man with silver-streaked dark hair; his gentle manner and smile seemed warm and authentic. His suit was expertly tailored, his shirt crisp and white. As Jonathan had indicated, he was an accomplished small-talker. As we climbed the wide marble steps that led to his offices on the third floor, he told me about the history of the building, and even found time to mention that he had read and very much enjoyed my study on the Bangladeshi sweatshops. If ever I had to cast someone to embody suavity in a film, my vote would go to Timothy.

His office, too, demonstrated quietly expensive taste (the kind acquired over generations, confident and not needing to show off): minimally furnished, it featured nothing but a large cherry-wood desk, a very orderly floor-to-ceiling bookshelf that held leather-bound tomes of legal literature, a black leather sofa and a matching armchair, a little drinks cabinet and a glass coffee table on which stood an empty fruit bowl. The floors were covered with a thick white carpet, and on the light-grey walls there were no pictures other than a colourful map of the world in a golden frame, probably dating from the fifteenth century. I noticed only one imperfection: there was a light, rectangular patch next to the map that must until recently have been covered by another picture.

Rose White was sitting upright on the edge of the armchair when we entered. She rose to shake my hand (a contact that felt strangely immaterial, as though I had been accidentally touched by a phantom). She, too, was tall and thin, and both her frame and her facial features gave the impression of excessive angularity. Everything about her seemed hard-edged and symmetrical, like a modern glass and steel building: her strong jaw, her sculpted cheekbones, her high forehead. She looked older than her husband, an impression that was mainly owing to her hair, which was ghost white, and her dark, tired eyes. Those eyes seemed to glide restlessly across the objects in the room, searching for something to take hold of, like a ship adrift at sea.

We exchanged a few pleasantries and Timothy offered drinks. Rose asked for gin. Timothy poured himself a glass of sherry. I opted for water. When we were all seated I pulled out my digital recorder. This changed the atmosphere; I could feel the two of them stiffening. I talked a little about the book project, how I was planning to put things together, and offered them the right to review and edit their interview transcript until they were fully happy with the result. Rose finished her drink while I was talking and got up to pour herself another one. She got up numerous times to refill her glass during our two-hour interview.

Two days after our meeting on 7 September, I received a handwritten note from them, in which the couple apologized for their behaviour during our session. Things did get a little out of hand, but I don't blame them for it. I think none of us can even begin to imagine the psychological impact of knowing that one's own child has committed an atrocity. How that must feel; where one would go from there; the energy it must take to continue to perform the simplest of routines and not to fall to pieces. But unlike their son, Rose and Timothy refused to change, delete or censor anything. Instead, they told me to do with the interview what I deemed best for the project, and I include our conversation unaltered, occasionally complemented by my observations at the time.

The direct exchanges between Timothy and Rose show most poignantly the corrosive effect the tragic events have had on their relationship.

IX

'Thank you again for agreeing to speak to me about your daughter,' I began. 'I know how painful this must be for you. I wonder whether you could start by telling me what your feelings are about the bombing?'

Rose stared into her glass. When Timothy, who had waited for his wife to reply first, realized that she didn't have any intention of speaking, he responded: 'Obviously, we're enormously shocked and saddened by Julia's actions. Our hearts go out to her victims. Rose and I have founded a charity to support the families of the bereaved and the wounded. We're trying to raise funds to help pay for their healthcare and psychological support. We just have to do *something*, no matter how small. It isn't much, it's just money, I know that, and it won't have the power to heal any of the victims' families' wounds, but we can't just sit back and do nothing – isn't that right, Rose? Darling?'

Rose didn't speak. Her eyes remained lowered and her body oddly stiff.

'Rose spends one day a week fundraising at the moment,' Timothy continued. 'She's reduced her hours at the hospital to make time for that. We sent cards to all of the victims' families. After all, it was our child who caused them all that pain. We feel responsible. I mean, how couldn't we? We can't just go on with our lives now as though nothing has happened. There must be some way to help and to make amends. Even if it's just by providing financial support. What else can we do?'

They both remained silent after this. Their sadness was almost palpable – it surrounded us like heavy fog.

'Can you tell me why you think Julia did what she did?' I asked them next.

Again it was Timothy who spoke. This time, he didn't meet my eyes but instead stared at the discoloured spot on the wall. 'I honestly don't know, Clare. I just can't understand at all what could have led her to commit this atrocious act. I simply can't comprehend it. It still won't sink in. I *know* that the attack really happened and that twenty-four people died as a result, but some part of me just can't accept it yet. I keep thinking that there must be a mistake, that Julia didn't do it, that there's some complicated mix-up that will be resolved soon... '

He paused and then continued. 'Killing people is not something I can reconcile with the Julia I know and have always loved and admired and cared for so very much. Not at all. It just doesn't make sense. It doesn't fit. Even as a young child Julia already had a finely developed social conscience, an astute sense of justice and a highly sophisticated conception of what does and doesn't constitute ethically acceptable behaviour. Julia was so talented. So beautiful. So *special*. So very different from Jonathan and Amy. She and I always talked so much, about all kinds of things, even in the past few years, when things had become more difficult between us. You know, I always felt that *I* was learning things from *her*, not the other way round. She had such a unique, perceptive vision of things. Rose, darling, don't you agree?'

Rose continued to ignore Timothy's attempts to draw her into the conversation. For most of the interview, she sat still and upright at the edge of her chair, and only ever moved to raise her glass to her lips and to refill it.

'Julia was always such a *good* person – the way she cared for Amy, the way she always fought for the causes of those less fortunate than us, the way she championed the plight of the disadvantaged... ' Timothy continued. 'You know, we're talking about someone who cared for her little sister like a mother. She took Amy everywhere she went; the two were completely inseparable. Julia was so mature and selfless about everything concerning Amy. It made me so proud to have raised someone like that. We're also talking about a person who spent most of her teenage years doing voluntary work in a rough and run-down homeless shelter. We're talking about a person who went to India for an entire year, once again to help the poor. I just can't understand what could have changed her so completely. It doesn't make sense. It just doesn't make sense.'

'Can you think of any specific events or experiences that might have led her to change?' I asked.

'Well, possibly, I don't know... Obviously we've thought about this question, over and over and over again, haven't we, Rose? Darling? Perhaps all the responsibility she took for Amy at such a young age was simply too much. Perhaps we should have intervened, insisted that she act more selfishly at that age, enjoy her carefree years more fully. I don't know. We were always very close, Julia and I, but she did seem different, more distant, when she decided to drop out of Edinburgh and during and after her travels. I felt that I'd lost touch with her and that she didn't really share things with me anymore. Not the way she used to, in any case. It was a real shock for us that Julia should have decided against an academic career. You know, she was predestined for it. But she gave it all up, more or less overnight… I never quite understood why. She didn't bother explaining.

'When she came back from her travels I still saw her fairly regularly. I really tried not to lose touch completely. I felt she was slipping away from me. We'd meet in town after work at least once or twice a month, and we'd have dinner, just the two of us. But our discussions had become more abstract, more political, less personal, somehow. She didn't really tell me much about her private life. In the last two years or so, we always ended up debating *ideas*. Or rather, she did. I mainly listened.'

Timothy paused, stared at the wall, and then continued. 'I believe she encountered some bad people on those travels. Or even before then, in Edinburgh. Radicals, disaffected types. She did seem so different after her return… Yes, I suppose we can say that with some certainty. We didn't care much for the friends she made when she got back to London, did we, Rose? Darling?'

His tone had become pleading, but Rose continued to sit silent and motionless on the edge of her chair.

'They seemed so coarse, so unkempt in a pathetic teenage-rebellion kind of way, and, if you don't mind me saying so, so *stupid*. I just couldn't understand how someone with Julia's intellectual abilities could tolerate, let alone seriously believe in all the utterly unoriginal and simplistic anti-globalization guff they were spouting. You know, she was a much more refined and complex thinker than the people she socialized with. That she, with all her talents, with all her idealism, had chosen to work in a run-down vegetable shop populated by resentful, dirty types with dreadlocks and piercings and no sense of humour whatsoever... '

Here I interrupted Timothy. 'What vegetable shop?' I didn't know anything about a vegetable shop.

'Well, when Julia came back from South America she lived on her own for a while, in a small flat in Camden that we paid for. But then, about a year or so later, we cut her allowance. We didn't do that lightly, I can assure you. But you know, she simply wasn't doing anything. She just seemed to be frittering away her time and talents, and went to all these demonstrations and occupations and gatherings... She wasn't working and she wasn't studying. It went on for far too long. We felt that funding this phase any longer than we already had was counterproductive. We felt it would just allow her to continue to drift. So we cut her allowance. She obviously didn't like that. But then she started to work in a dismal little organic vegetable shop. And she moved in with one of her colleagues – I can't remember her name, a pale, morose girl.'

I asked him for the address of the vegetable shop, which he still knew by heart.

'Mind you, they won't be very welcoming there,' he warned me. 'They don't have much time for people like you and me. They think we're the enemy. When we found out that Julia had a job, we went to see her at the shop a few times. Obviously we wanted to support her in any way we could. Although we didn't like the kind of job she'd chosen, at least she had chosen to do *something*... We even made an effort to buy our vegetables there for a while, although it was at the other end of town. But we were so clearly unwelcome in that place that we soon stopped trying.'

And then Timothy, whose voice had been sad but calm until that point, became agitated.

'Do you want to know, Clare, what I really think? I think someone must have corrupted Julia, someone must have incited her, someone must have turned her into this... *monstrous thing* she's become. She must have met some terrible characters on her travels and then fallen in with the wrong crowd when she came back. I'm convinced someone made her do it. She wouldn't ever kill anyone. Not Julia. There must have been others, radicals, terrorists, fanatics, lunatics... She can't have planned and executed that pointless carnage all on her own. It's impossible. My beloved child building a bomb and setting it off in the full knowledge that it would kill all those innocent people? People who were doing nothing other than *drinking coffee*? No, it's simply not possible.'

Timothy had risen from his seat and begun to pace up and down.

'How anyone could have convinced her to do that I don't know. I just don't know. We've both done our very best to teach our children the difference between right and wrong. We thought Julia, of all of them, had the strongest defences, the strongest ethical convictions and values. I can't even begin to imagine how someone could have turned her into a killer. She can't have been well. Perhaps she had some mental problems we didn't know about. God, I so wish she'd let us see her. It's *hell* not to be able to see her, not to be able to help her! It's hell, Clare! She needs help. She needs our help badly.'

And when he addressed Rose once again, there was a desperate fierceness in his plea. 'Rose, say something. Please. I can't do this on my own. Can you just say *something*? Please, darling!'

But Rose just sat there, her gaze sliding across the room unable to fix on anything, as though all surfaces had become slippery. Timothy took Rose's lifeless hand and pressed it. He looked utterly despondent for a moment. Then he got up and filled her empty glass. Having sat down again, he turned back to me.

'Rose isn't well. She isn't coping with the situation. Forgive her,' he said.

Shaken out of her stupor by the remark, Rose burst out: 'Of course I'm not well. Of course I'm not coping. How could I? How could anyone? We've raised a mass murderer. Julia killed twenty-four people! Obviously, we must have done *something* wrong.'

Then she started sobbing. It was a dry, hard and fast

kind of sobbing, unaccompanied by tears. It lasted for about a minute. I didn't know where to look. It was painful to witness. When she spoke again she addressed Timothy.

'Just yesterday I dreamed that dream again. I'm in front of a tribunal, hundreds of men and women in white who are standing on a platform, and everyone is staring down at me, full of contempt. I feel like vermin. Then a small woman with round glasses reads out a list of my crimes and the verdict – I've breached the Hippocratic oath by raising a monster. My licence to practise medicine is revoked, and I'm chased away by angry shouting and hissing and seek shelter in the nearby woods.

'I mean, the bitter irony of it all. I've dedicated my life to saving and protecting the lives of others, but have brought up someone who took twenty-four lives without even blinking an eye. I'll never forgive her. Never! She destroyed us. Everything we've lived and worked for: our lives, our family – all is in tatters. All is lost. And you… Of course I'm not well!'

Timothy looked pained. 'Don't say that, Rose, darling, don't go there, please. We've been through this so many times… It's *not* your fault. It's not *our* fault. Don't you remember what our counsellor said? We've loved and supported each one of our children to the very best of our abilities. That's all parents can do, and we did our job as well as anyone else I know. In fact, I'd even say better. You're a fantastic mother, you always have been. Our children lacked nothing. They've had the most loving and privileged upbringing anyone can dream of.'

Rose laughed. 'Violence doesn't come from nowhere, Tim – you know that just as well as I do. People from happy homes don't turn into killers. They just don't. We must have done *something* wrong. All of us. This kind of thing just doesn't happen to normal families. But what? *What* on earth can we have done to have caused *this*?'

She got up and poured herself another drink. Nobody said anything for a while. Then I asked: 'You must have thought a lot about this question. Do you think there might be something – anything at all, even if it is tiny and might seem unimportant – that could have adversely affected Julia's development?'

Timothy and Rose looked at each other. He very gently shook his head. Then he stared again at the discoloured patch on the wall, and responded: 'Well, there's one episode that I keep mulling over in my mind, over and over and over again, actually. I just can't help it. It's a bit like that dream you keep having, Rose. Forgive me for talking about this to a stranger, darling, but… I feel I need to share it. It was many, many years ago. Julia was six. She'd started school the previous year, and she was taking violin lessons at that time. Rose is very musical, aren't you, darling? She has the most beautiful singing voice, ethereal, light and airy, and yet incredibly powerful… We used to sing a lot when we were younger. Anyway, Rose always believed that learning an instrument was important for the development of children. Jonathan learned the piano, but he was rather hopeless at it. He really doesn't have one musical bone in his body. He gave up after just two years.

'Julia, however, had her heart set on learning the violin – she'd seen a beautiful woman in a long, black dress perform Bach's violin sonatas in our local church one evening when she was four or five, and this image had made a lasting impression on her. When we thought she was old enough, I made some inquiries, and a friend of ours recommended a Ukrainian concert violinist who was teaching other pupils at Julia's age. She was called Alina Abramovich. She, too, was beautiful, a bit like the woman Julia had seen perform in church – I hope you won't mind me saying that, Rose.

'Alina came to our house every Tuesday evening before supper, and she and Julia practised together in our living room. Julia was a very gifted student and made rapid progress – I believe had she set her heart on it she could easily have become a professional musician. You know, she had such talent, such drive; she excelled at everything she did. I always tried to get back from work early on those days, so that I could stand in the door and listen to the two of them. It gave me such pleasure. Their duets made my heart sing. Alina did of course notice my enchantment, and we started to talk after her lessons, about Julia's progress and music at first. We were both ardent admirers of Bach and of Beethoven's late quartets. Then we started talking about other things. It soon became a habit that she and I would have a glass of wine after the violin lessons. Rose was working very hard at that time, and often returned late from work, just in time for a late supper. A few times Alina stayed to eat with the entire family.

'One evening – I still don't know what possessed us – Alina and I drank more than usual. You were late that day, Rose, very late. Too late... If only you'd arrived earlier. Alina became drunk and sentimental, and she talked about the friends and family she had to leave behind in the Ukraine when she came to the UK to pursue her career. She remembered her parents and how frail they'd looked when she last saw them, and she suddenly started to cry. I took her hand, just to comfort her. But she misunderstood the gesture. She pressed my hand firmly and then she leaned forward to kiss me. She kissed me on the lips and put her hands around my head and interlocked her fingers so that I couldn't withdraw as quickly as I'd have liked to. I was terribly surprised. Perhaps I hesitated just a moment too long before I gently began to loosen her hands and pulled away from her mouth.

'"No, Alina, no," I said. "Don't, please."

'But at that moment, I noticed Julia. She was standing in the kitchen doorway and looking at us. I still remember everything so vividly... Julia was wearing a blue cotton dress with a small white collar, white tights and ballerina shoes, and her hair was braided in two pigtails. All colour had drained from her face, and before I could get up and catch hold of her and explain the situation she ran away and locked herself in the upstairs bathroom. I knocked on the bathroom door for at least forty minutes. I used all my skills to persuade her to open up and to let me explain, but she was as stubborn as a mule. I could hear her crying hysterically behind the door, and got increasingly worried. It was only when I started to try to force open the lock that she finally let me in.

'Rose had arrived by then, and understandably wasn't very happy about my explanation of what had happened. But she hid her anger for Julia's sake. You know, Rose is always very professional about everything, including mothering. Anyway, we tried to talk to Julia and to reassure her. We talked about how much Rose and I loved each other, and we tried to explain that Alina had misunderstood something and was terribly lonely and unhappy, and so on. Julia seemed to grow calmer and eventually appeared to accept my explanation. We felt confident that all was well again when she finally went up to her room, tired out by all the crying. I helped her change into her pyjamas and tucked her in and kissed her goodnight before I switched off the lights in her bedroom.

'Once Julia was in bed Rose and I had an argument in the kitchen that lasted for a long time, probably two or three hours. You know, Rose didn't quite believe my version of the story, and it took me for ever to convince her. It was well past midnight when we heard loud crashing sounds from the living room. When we rushed over to see what was happening we found Julia with the broken neck of her violin in her hand. She must have smashed it repeatedly against the grand piano until it was in pieces and all its strings had snapped. She looked at us with her big green eyes, and her pale, small face radiated a strange calmness that I found almost more unsettling than her destructive act. Then she said: "Dad, Mum – I'll never play the violin again." And she didn't. She never touched any musical instruments again in her life.'

'I really don't understand why you had to tell that sorry story,' Rose said, after another uncomfortable silence. 'What does that have to do with anything?' She didn't even try to hide her anger.

'Well… I don't know, darling. I've been thinking about that episode a lot lately. I just can't forget Julia's face when she saw Alina and me, that white, frightened little face. I keep thinking that seeing her father kiss another woman at such a young age must have broken something in her, that it did some kind of damage. That I'm to blame for what has happened, somehow. I don't know. I can't really explain.'

Timothy covered his face with his hands. Rose didn't say anything. Eventually, she got up to pour herself another drink. Then she started to speak. Again, she only addressed Timothy. It was as though I wasn't even in the room.

'If anything did do damage to Julia, it was the way you spoiled her. The way you so clearly favoured her over our other children. The way you always made her feel special. The way you always sided with her, no matter what she'd done – even if it meant siding against me and undermining my authority. The way you fostered in her a sense of being better than everybody else. *That* – all of that – messed her up, not that silly kissing episode. It means nothing; it explains nothing. But you spoiled that child. If anyone has corrupted her, it's *you*, Tim. You! You alone.'

Timothy raised his head. 'Don't say that, darling. I know you don't mean it. We're all tired and at the end of our tethers.'

'But I *do* mean it,' Rose said. 'You spoiled that child. You completely idolized her! It just wasn't *natural* – it was sick, obsessive! Just look at Amy! She's a wreck. Look at Jonathan! He never got over the feeling that his father didn't really love him. He desperately tried to copy you, in all kinds of ways, just to get your attention and win your respect. And look at me, just look at me now! All you ever really cared about was your beloved Julia. You didn't give a shit about the rest of your family. She could do anything, she could get away with murder. Ha! Hang on. She just did! You'd always support her and tell her how special she was. You never criticized her. Never, not once in your life. All Julia did and said was goodness and wisdom incarnate for you. You never showed her any boundaries. It just wasn't right. And look at the result of your sick idolatry! If Julia let you see her now you'd probably still try to "understand" her motivations. In fact you'd probably applaud her for what she's done.'

'Rose, darling, that isn't fair. Please stop it.'

'"Rose, darling, that isn't fair. Please stop it." Oh, you and your cowardly liberalism and your eternally understanding nature make me so *sick*. You make me want to vomit, Tim. Vomit! I detest your hypocritical tolerance. I detest your saintly lenience and your "decency", and your blindness. It makes me want to vomit my heart out.'

'I think it's the drinking that makes you want to vomit, Rose,' Timothy said. 'You've really had enough now. You should watch your alcohol consumption. You're not well, Rose.'

But Rose had no intention of stopping. 'There were so many warning signs that something wasn't right with Julia. But you just weren't prepared to admit it. Never. You always defended her, no matter what she did. Even after she ruined your son's wedding day. Even after that speech she gave at your birthday. Do you even remember that? Just a few months ago? It was so cold and inappropriate, that speech – everyone was shocked by it but you. You just spouted out your eternally understanding babble: "It's a bad phase, Rose, darling, she'll regret it soon, darling, she's not herself at the moment, darling, let's be patient with her, darling, I'm sure she'll turn a corner soon, darling." Ha! Well, so much for your powers of insight. Christ!'

And then, for the first time, Rose looked me in the eye and addressed me directly. 'Clare, let me tell you about that day. Now *that's* a story that is relevant. It was Tim's sixty-fifth birthday, and Julia had very reluctantly agreed to come and celebrate with us, the rest of the family and a few friends and business partners. I'd booked a room and two big tables in a French restaurant in Knightsbridge. It was Tim's *sixty-fifth*, after all. Of course, straight after her very late arrival the oh-so-politically-correct avenger of all the downtrodden stuck her nose up in the air and made some biting comments about the haut-bourgeois surroundings and the fact that the produce on the menu wasn't organic. She made a massive fuss about her order, and demanded reassurance that her dish wouldn't just be vegan but that the chef would only use locally sourced bio-dynamically grown ingredients, and so on. It was ridiculous and embarrassing. I was really shocked by her dogmatism. Honestly, a religious fanatic afraid of being fed pork would have been a pussycat in comparison.

'While everyone was eating their main courses, she stood up to give a speech. Not a single word about her father, his birthday and his numerous achievements. I don't think she even remembered to congratulate Tim! Instead, she launched straight into a very graphic diatribe against meat consumption. Most of us had chosen meat, of course – it was a French restaurant, after all. Julia went out of her way to describe the gory, inhumane conditions in which European farm animals were kept and the horrible sufferings they had to endure – the diseases, the transport issues, the slaughtering methods, and so on. She fully succeeded in spoiling everyone's appetite. I don't think anyone finished their plate after she was done. Then she stormed out in a huff during the dessert course, because she was convinced that, in spite of her detailed instructions to the waiter and the chef, her dish had pig-skin gelatine in it.'

'I think you're misrepresenting this event a little, Rose,' Timothy interrupted. 'She did congratulate me, she even gave me a hug, and I was really grateful that she came at all. She hates gatherings like that. And you know very well that Julia takes her veganism seriously, and feels passionately about meat consumption. A lot of her arguments were actually very convincing, and her speech wasn't at all as extreme as you make it sound. And she had every right to insist that her dietary requirements be taken seriously: a Michelin-starred chef should be able to respond to personal dietary requests, don't you think? I was actually quite shocked that this particular chef didn't. And her pudding *did* have gelatine in it. Even I could see that. It quivered and wobbled on her plate like a lump of pure jelly.'

'That's not the fucking point!' Rose shouted. 'See what I mean, Clare? Can you *see* what he does? He always takes Julia's dogmatic outbursts seriously; he always engages with the *content* of her diatribes. He can *always* see her bloody point. What he can't see is that there is something *pathological* about her fanaticism. It was his bloody *birthday*, for fuck's sake. She should have tried to say something nice and loving about her father, with all his friends and colleagues there and all that, instead of ranting about the bloody food.'

'I think you're being unfair, Rose. Julia happens to have very strong political convictions – that's just who she is. You've always been too harsh on her; you always assume there are darker motives behind her actions... '

'There we go – *I* have been too *harsh* on her? So you think it *is* my fault that Julia turned into a killer? I knew it! But guess what: I happen to disagree with your assessment, Tim, I disagree profoundly – I think you bloody idolized her, and if anyone is responsible it's you! You with your blind faith in her and your sick veneration complex! You rotted her soul!'

'Perhaps I simply tried to make up for your coldness, Rose.' Timothy suddenly looked incredibly tired, as though he hadn't slept for weeks.

'What do you mean by that? I've never been cold to any of our children – never!'

'Let's not go there, Rose. I'm sorry. Let's stop this, please. This won't lead to anything.'

'Oh no, no, no, I want to hear. Tell me in what ways you think I've been harsh and cold to our children. I demand to know.'

Both of them had stood up and were facing each other.

'Fine,' Timothy said, 'since you're not holding back any of your own resentment... I think you've always overemphasized the importance of achievement. The children always felt they had to perform well and behave impeccably in order to be worthy of your love. Your affection could never be taken for granted. It had to be *earned*, you know? It always struck me as... well, conditional rather than unconditional.'

'You mean I didn't just sit back and say "Great, do go ahead and hit boys on the head with beer bottles when you feel like it, Julia, darling", and "Great, well done for dropping out of Edinburgh to go travelling, Julia, sounds like a brilliant idea to me"? Is that what you mean?'

'No, that's not what I mean, obviously. And she did that to defend Amy, Rose, who'd just been sexually *molested*, remember? Don't twist the facts, please. I'm not talking about placidly agreeing with every one of our children's actions and choices. I'm talking about a more general lack of... I don't know... warmth. Compassion.'

'Hear hear! The good old cold mother narrative – how original, Tim. *Please.* Unlike you, I had to earn my privileges – I had to work my way up from the very bottom. I achieved what I achieved through discipline and hard work and by putting in *very* long hours. I wasn't born rich – as your bloody family doesn't tire of reminding me. They never liked me. They thought you were marrying beneath you and that I wasn't good enough for their precious son. Can you even *begin* to imagine how hurtful and humiliating that was? Yes, I believe that a good work ethic matters, I'm the first to admit that, and I won't apologize for it either. And guess what: I sincerely hope I passed this value on to my children. But that doesn't make me *cold*!'

'You just don't get it, do you?' Timothy's voice had become hard. 'You know the way you garden, Rose? You focus exclusively on weeding, on cutting back trees and hedges, on stripping down and ripping out bad seeds. You never plant stuff, or design new beds, or even nourish the existing plants sufficiently. And as you garden, so you mothered: you always focused on what you didn't like in our children, on their perceived negative qualities, which you tried to eliminate. I don't think you ever concentrated enough on nurturing them and on helping them to blossom.'

Rose sneered. 'That is such a fucking preposterous analogy. My gardening style has nothing to do with any of this! Nothing! But given that you insist on pursuing that idiotic comparison, you clearly *should* have weeded out the bad tendencies in Julia while it was still possible, before they stifled all her good qualities. You can't just let bad things take over your garden without putting up a fight. You *should* have shown her boundaries. You *should* have cut out her cancerous fanaticism while it was still possible to operate without killing the patient. Instead, you *encouraged* those tendencies in her by always taking her arguments seriously, no matter how crazy and absurd and hurtful they were.

'When she decided to abandon her studies, all you said was "That's fine, Julia, darling, if you want to, please go ahead and become a drop-out; your oh-so-tolerant Daddy is happy to finance your world travels. Don't worry about the future and about ruining your career prospects! Don't worry about breaking your parents' hearts! Just follow your whims and indulge in your teenage anti-everything rebellion – Daddy will finance you! Daddy loves you so very, very much!"'

'You know very well that isn't what I said to her,' Timothy said. 'That's just not fair. I tried my very best to persuade her to continue with her studies. You know that! It hurt me more than anyone else that she threw away her academic prospects. I even flew up to Scotland to talk her out of it. Don't you remember that? But given that I could neither persuade her nor force her to stay in Edinburgh, I did at least want to make sure she'd be safe on her travels. I couldn't let her head off to South-East Asia without any money now, could I? It was our obligation to ensure our daughter's safety. The less money you have to spend in those countries, the cheaper the places you stay, the greater the risks of kidnapping, rape, robbery and all that. You know that, Rose; we agreed to do this together. Don't you remember that? Can't you remember anything right? Has the bloody gin impaired not just your judgement but also your memory?'

'My memory works just fine, thank you very much. I wasn't in favour of funding that trip. Never. I just thought it pointless to object, because I knew you'd give her money anyway. I mean, *come on*. Of course you would have. I know you and your sick obsession with your golden girl. But what you didn't consider is that without your money Julia would have returned much sooner. I'm convinced that it was *precisely* the squalor and misery and danger abroad, from which your money protected her, that would have curbed her desire to stay away for that long. I think funding her travels was a very bad idea – look at what has become of her. I mean, just *look*, Tim. She came back even more alienated and fanatical than before. If anything, her travels made everything so much worse.'

'Well, hindsight is always difficult to argue against, isn't it? But it was our decision, Rose, not just mine.'

'You know what I think? Your love was never properly paternal. I think you *overcompensated*. You were so afraid that you wouldn't be able to love Julia enough that you ended up...'

'Stop!' Timothy's voice was suddenly piercing, like the cry of a bird of prey, and Rose rubbed her eyes, shook her head and then smoothed her hair, as if trying to brush off a bad dream.

Then they both fell silent, their faces sad and tired, their energies spent. Timothy poured all of us another drink, and the two of them sat back down again. We were silent for a few minutes, before I dared to ask my next question.

'Can you tell me a little bit more about the ways in which Julia had changed when she returned from her travels? And how was your relationship with her in the past few months?'

Timothy cleared his throat. 'Well, that's quite difficult to describe. When Julia finally returned to the UK we were all really excited to have her back. The whole family, with the exception of Jonathan, who was still sore about her wedding speech, went to the airport to welcome her home. Amy was elated by the prospect of regaining her beloved sister. We just couldn't wait for her to walk through the arrival gates. When she finally did come through, though, I was quite shocked by her appearance. You know, we hadn't seen her for two years. She'd grown haggard, her face looked thinner and her mouth harder; she was wearing cargo pants, army boots and an old pullover with holes in it, and her once-so-pretty hair was dishevelled and had clearly not been cut for a very long time.

'We hugged, and I was overjoyed that she was back home safely. She, too, seemed very pleased to see us, and for a few days she talked almost non-stop about her experiences during her trip. But she mainly told us about facts. It was curiously impersonal... Economic, political, ecological questions, that kind of thing, you know? We got a pretty clear sense of where she'd been, what she'd witnessed, and that the abject poverty and working conditions in these places had made a profound and lasting impression on her. She seemed angry and distressed, and very restless – all at the same time.

'I think Amy was very disappointed that Julia didn't really appear to be particularly interested in her own news. Amy had just won a scholarship to study for a PhD, and was really excited about her project and all that, and had so much been looking forward to discussing it all with Julia. Julia stayed with us for about two weeks or so, and then moved to a flat in Camden to live on her own. She must have arranged that before her return. It was a rather shabby flat, in a building that looked as though it was about to fall down. I didn't like what I saw at all when we delivered her things there. We agreed to pay her rent for a while, until she knew what she wanted to do next. But, as I said, after a year or so we decided to stop doing that.

'Then she began to work in that ghastly vegetable shop near Camden market, and moved in with a friend she'd met there. That shop was a terribly run-down place, utterly unhygienic, populated by smelly mongrels that had never been properly trained and that didn't follow orders. The people who worked and hung out there were all aggressive, joyless fanatics, not friendly laughter-loving hippies, you know? They always looked at Rose and me as though they thought us the bourgeois enemy incarnate and would like nothing more than to stake us with the meagre organic carrots we bought from them. Instead, they begrudgingly wrapped them in ancient left-wing newspapers and handed them over in the most contemptuous manner possible.'

Then, to my surprise, Rose giggled. After their painfully acrimonious sparring match, I hadn't expected this at all. Timothy clearly didn't, either. His features softened instantly. He, too, smiled, and then looked at his wife so tenderly, and so full of sadness, that it made my heart melt.

'Yes, that's true,' Rose said. 'Julia's friends in that shop really did treat us with such ridiculous disdain that it was almost funny. After a few visits, we stopped going there, though. It was just too awkward. Besides, their vegetables were dreadful – ugly as sin, sour and small, either unripe or rotten, often worm-infested, and really completely unfit for human consumption. I mean, who on earth grows that stuff? Do you remember the so-called "pumpkin" we bought there, Tim? That foul little ball of mush, for which they charged us eight pounds or something ridiculous like that?'

Timothy nodded, and smiled at Rose. She smiled back at him. But then his face became serious again, and he continued: 'Julia also went to a lot of anti-globalization events and got very engaged with the Occupy movement. She travelled across the UK to take part in various campaigns, and even went to Europe a few times, to protest wherever representatives of the World Bank, the WTO, the IMF, the G8, and so on were meeting. She'd always tell me about these gatherings in quite some detail when we met.

'She didn't come to see us at home very often at all. Mainly for family celebrations and things like that, and very reluctantly. Once, she brought along her friend from the shop whom she was living with, a sullen, pale girl who didn't say a single word to us, and refused even to accept a cup of tea – presumably because it wasn't organic or something like that.'

'Yes,' Rose added. 'That girl just stared at us in silence, as though we were the scum of the earth. It beggared belief. Utterly discourteous!'

'Well, and then there was my birthday this January, which Rose has already mentioned. After that I only saw her a few more times before the attack. And obviously, we haven't seen her since. She won't let us visit. Rose felt pretty sore about the birthday dinner incident, and had finally given up trying to convince Julia to come and see us. For quite a while, it had been a rather one-sided pursuit, the attempt to stay in contact. We got the impression that she didn't care very much whether she saw us or not... But I just couldn't stand the idea of losing touch completely. I insisted on our monthly dinners, even though they had become rather tense affairs. She'd completely ceased to be dialogical. Whenever I posed a question or an objection to her, she just broke into long, angry monologues. But still... I mean, I would never, in a million years, have imagined that... '

One last time, Timothy and Rose fell silent. Then Rose checked her watch. 'Gosh,' she said, 'look at the time, Tim. No wonder I feel so awfully tired. We've kept Clare here for far too long. Let's go home now. It's been a very tiring day.'

Then we all got up to leave. Timothy helped Rose into her coat, and then the three of us went down the stairs to the lobby in silence. Having said our goodbyes, I watched them walk down the street to their car. Timothy put his arm around Rose, and she let her head sink on his shoulder.

X

I felt strangely disappointed after the interview. I had expected something else – some definitive pointers, or at least some clues, and I couldn't help but feel that there was something important they hadn't told me. I had hoped to meet more extreme characters – narcissists or psychopaths; authoritarian right-wingers or religious fanatics; passive-aggressive manipulators or irascible tyrants. Instead, I encountered two likeable people with a few completely ordinary human flaws, who were utterly heartbroken by what had happened. I had no doubt that Rose and Timothy were caring, well-intentioned and, by and large, good parents. Yes, Timothy was probably too enamoured with his daughter, while Rose might be on the colder side of the motherly spectrum, but that didn't explain anything. On the contrary, I thought, those tendencies actually balanced each other out rather neatly.

I felt for them, George. It was painful to watch them turn on each other so viciously, like characters in a late Bergman film. It was my impression that the scene was out of character, but then again, we simply can't ever know how couples interact with each other behind closed doors –

whether they are loving and gentle, bored and indifferent or cruel and constantly at each other's throats. Public coupledom is always a performance, a way of presenting a specific image to others that may or may not correspond to authentic feelings. We only ever catch theatrical glimpses of the lives of others. For a long time, I had assumed that your marriage was a haven of bliss, before you confessed to me one day what was happening behind the scenes.

It's possible that Rose and Timothy's dark blame game was just an expression of raw grief and helplessness. But then again, some of the things they said to each other seemed to refer to older grudges. Some of the reproaches attacked the very core of their characters: cold Rose and Timothy the liberal weakling. The achievement-obsessed mother and the blindly adoring, all-too-forgiving father: I have seen this constellation in many a family, and the gender roles are flexible.

I have always felt uneasy when forced to witness the poisonous afterlives of disappointed expectations. They disturb me, these ugly acts of mutual recrimination, the bitter fruit of years of repressed resentment. I have seen what it can do to people. I have seen how Amanda battled so hard (twice) against her husbands' gradual falling out of love with her; how she desperately attempted to change in order to please them and thereby halt the process. The first disliked her timidity in public, and eventually left her for an actress. The second wanted her to be thinner and more glamorous and didn't hide the fact. He always struck me as shallow and as a woman-hater who didn't even bother to pretend he felt otherwise.

But the corrosiveness works both ways, not only when you're at the receiving end, but also when you're the one who is easily irritated by trifles. I felt like an ogre every time I realized that I simply wouldn't be able to stay in a relationship any longer with the men I've dated, and I usually kept my reasons secret, since they worried me. I am sure they were only symptoms in any case: it's more than likely that I didn't just break up with Alan because I disliked the way he constantly swallowed consonants that I deemed important, and that there was more to my refusal of Oscar's proposal than the fact that I could no longer bear the sight of his pink comedy socks. I found the way in which Theo cluttered up my apartment with his many pointless gadgets insufferable; I couldn't bear the way in which Sean kept scratching his left knee whenever he got excited about something. Even one of your habits, George, irritated me during our two happy years, but I won't tell you what it was, as the fault doubtless was in the eye of the beholder.

Deep down, I often feared that there was something wrong with me – why else would I have let these banal things get in the way of relationships that were genuinely important to me? The only person with whom I ever talked about this was Laura.

'Do you think I'm mad, or just sad?' I asked her two days after my interview with Rose and Timothy, over tea in the Blue Nile. I'd just confessed to her the story about Sean and his irritating knee-scratching habit, and how I'd told him the night before that it was over between us, after just two months.

Laura laughed out loud. I think she always enjoyed hearing about my rather teenage love life. 'No, neither. You're just a totally classic workaholic commitment-phobe, whose excuses for dumping people are becoming increasingly desperate. Why don't you just admit it? I'm sure Mum can sort you out. Just embrace the diagnosis and stop pretending, Clare.'

I know Laura didn't mean to upset me, but her comment struck a nerve. Obviously there was some truth to it – after all, my only long-term relationship was with my cat. Besides, I was still reeling from the fact that I appeared to have lost any chance of a future with you, that I'd realized far too late how much I cared for you. But Laura's remark also reminded me of another, much less kind assessment of my character, one that had wounded me very deeply at the time.

And then, on 12 September, at four o'clock in the afternoon, the news broke. I was working on the transcription of Rose and Timothy's interview and had just scanned the *Guardian* headlines online, and there it was. I tried to stay calm but failed miserably. My hands started shaking, and then my entire body followed suit. I got up and poured myself a large drink, and then another. Then the phone rang – Amanda checks the news as compulsively as I do. She told me she'd come over as soon as she was free. She still had to see one more patient that day.

Having downed a third glass of whisky, I returned to my computer and read the rest of the article. Adrian Temple, it announced, was to receive a silver trophy industry award from the British Banking Association for 'outstanding achievements' in the sector. The prize, endowed with £500,000, would be awarded at a lavish do at the Institute of Directors on 7 November. Prominent guests were rumoured to include the governor of the Bank of England and various high-ranking City figures. The article mentioned that before his meteoric rise, Temple had worked as a humble clerk in a small Royal Bank of Scotland branch in Sheffield in the 1990s. In 2001, he had become one of RBS's most successful traders. A spokesperson from the British Banking Association claimed that the profits he secured between 2001 and 2006 for his employer amounted to £800 million. They also briefly mentioned a 'not entirely successful but well-intentioned attempt' to 'open up the exclusive world of trading to ordinary citizens', before moving on to praise Temple's most recent achievements as a CEO at HSBC, where he was now in charge of their overall investment strategy.

I couldn't believe what I was reading. It simply didn't feel real. After all, it was public knowledge that only four years ago Temple had *knowingly* defrauded 512,459 eager British investors of the eye-watering sum of £15 billion. Most of them lost their entire life savings; 24 per cent had to declare bankruptcy; one in ten lost their homes; and at least six people committed suicide. Had the world already forgotten the sordid details of this case? The scandal had been discussed on the front page of every national newspaper. Had everyone forgotten how Temple launched his treacherous *SmartInvestmentVenture* campaign that loudly promised dream returns for every investment over

£20,000 (of course, nobody bothered to read the small print)? Had everyone forgotten how the trader Temple, slick as a sea snake, popped up again and again on our television screens in an aggressive ad campaign, how he made it all sound so simple and safe? How he bragged about his ability to turn ten into a hundred pounds, very deliberately appealing to vulnerable people's dreams of quick and easy money? How he talked the insider talk, mentioning margins, maturities, return rates, redemptions, securities, yields, and so on – enough to intimidate the uninitiated and to give the impression of secret knowledge that only he possessed? How he then promised to guide you through the trading jungle, if only you would trust him with your money?

He presented himself as part magician, part businessman and part prophet, as a self-made rags-to-riches man who could make everyone's wildest financial dreams come true. He promised nothing less than the democratization of investment banking: Temple would be the people's broker, their spiritual guide in the world of glitzy deals and lucrative trades (if only you would trust him with your money). As of now, his message went, the highly profitable world of hedge funds, bonds and portfolios was no longer the exclusive territory of the privileged few who were trained to trade – no, you, too, the viewer, could partake in this bonanza! If enough people participated, he, Adrian Temple, would create a super-national portfolio and turn everyone into a millionaire.

He seemed to be the ultimate clichéd representative of the much-maligned banker figure (he even wore shrill ties with knots as thick as fists, and slicked his hair back with so much gel that he looked like a wet rat). He was a poor man's version of Gordon Gekko, but without the charisma and the wit. I thought this guy couldn't be for real. But he was, and unfortunately not everybody was as appalled by his persona as I was. His scheme instantly proved to be a massive success. *Can you see nothing?* I wanted to shout. *Do you understand nothing?* Can you not see that this man is a Mephistophelian Pied Piper of the first order, just another poisonous spawn of the Charles Ponzi, Nick Leeson and Jordan Belfort tribe?

But I, like everybody else, underestimated him. As I later found out, everything about his campaign was meticulously calculated. He had created the persona he embodied in these ads (in real life, he wore his hair slightly ruffled, floppy and entirely gel-free); he knew which keywords to drop in and when; he knew when to look into the camera and when to look away; he knew exactly who his target group was, and how to manipulate it. He had designed his campaign scrupulously, with the best market researchers and smartest advertising psychologists available. He wasn't an idiot at all. And, as I would find out, although he knew that his investors would sooner or later lose all their money, the whole thing was also legally watertight.

Yet the number of people who fell for this 'dream' scheme and who were prepared to hand over their savings probably surprised even him. It rose further when, in the first year, Temple's 'super-portfolio' yielded a modest profit to its investors. But then, of course, things started to go wrong.

A first loss here, another one there; a badly judged trade here and a crazy gamble there; a junk bond that dragged others down and a dead-cert insider trade that went belly up; problems in the Eurozone; a minor disturbance on the Asian markets; and puff – it all melted into air. After only eighteen months, Adrian Temple had gambled away the entire £15 billion that had been put into his care by the hopeful and the destitute. Just like that. His own fortune, however, amassed through a flat-rate trading fee of 5 per cent, which he conscientiously deducted from every payment into the *SmartInvestmentVenture* fund, was safely stowed away in his personal offshore account. It turned out that he never invested a single penny of his own money in his so-called 'super-portfolio'. He knew all too well how risky it all was.

My favourite part is still that he never even apologized to the people whom he defrauded. 'Shit happens,' he said in a now notorious interview, in which he came across as so callously unrepentant that his attitude shocked even Jeremy Paxman. 'Trading is a high-risk enterprise – sometimes it goes well, and sometimes it doesn't. *C'est la vie.* The people who are moaning now should have read the small print.'

There were many out there who were keen to get him after that. The basic architecture of his scheme as such wasn't illegal, but various lawyers and activists and I were hoping to find other, smaller, procedural errors on which to build a case against him. Anything, really. What I did uncover during my research – that everything was meticulously planned from start to finish, and that Temple never expected his super-portfolio to last for more than twelve months, and was only ever interested in his commission – did of course surpass all expectations. And everybody knew it was the truth. And yet, as I learned the painful way, even intentionally gambling away the money entrusted to him appears not to have been illegal. And now he would receive an award for outstanding achievements in the finance sector. It just beggared belief. What would be next? A knighthood?

Thank God, not too much later, the doorbell rang and Amanda arrived. I could see the relief in her eyes when I opened the door. She was out of breath and must have feared the worst. She hugged me so hard that I thought she would break my back, and then, probably repelled by the smell of the not inconsiderable amount of whisky I had consumed in the meantime, she took my chin in her hands to look me in the eye. It was only at that point that I noticed I had difficulty keeping my balance.

'You're drunk,' Amanda said. And then she added, much more gently: 'Have you taken anything?'

I hadn't. Amanda guided me to the kitchen table and made some coffee. And then – and I still feel bad about it – I subjected my poor, patient sister to a rant of epic proportions, an angry, slurred diatribe, until, in the early hours, when I had run out of steam, she gently guided me to my bed, helped me out of my clothes and tucked me in.

XI

All of a sudden I found myself in a dark place again. I really believed I had come to terms with my defeat. But I simply wasn't prepared for this blow. After all the slow and difficult healing, just when I felt I'd reconnected with my old writing self, the plaster that I'd mistaken for new skin had been brutally ripped off, exposing a wound that was still as raw as when it was inflicted. The small, narrow row of too-neat and too-white teeth exposed by Adrian Temple's victory grin in court once again haunted my dreams.

In the days following the announcement, I slept badly and drank too much. Amanda came round to check on me every evening, and every evening I repeated my frenzied ranting. I think she seriously feared I might snap, this time. I couldn't stop talking about the cynical sickness of it all. But after a week or so, I calmed down a little. I had to. I had work to do, a deadline to meet, a promise to keep. I could see Amanda was beginning to lose patience with my seething sermons, and she implored me not to let Temple destroy my career a second time. Some of the other things she kept saying to me must have helped, too. In crises, Amanda's instincts really are amazing.

I also thought of you, George, and that I simply couldn't let you down. When you called me right after you heard the news, we both knew that I was lying when I told you I was fine. You listened patiently to my performance, and you didn't interrupt my monologue on the degeneracy and shameless cynicism of our apolitical age and its perversely twisted values, where vulnerable so-called benefit 'scroungers' attract unprecedented degrees of hostility and stigmatization, but tax-dodging multimillionaires and fraudulent investors do not just walk free but are applauded. And so on. I continued in that vein. I made some tired jokes, at which you laughed politely. But after a while you gently interrupted me and said, 'Call me any time you need me, Clare. I mean it. And next time, let me know how you really are.' It was only after you'd hung up that I started to cry, no longer able to control my overwhelming sense of impotence and self-pity. But I kept up the pretence, even the next time you called. I didn't want you to see me so weak. Although, had you not been there in court when the verdict was read out, right behind me in the gallery (even Lailah had left her bedroom that day to support me), and had your gaze not held mine when I turned around to look at you, who knows what I would have done.

Optimistic as always, Amanda had booked a table in our favourite restaurant in Mayfair that day – our parents used to take us there whenever one of us had something to celebrate. Like everyone else she thought we would be raising our glasses to toast victory that evening. Instead, the meal was the most sombre of affairs. I think we were all shell-shocked, and nothing could lessen the horror of the catastrophic facts with which I found myself confronted. I had no idea where to find the £150,000 I had been ordered to pay Temple in damages. In addition, I'd been sentenced to pay a proportion of the court costs, which my lawyer estimated would amount to another £150,000. In total I owed £318,894.32.

That night, Amanda suggested we sell our parents' cottage, which I refused to do. The two of us had decided to pass it on to Laura a long time ago, and there was no way I would allow my mistakes to eat into my niece's inheritance. It was so kind of you to offer me £50,000 from your daughter's education fund – your generosity made me cry, but I obviously couldn't accept that sum, either. Even Lailah offered to ask one of her wealthy relatives for an interest-free loan. It was a truly noble gesture on her part, considering she knew what had happened between us, both before and after your marriage. But that evening, I wasn't in a position to appreciate these demonstrations of kindness. It wasn't so much the prospect of financial misery that depressed me most. It was that my belief in institutional justice had been injured, possibly destroyed for ever. Until that day, I'd been a passionate believer in the theoretical and practical fairness of our legal system. I used to believe in the power of the word, and in the power of the truth: my work, my books, my journalism – I used to think of all of these things as forms of political engagement that could change the world for the better. But after the verdict, I was no longer so sure.

What is more – and I haven't told this to anyone yet, George, not even to Laura – I had a run-in with Temple following the pronouncement of the verdict. After the judge dismissed us, we must both independently have headed to the loos to prepare ourselves to face the media who were waiting outside the Old Bailey. When I left the ladies', Temple came out of the gents'.

'Clare,' he said and grinned. 'Trying to repair your tear-smudged make-up before your long walk of shame?'

'You wish,' I said. 'People like you don't make me cry, they just make me angry. And sick.'

'Of course. You're not the crying kind, are you?' And then Temple shoved me against the wall and whispered in my ear: 'Frigid, bitter old bitches like you – you're dead inside, too dried up even for tears. I bet you live alone, don't you, Clare? Single and childless? Tell me I'm wrong. I bet your cunt is just as dry and cold and bitter as your prose. I'm right, aren't I? I mean, where's all that venom coming from, if not from sexual frustration?' And then he laughed. 'You pathetic old cow. Did you really think you could mess with *me*?'

I moved away from him. I could feel the impact of his words reverberating through my body; I could feel myself blushing against my will. I tried to steady my voice before I responded, but I fear it sounded squeaky when I said: 'My private life is none of your business, Temple. And I'd also ask you to go and share your highly original thoughts on the private parts of older women with the media outside, if you dare.'

I got drunk that night, very drunk. You all just continued to fill my glass. It was the kindest thing you could do. The only thing you could do, really. I remember trying to articulate my despair at some point.

'Why work, why write, why care? What use are any of the things we do? What's left, now?' I slurred.

You all chipped in with answers.

'Relationships,' Amanda said. 'Meaningful interpersonal relationships. That's all there is. And that's all there ever was in any case. Working on your own happiness and the happiness of those you can reach around you. Move from the macro to the micro level, Clare. It's the only one over which you can have any control. Don't try to change the world. Focus on the small things. Everything else is an illusion.'

'Pleasure and passion,' Laura said. 'And *fun*. Why's that concept so taboo these days, almost as though it's a dirty word or something? As long as you enjoy what you do, and it gives you pleasure and purpose, go for it. Have more humble aims – do what you love, and do it as well as you can. This desire for exceptionality, fame, impact – I think that's just immodest. I know I'll never be Nigella Lawson, or Jamie Oliver, or Michel Roux, but I don't care. I adore what I do, and I aim to do it to the very best of my ability. I can put a smile on people's faces when they eat my food, and you know what? That's enough for me. Joyful moments, as many of them as possible, is all we can hope for.'

'Faith.' That was Lailah's short, sharp answer, on which she didn't elaborate. She didn't have to. We all knew she'd lost hers (and not just theologically speaking), and that she mourned for it as one mourns for a dead child.

'Thought.' That was yours. 'Art. Literature. Truth. Beauty. They don't have to serve a purpose, or cause a revolution, or impact on our socio-economic environment in any measurable way. They have every reason to exist in their own right. They can reach people's hearts and souls. They're what gives our lives meaning and makes us feel less frightened and alone. They allow us to step into another's shoes, and open up worlds that would otherwise remain for ever hidden. That's enough.'

'But,' I began, 'but... ' I was too drunk to finish my sentence, and I poured the final drops of wine into my glass instead. What I'd wanted to say was that all these solutions struck me as profoundly apolitical and ultimately as defeatist. This unambitious retreat into the pursuit of personal pleasure and insight, it really jarred with me. I'd always wanted so much more than that.

Ultimately, Temple's legal team was quite simply cleverer than mine. Nobody queried the accuracy of the facts pertaining to his business practices as I had presented them in my book. Nobody questioned the gross immorality of his financial transactions and the callously premeditated greed that drove them. The judge even admitted that Temple's 'utterly shameless' scheme constituted an 'abuse of trust on an unprecedented scale' and had wreaked 'incalculable devastation' on his victims. But unfortunately nothing he had done was technically illegal.

I, in contrast, had made two mistakes – small but significant ones. Although Temple sued me for libel and for 'damaging his reputation', ironically he wasn't referring to my exposure of his cynical investment scam. Instead, his team homed in on the fact that I'd described him as an adulterer and a class A drug-user. I hadn't even done so in my book, but in some of the interviews I gave to promote it. It was a very clever strategy. I had no hard evidence to prove his cocaine habit, and none for his affairs, either. I had considered these points to be trivial asides; private matters, really, and not even interesting ones, given that they are so common. I (for reasons you know well) would never sit in judgement on people for marital infidelity, and I have always considered the division of stimulants into legal and illegal as an arbitrary and hypocritical exercise. I see no qualitative difference at all between getting drunk and getting high; our soul-aches are unique and we should all be allowed to medicate them with whatever substances work best for us.

But I do think that the kinds of highs we seek can say something about our personality, just like the cars we drive, the clothes we wear, the interiors of our homes and the books and music we are drawn to. I dropped Temple's cocaine use into the conversation only to draw a fuller picture of his character, in the same spirit in which I commented on some of his other habits and predilections (his penchant for wearing primrose-yellow and lime-green cashmere pullovers, for example; his collection of showy watches; his habit of flipping his hair from his forehead with a brisk jerk of his head; and the fact that, to my great astonishment, he didn't play golf, but instead practised archery and was actually rather good at it, too). At best you could accuse me of having opted for a lazy shortcut – but then again so much about Temple did seem to be utterly clichéd. Although in some respects he did surprise me, above all in the way he expressed his love for his daughter: he didn't shower her with white ponies and pink Chanel tutus, but instead actually spent time with her. They visited museums; they went swimming and fencing; and – most remarkably – they did regular voluntary work in a bird sanctuary in the Bretton Woods.

Knowing how the whole publicity circus works, I'd also quite consciously decided to feed it some morsels of the kind I knew would help me promote my book. I didn't really suspect that these little details would cause such a stir – optimistically, or maybe rather naively, I'd assumed that the public would focus on what really mattered, on all the other things I uncovered and which I did document meticulously and conscientiously. But I was wrong. And really, I should have known better. Almost every interviewer I met after the publication of my book wanted to talk about Temple's private life and his character. It was the gossipy, frivolous elements that interested people most. They wanted to hear more about Temple's Chinese mistress (a twenty-three-year-old escort of bamboo-stalk suppleness and legs that went on for ever); they wanted sordid details on the themed orgies in secluded mansions in the Cotswolds which the two of them appeared to have frequented. They kept asking questions about his cocaine use, while I desperately tried to move on to his *actual* crimes.

I grew so upset that I refused to continue with the promotion activities. Do you remember, George, how you convinced me to carry on by excusing, even ennobling, all this personal prying with the pull of the human-interest factor and our innate desire for stories? How you told me that I had to allow people to imagine the monster in more concrete terms? It was on a rainy summer evening, we were drinking a glass of wine in the BFI bar after having seen *Nosferatu*, and it was the evening on which our second liaison officially ended – I still think 'affair' is not the right word. We were lovers, plain and simple. We loved each other. But you were wracked with guilt; you kept talking about your daughter and Lailah, and how you didn't have it in you to leave her, in spite of the fact that she'd by then succumbed completely to her severe depressive disorder and was refusing treatment, and that her unbridled hostility towards you had destroyed all that was left of the love you once felt for her. But you cared for her enormously (and you still do). It was a cruel reversal of roles – the second time round, I wanted you more than you wanted me. I would have taken you for good, George, I was ready then. I would have committed to you, properly this time. But you didn't trust me anymore; you said I only wanted what I couldn't have, and that I would grow bored and restless and get cold feet just like last time. You said that there was simply too much at stake for you, and that you knew my patterns. When I asked you what patterns, 'Ach, Clare' was all you said, your voice heavy with sadness, and then you took my hand.

But enough of that – that was all a long time ago, and we were both terribly grown up about the whole thing and we managed to remain close and caring and continued to work together. Except that I coped slightly less well with it all than it might have seemed on the outside. You, by contrast, really did seem fine. Most of the time, at least.

But I need to return to Julia's story. In September last year, having spent an entire week more or less permanently drunk and feeling very bitter about the state of our rotten age, I decided to pull myself together. I didn't want to let Temple defeat me a second time. The submission deadline was drawing closer (seven of my precious fourteen weeks had already passed, and I had so much work to do; I realized I was nowhere near where I should be with my research).

And perhaps there was some benign force watching out for me after all, one that didn't wish me to go under in this sea of bile – at least not quite yet. On the morning of 23 September, having just returned from a long walk in Regent's Park to calm my mind in preparation for the day's work, and during which I even caught a glimpse of the golden autumn sun, I found an email in my inbox. The subject line simply read 'Julia', and the sender was someone called Alison Fisher.

The email didn't come entirely out of the blue. About two weeks earlier, I'd sent a message to a range of people who had studied with Julia in Scotland. Having got a First in PPE at Oxford, Julia had studied for an MSc in Political Philosophy at the University of Edinburgh, from October 2009 to January 2010. I found the names of her twelve fellow students on the university's alumni website, and was able to track down the email addresses of eight. Once again I explained who I was, as well as the exact nature of the project, and asked whether they would be able to get in touch with me to share some of their impressions of Julia while she was in Edinburgh. Alison's was the only response I received from the Edinburgh cohort.

Alison wrote that Julia and she had been friends for a few months, and that she'd be very happy to talk to me. She now lived in Canterbury and suggested I meet her there the next day for an after-work drink. Immensely grateful for this opportunity, I responded at once to confirm the time and place of our meeting. The next day, I left London a few hours too early. I had decided to wander through Canterbury for a while, as I hadn't seen this quaint little cathedral town for many years. In fact I had last visited with my parents more than a decade ago, and I longed to see the cathedral gardens and the cloister again. I was too restless to read on the train, and instead stared out of the window for the entire journey. The sky was cement grey and the clouds were hanging low. We drove past the enormous King's Cross development site, where new, scrawny-looking buildings were climbing weed-like towards the heavens; we passed the desolate swampland that starts just where the city ends, and then numerous orchards and bright green hills speckled with sheep and other cattle, which reminded me of the lost days of my childhood in the countryside.

When I arrived in Canterbury I immediately saw the building near the station that Alison had suggested for our meeting, a large, shed-like structure that must once have sheltered train carriages and hay wagons, and that now housed a farmers' market and restaurant. But I was three hours early, and so I walked on, through the narrow opening of Westgate Towers into the city centre, down the cobblestoned high street and past numerous low red-brick buildings and timbered medieval cottages, with their rose- and camellia-studded front gardens. I crossed a shallow, overgrown canal, and then turned left into a square teeming with tourists and field-tripping students from France who were admiring the grand entrance to the cathedral precincts.

I found that I still remembered the layout of the place, and headed straight to the cloister. I have always found cloisters calming – there is something soothing about the splendid symmetry of their criss-crossing Gothic arches and the overgrown gravestones. For a moment, I rested my forehead against a cold, smooth stone pillar and closed my eyes. Then I explored the herb garden, and, having walked around the precincts, I returned to the west-facing facade to examine the impressive collection of grinning gargoyles that protruded from the surface like demonic pustules.

Then I ordered a Leffe in a café-bar around the corner and watched the swarming tourists. I was still about half an hour early when I returned to the venue by the station, and I found a table for two on the upper deck where the restaurant was located. I watched the market people below covering their stalls and wares with hessian sackcloth, until the entire place conveyed a sense of absence and loss, like the home of someone who has recently passed away. When the hustle and bustle of the market had died down, early diners began to flock in. I read through my notes and ordered another beer while I waited for Alison to arrive.

Alison was twenty minutes late, for which she apologized profusely. She was wearing black jeans, black, flicked-up eyeliner and a lumberjack shirt, and was carrying a selection of heavy-looking old leather bags. I was immediately struck by her warm smile, her big azure-blue eyes, her tiny nose splattered with pale freckles, and her poker-straight raven hair, which shone like molasses. Her voice was deep and husky, and she spoke so quickly that her words tumbled over each other in their excitement. Hers was a bubbly, infectious, monkey-liveliness – she was the kind of person you couldn't imagine sitting still for very long. She asked me whether I'd eaten, and when I shook my head she cried out: 'Oh good! I'm so glad. I hate eating alone and I'm starving. I haven't even had time for a sandwich today. You wouldn't *believe* how crazily busy things were at work.' I liked her immediately.

Then she emphatically urged me to choose the vegetable platter, swearing it was 'by *far* the best thing on the menu'. I didn't dare to ignore her recommendation, and luckily she was right – our meal was superb. Alison, too, ordered a beer, and when we'd both finished our aperitifs we decided to have a bottle of red with our main course. She chattered away in her throaty, hurried way as though we'd known each other for decades, and in the space of less than half an hour I learned that she was working for the council as a social services adviser, that her partner, Carlos, was a fitness instructor who was deeply disappointed by her complete lack of interest in all things sport-related and in her refusal to further enhance the firmness of her thigh muscles. She jumped up and turned on her axis, asking me what I thought of them, and I laughed and said I thought they looked just perfect. Luckily, she and Carlos did share a passion for dancing, and had recently bought a flat together, close to the city walls right by the canal. They were thinking of getting married and having kids – but not *too* soon, she hastened to emphasize. Alison also told me that there were some pretty deprived places in and around Canterbury, very different from what the tourists saw, and recounted some harrowing tales of cases she'd recently had to deal with, including that of a gang of chain-smoking, vodka-drinking pregnant teenagers. We only started to talk about Julia once we'd finished our meal, and most of the wine.

XII

'When did you first meet Julia?' I asked, having switched on my recording device.

'I remember that as though it were yesterday. It was at the social and political science welcome meeting at the beginning of term, in October 2009. We were all in a totally packed lecture theatre in the school's main building on George Square, but I noticed Julia right away. I don't know, there was *something* about her that immediately drew me to her. She always held herself very upright, you know, like this.' Alison straightened her back and threw her head back, cocking it to the left to illustrate Julia's usual posture.

'So she sat very straight like that on the edge of a chair in the back row with her arms folded across her chest,' she continued. 'She reminded me of one of those film noir heroines of the thirties and forties. There was something very feline and a bit masculine about her, you know? I sat down a few seats away from her. But after only ten minutes or so of listening to a pretty ill-judged and condescending welcome speech by a young male professor called George Williams, she left the theatre. Like, deliberately and loudly, so that everyone noticed. She pulled the door shut behind her with a bang. I thought it was very brave of her, and soon a few others got up and left, too.'

Alison took another sip of wine, stretched her back and then continued. 'I saw her again two hours later, at a buffet lunch organized for the new MA students in political philosophy. I was really excited that she'd be in my class, and I went straight up to her. I made a joke about the bad speech and we both laughed about how inappropriate it had been. Then Julia studied me carefully, and grilled me with lots of questions: where I came from, what I'd studied before coming to Edinburgh, what modules I'd chosen, what books I was reading. We seemed to have a lot in common, and we clicked from the start.'

'Would you like another glass?' I asked Alison, since we'd finished the wine by then and she had tried twice to coax more out of the empty bottle.

'Will you join me?' she asked.

'Sure,' I smiled.

'All right then,' Alison said, and signalled to the waiter.

'So you and Julia became friends?'

'Yes, almost instantly – I've never felt so close to anyone so quickly. And I've never lost contact with anyone so abruptly, either. I mean, I like people and I get on with most of them, but with Julia it became deep and intense *very* fast. After that brunch we decided to go elsewhere together to continue talking, and Julia took me to a small, totally run-down pub on one of the steep, winding side-streets that branch off the Cowgate. Its windows were boarded up and covered with graffiti of a vaguely political nature. Inside, too, everything was derelict. The floors looked as if they hadn't been cleaned for decades and the black walls were barren apart from a crudely painted red anarchy sign. The place was run by a bald, bulky and pretty scary-looking Glaswegian whose face was covered with tribal tattoos. His name was Mo. To be honest, I couldn't understand a *word* he said, but he and Julia clearly already knew each other, since he broke into a smile when she came in. Mo's was Julia's favourite haunt in Edinburgh. It was usually empty and too rough-looking to attract other students. They all preferred the safer, glitzier boho places in the vicinity. As did I, actually, but I found going to Mo's with Julia really thrilling. Obviously I'd never have dared to set foot in there without her. It was the kind of place in which you'd fear getting beaten up for reading a book, or for having an English accent.'

Our extra wine arrived. We clinked glasses, and then Alison continued.

'Julia didn't drink alcohol, did you know that? I never *once* saw her with a drink, in the entire three months I knew her. Anyway. That didn't stop me from having the odd one. Or five.' She laughed.

'Do you know why Julia didn't drink?'

'She said she disliked both the taste and the effect. Mad, isn't it?'

'What did you and Julia talk about when you met?'

'Oh, all sorts of things. Our modules, the other students, our lecturers. *Crushes*, obviously. Our families. She told me quite a lot about her sister. I think she was called Annie, or Amy, or something. Julia was very worried about her;

she had a serious eating disorder, apparently. Julia felt quite torn about how to respond to it. I've got a cousin who suffered from anorexia – still does, as it happens, so I could completely relate to her dilemma.'

'How do you think Julia felt about her parents? Did she talk to you about them?'

'Hmm, not that much, really. I think I probably ranted on about mine quite a lot, but she didn't really say that much about hers. From the few things she did say, I gathered that she found her mother a tad cold and her father a bit over the top. But I don't think she was particularly preoccupied with them.'

'What topics did interest her?'

'Ideas. Definitely. She was very interested in theories and big questions – justice, ethics, equality, that kind of thing. She'd always talk about ideas if you didn't stop her, and obviously she was extremely sharp and articulate and all that, so I wasn't ever bored when she went on about political and ethical dilemmas and so on. Obviously I was interested in these topics, too, but perhaps not *quite* as obsessively as she was. She *was* really serious about it all, you know? Like really intense.

'Luckily, we'd chosen exactly the same modules that term – one on political philosophy, one on ethics and markets, one on globalization and its discontents. I can't remember the name of the fourth. We always sat together in class. We had so much *fun* together. We'd send each other silly little notes and whisper things to each other, and we both fancied one of the lecturers, the one who taught globalization and its discontents, so we deliberately flirted with him to try and make him blush. I think we must have been pretty annoying!

'But then Julia always made up for those moments. I mean, she was just so fiercely, *scarily* clever – even the lecturers were in awe of her. And whenever she said anything during the seminar discussions everyone else just sort of agreed and nodded their heads.'

'Really? I would have thought that her views wouldn't necessarily appeal to everyone... '

'Oh, they did! Well, except for one person – I almost forgot about her. There was one student Julia didn't get on with at all. Mia something... Meyerowitz, I think it was. I'm pretty sure no one in the seminar liked Mia that much. She had an incredibly shrill, tinny voice and tried to dominate seminar discussions. She looked like a Japanese teenager who'd just returned from the future: she was small and wiry, and wore her pink hair in two braided buns over her ears, separated by a sharp-edged fringe. Usually, she was clad in wetsuit-like rubber outfits paired with absurdly high boots, or else she was dressed like a schoolgirl in an Asian horror film. Like, *totally* over the top, you know? Mia was a big theory-lover, a highly articulate advocate of identity politics, for whom Foucault, Derrida and Butler were gospel. You know the type? Julia had real issues with Mia's views – she thought that the politics of representation and the concern with symbolic structures that was so fashionable in academia at that time was narcissistic and a dangerous distraction from the only thing she felt really mattered: a fairer distribution of wealth. She took that kind of stuff *very* seriously, and Mia *really* bothered her.'

'How would you describe Julia's political views at that time?'

'I don't know. They were hard to pin down. She read a lot of stuff on decolonization, all kinds of political resistance movements and guerrilla warfare. There was definitely a neo-Marxist streak. For example, she thought that the only cure for the crude economic and ecological exploitation on which Western privileges were built was the radical abolition of private property. I remember her explaining all that to me in more detail in Mo's bar one evening.

'Anyway, Julia and Mia clashed from the start, and their quarrels grew ever more heated. Mia really *was* quite annoying, with her Mickey Mouse voice and endless theory-speak, and I think pretty much everyone in the class sided with Julia when they argued. Soon the Western political thought module was completely dominated by their verbal duelling. Things really came to a head when Mia gave a presentation on Judith Butler's *Gender Trouble*. About five minutes into the presentation, Julia pulled a face and rolled her eyes at me. But unfortunately, Mia had seen her do it too. She asked Julia really aggressively if there was something she had to say, and as you can imagine, Julia did.

'They really laid into each other. Julia went on about how taking these paradox-peddling obscurantist rhetoricians seriously was like contemplating which wallpaper to choose while your house was burning down. Mia in turn called Julia a spoiled upper-middle-class white bitch who didn't know the first thing about poverty or real suffering. And on they went, you can imagine it. The rest of us were in stitches, except for Mia, of course, who was fuming.'

'It does all sound a bit crass, Alison,' I said.

'Yes, but it was really funny. I don't know. Maybe I haven't told the story very well. Julia did have a funny side, you know? She made me laugh. A lot. All of us, in fact. At the start of the year, our seminar group went out regularly for drinks. One evening, we went on a pub-crawl that ended up in a place called The World's End on the Royal Mile. After we'd been there for a while we all agreed to walk up to the castle to enjoy the view of the city at night. Julia was the only one who was sober. The rest of us were completely rat-arsed by the time we reached the cobblestone-covered car park at the top of the hill. We stumbled across it towards the castle gate, which we planned to enter so that we could inspect the infamous Stone of Scone. But to our great disappointment we found it guarded by a soldier, who was standing stiff and still, blocking the way in. He was around eighteen or nineteen, clad in a traditional Scottish ceremonial kilt, and his white, round face, which was decorated with an unflattering cap, shone brightly in the moonlight. I remember we all thought he looked absolutely hilarious, and we took lots of silly pictures of him on our phones.

'Then we started pleading with him to let us in, but he just ignored us. He stared straight ahead, never even acknowledging our presence. We came up with all kinds of reasons why we urgently needed to go into the castle. We even tried to bribe him with whisky and shortbread, but to no avail. Then the girls in the group became more daring, calling him names, commenting on the shapeliness of his legs, promising him kisses, finally threatening to lift his kilt, but the boy remained standing to attention. Amazing!

'Julia watched the spectacle from afar. Then she joined us and declared that she could make him move. We all jeered and laughed, but Julia insisted. Mia didn't believe her, and suggested a bet. I think they bet fifty quid each – and the rules were no touching and without throwing anything. They shook hands on it. Julia smiled and walked up to the soldier. Then she pulled down her trousers and knickers, squatted down next to him and started to pee. Just before the puddle reached his feet, the boy stepped aside, his face as red as the feather in his cap. We were dying of laughter. It was *so* funny, Clare. Only Mia was peeved, of course.'

I thought about that scene while Alison went to the loo.

'How did Julia feel about academia more generally?' I asked her when she returned. 'And how did she get on with your lecturers?'

'Well, really well, at the beginning. There was this middle-aged professor, Robert McMullan, whom we both kind of fancied – you know, softly spoken, rolling his "r"s in that sexy Scottish way, sensitive and quietly elegant, with melancholic brown eyes and floppy grey hair, and so on. Although I wouldn't have admitted it then, he obviously fancied Julia, too. He always looked as though he was about to sink down on his knees and propose marriage whenever she opened her mouth, like he was totally bewitched. He'd stare at her for ages and forget to respond until people started to giggle. He'd constantly cite her in his lectures: "As Julia put it so lucidly the other week", and "as Julia has pointed out so perceptively" – that kind of stuff. Embarrassing! The other lecturers were a bit afraid of Julia, I think, because she was obviously so much brighter than they were, and they must have felt threatened by that. You know, most academics are dreadful narcissists.'

'So why did your friendship with Julia end?'

Alison laughed. 'Well, why do friendships between women usually end? A *man* came between us. He stole my best friend. Seriously, that's *exactly* what happened. To this day I'm not sure where he came from, what he was doing in Edinburgh, or even what his real name was. All I know is that he called himself Chris, and that she met him at Mo's place. We were sitting at our usual table, and Julia was talking about the social repercussions of lowering capital gains and income taxes when I noticed that she became distracted. She kept glancing over her shoulder, and finally I, too, craned my neck to see who or what was diverting her attention: it was a tall, very good-looking man, in his late twenties or early thirties, who was standing at the bar and chatting to Mo.

'He *was* very good-looking, I'll admit that: lean and muscular, with short, sand-coloured hair, tanned skin, fine features and dark-blue, dancing eyes. In spite of his rather shabby outfit, he looked sophisticated, and he had a posh voice. Mo, who'd also noticed Julia's interest, called her over and introduced her to him. They immediately started to chat and were so absorbed in their conversation that Julia forgot my presence altogether. After half an hour or so, I'd finished my drink on my own and got up to leave. She did give me a quick peck on the cheek when I passed them, and half-heartedly introduced me to Chris, but I know when I'm not wanted, and I let the lovebirds get on with it.

'I saw her only a few times after that. It was obvious that she'd fallen really hard for this guy. She stopped responding to my calls and left most of my emails unanswered. I felt a bit hurt by her sudden rejection – after all, we'd been such close friends. But you know what? In the end I understood. I mean, we've all been there, haven't we? When you fall in love, you fall in love. I got over it. I knew it wasn't personal. I'm sure I've behaved like that myself.

'She told me a little bit about Chris when I did see her, that he was involved with some political groups, but what their aims were I don't know. When he wasn't at Mo's, he seemed to spend most of his time in a bookshop in Windmill Street, talking to the owner and his friends. Apparently he'd caught the attention of quite a few other women on our course, and rumours were circulating among them. Some said he was a dealer, some that he was a gardener, some that he was working on a radical philosophical treatise. One girl was convinced that he robbed banks and gave away his spoils to the poor. I saw him with Julia in town a couple of times; they were walking hand in hand, looking totally enraptured with each other.

'The very last time I saw Julia was in mid-January 2010. I'd just returned from my parents' where I'd spent the Christmas holidays. She called me out of the blue on a

Wednesday afternoon and asked if I could come to her flat. She said she wanted to give me something. When I arrived I found her in an almost empty apartment with only a few boxes and plastic bags. We hugged, and she said she was moving out of her flat. I asked whether she was moving in with Chris – it seemed the obvious explanation. But Julia told me that they were going travelling, that they'd had enough of academia, of Edinburgh – of everything, really. I was completely shocked and asked her about her studies, her degree, her parents, how they would finance it all – I was really worried for her. I mean, dropping out is *such* an extreme thing to do, don't you think? And it felt like a terrible waste – she was by *far* the most talented of all of us.

'She looked at me very seriously. And she sounded genuinely sad when she asked me why she should stay, what for. She said she had no desire whatsoever to work for her daddy in his law firm and to facilitate yet more unappetizing corporate mergers, or to join an investment bank and help some greedy, testosterone-driven cokeheads to gamble away the nation's savings. Then she handed me two heavy plastic bags filled with books, hugged me hard, and that was the last I saw of her. I still have some of her books, including her copies of Fanon's *The Wretched of the Earth*, Che's *Guerrilla Warfare*, Debray's *Revolution in the Revolution?*, and Marighella's *Minimanual*.'

'What do you think happened to Julia?' I asked. 'How do you explain what she did?'

'I really don't know,' Alison said. Suddenly, she looked drawn and tired. All her liveliness and energy appeared to have evaporated into thin air. She listlessly folded and unfolded her napkin, and then folded and unfolded her legs. 'I mean, I've thought about it a lot, obviously. I was totally shocked when the news came out, utterly shaken. When someone you knew and very much liked does something like that, I don't know, it really affects you. But even today I find it impossible to reconcile my memories of Julia with what I've heard and read about her. It's like we're talking about two completely different people. I remember her as warm, funny, caring and engaged. Very serious and intense about certain political issues, yes, but, you know, in a completely reasonable way. Most of what she said made a lot of sense to me, and to everyone else in our class, too.'

Alison finished her wine. 'The only explanation I can think of is that someone must have corrupted her – that she met someone on her travels, someone evil, someone who messed with her head. Perhaps it was that Chris guy. I don't know. But I know for sure that the person I met in Edinburgh was neither evil nor a sociopath. Far from it.'

When we left the restaurant, Alison accompanied me to the train station, where we hugged goodbye. I turned around just before boarding the train and saw her still standing there, behind the gates, waving.

XIII

Who was this woman? The more I learned about Julia, the blurrier my image of her became. This was strange – usually, the opposite was the case. In the course of all the previous biographies I had worked on, the pieces of my subjects' personality puzzles gradually began to merge into a bigger picture, until they formed a coherent whole. It always took patience, and hard work – it was never an easy process – but at some point there was always *something* I could use, some theory that emerged organically, some kind of pattern of cause and effect. But not in this case. I was beginning to worry about how to reconcile these different visions of Julia – I would have to take sides at some point. Had Julia been seduced and corrupted by someone, as Amy, Alison and her father seemed to think? Was she simply evil, as Jonathan suggested? Had her character been spoiled and damaged by bad parenting, as her mother believed? Or was there a cold, perhaps even sociopathic streak in her personality?

What is more, I found myself questioning the ways in which the people I had interviewed interpreted Julia's actions. They appeared to me such unreliable narrators, all of them, blindly adoring or else aggrieved and resentful.

But most disturbingly, listening to their stories, even the ones that were supposed to cast Julia in a bad light, I had caught myself more than once thinking that I could actually see Julia's point.

Very soon, I would have to make a decision about what line of argument I was to adopt – otherwise, without a strong story, I knew you would send it all back, studded with the piercing comments in Bordeaux-coloured ink for which you are so famous, and lose faith in me completely. And without your support, George, I may as well give up.

Readers of biographies want above all a sound narrative that imposes meaning on the seeming chaos of life. They don't like unresolved ambiguities. They expect biographers to be their spirit guides in the murky territory of character and motivation. But how was I to accomplish this, given that my subject wouldn't let me speak to her, that there were no letters, diaries or other textual traces of her psychological and intellectual development, and that everyone I had interviewed so far seemed to have very different opinions on Julia's true character? I wished Mia Meyerowitz would get back to me – Alison's description of her sounded intriguing. I kept thinking that she must have some interesting thoughts on the case. I Googled her and found out that she was an Associate Professor of Queer and Gender Studies in Berkeley, California. She sounded like she was the only person so far who even came close to being Julia's intellectual match. I sent her a follow-up email, urging her once again to get in touch.

Did Julia really mean any of the things she said to Alison, to Mia and in class, I wondered, or had she just been sharpening her rhetorical skills, exploring how far her verbal powers would take her, and whether anyone had the ability and the guts to stop her? Was Julia just pulling the wings off her opponents out of boredom, or did she get some kind of pleasure from watching them suffer?

When I got back late that evening from my trip to Canterbury I felt nostalgic for my childhood. I miss my parents so much that sometimes the pain completely overwhelms me. I took out a box of old letters and photographs. There were pictures of them standing proudly hand in hand in front of our cottage; pictures of Amanda and me playing in the orchard; pictures of our first school days; and of family holidays in Brittany and Cornwall. While I browsed, I also came across the letter you wrote me after we broke up, the first time. I must have read it a million times. I still think about it, often, in fact, and whether there is any truth to your allegations. I still haven't quite made up my mind. You called me an enjoyment-averse workaholic, a commitment-phobic coward, stubbornly determined to reject the only things that really mattered in life – intimacy and love. You called me cold. An 'arctic intellectualizer' who sent shivers down your spine, a 'pathological run-away bride' with a 'refrigerator mind that chill-blasts the life out of all things of beauty' – these were your very words. People like me, you wrote, are the worst: cheating refuseniks, too afraid to embrace love when it stares them right in the face. We, you prophesied, will be left with nothing in the end. We're the ones dying alone and afraid in the dark, with the bitter taste of regret in our pinched mouths.

I know you wrote this in anger, and you have apologized for it. But I am still not sure which parts of it you really meant, and which ones were simply designed to hurt me. I do rather hope you did (and do) not actually think of me that way. Apart from your apology for your 'very upset and childish outburst', and your assertion that you still hoped we could continue to work with each other as before and remain good friends, which followed (in writing and with flowers) one week after the letter, we never spoke about it again. Your accusations continued to haunt me, though. They still do.

Thinking back, now, remembering the good bits in what we had, I find it difficult to understand what it was exactly that drove me to drop you. We saw eye to eye on almost everything; you made me laugh and you made me relax; we had so much *fun* together. Do you remember how often we giggled? You would only have to raise one of your eyebrows, which always made you look like Mephisto, and I would crack up. I loved your wit and your curiosity and your caustic comments on things you didn't like, and your unruly battleship-grey hair; your slow dark laughter that reached its climax in such a leisurely manner, like cumbersome Pacific waves crashing on the shore. I loved your cinnamon scent and your crankiness. We were so good together, George. I think we brought out the best in each other. I still miss you and me, how we were back then.

I don't know what changed between us, and when, and why – these things happen so gradually. I only know that at some point, towards the end of our first liaison, your laughter no longer reminded me of the sea-shore but just struck me as too loud. And the enchanting eccentricity of your crankiness had, in my mind, been transformed into moodiness and wearisome petulance. But that wasn't it, of course. Above all, I felt increasingly stifled by your expectations; I felt you were beginning to eat too much into my time, distracting me from my work. You constantly wanted us to *do* things – to go to exhibitions, to see films, to explore new restaurants, to attend dinner parties; you wanted me to meet your mother (which I did, and, as you know, I didn't like her much and neither did she take to me) and all your friends, of which you had so many, far too many for my liking – you always were much more gregarious than me. You expected me to take five days off around your forty-fifth birthday (just like that – two weeks before I had to submit a manuscript) to explore your favourite Parisian galleries and cafés with you, and you were angry and upset when I declined. Although you worked in publishing yourself, you never quite understood that writing takes time and discipline and real commitment. Every time I had to work evenings and weekends, you considered it a personal insult. You were relentless. And the more you asked and pressed me to do things with you, the more often I had to say no, which made me feel guilty and you unloved. I became irritable; you became morose. One day, I woke up and just knew it wouldn't work.

Thinking about all of this upset me so that after dinner, rather than returning to my cell, I spent some time in the TV room, just to avoid being on my own with all these thoughts. Anyway. I should move on; it is getting late. Towards the end of September, I found another email waiting in my inbox.

Mia Meyerowitz had responded to my second message, in which I had told her that Alison had reached out to me and that her name had come up in her account, and asked again whether she could share some of her thoughts on Julia. I added some flattery around the edges, too, which tends to work with a surprisingly large number of people, especially with academics. But evidently not this time – my heart sank when I saw how short her message was. This is what she wrote:

Dear Clare,

Thank you for getting in touch and for your kind words. You asked me to describe my impression of Julia White's character based on our shared time in Edinburgh, and I am happy to comply with your request. In fact, I can do so swiftly and succinctly: Julia White is a psychotic of the first order, and I sincerely hope that she will rot in prison for the rest of her life. I am not sure how (and why) you are planning to write an entire book about this person; the analysis of socio-pathology is best left to those properly trained to do so. What is more, it is, ultimately, not a very interesting subject.

I wish you the best of luck with your endeavour in any case.

Yours,
Mia

Mia was unfortunately not prepared to elaborate further on her statement.

XIV

Whenever I'm alone these days, the guilt I feel about what I have done becomes almost unbearable. I have come to fear being on my own so much that I look forward to the daily outings, headcounts and chores now – they provide some respite from my troubling memories. Since last week, I have had to work between breakfast and lunch, and from two to five except on days when I have visiting rights. I was able to choose between service in the kitchen, the laundrette, or the workshop. I chose the latter. I always liked making things with my hands. With my very first pay cheque, I bought myself an electric screwdriver and a set of sturdy stainless steel tools. I always thought it important that I should be able to fix things that needed fixing on my own – I don't like being dependent on others. I taught myself a whole range of things, and I can fit shower curtain rails and ceiling lamps, bleed radiators and re-pressurize boilers, and I am an expert assembler of all kinds of Ikea furniture.

In the workshop, we're supervised by a taciturn Asian man with a saffron-coloured turban, which jars oddly with his blue uniform. He barely ever speaks, and appears to be working on an elaborate and really rather impressive-looking wooden shrine. We inmates either have to repair small electrical appliances, or else assemble simple pinewood furniture: bedside and sofa tables, footstools, chairs and flower stands. They are not too bad looking, actually. Each day, I find a new task on my workbench, along with a manual and a set of tools, the contents of which the guard controls rigorously to make sure nobody steals anything that could be used as a weapon. There are about twenty other women in the workshop to which I have been assigned. They all seem quite friendly. I have come to look forward to the hours I spend there. Usually, the radio is on, or else we talk or just work in silence. It's good to have something to do, and it's good to be able to chat to others. I'm slowly re-learning how to do that. Here, things are really peaceful, possibly because they only allow mentally stable inmates near the tools and machinery. I suppose it is a compliment that I have been classified as one of them.

I have begun to pay more attention to what is happening around me here. Sarah – the shy new girl with the shaking hands – never says a word, but she always seeks my company. During meals, she sits next to me, very close, like a freezing bird in need of warmth. I try to get her to talk a little, but apart from her name I haven't yet managed to get much out of her. She worries me – she hardly eats anything and her skin is a sickly shade of yellow, like a fading bruise. Her hair looks medieval, as though she chopped it off herself in a moment of despair or self-punishment, and her dark eyes are moist and feverish.

I also found out more about the black woman I mentioned. One of the guards told me that her name is Amelia and that she used to be a teacher. Four years ago, she apparently smashed her husband's brain to pulp. It's very hard to believe – she has such a kind, wise face. She's the only other person who frequents the library, and now, whenever she sees me sitting in my usual place by the small window, reading the papers, she acknowledges my presence with a short nod. Yesterday, she even smiled. I smiled right back at her. Perhaps, one day, we'll actually speak to each other. I would love to hear her story.

But time is precious – even more so now that I work most days. Having read Alison's account, it became obvious to me that I had to find the man who called himself Chris. Julia's parents, moreover, had also mentioned a male friend, whom Julia had occasionally referred to in the postcards she sent them from the various countries in South-East Asia and Latin America that she had visited on her trip. From her parents' and Amy's remarks, I also gathered that Julia returned to the UK on her own, and that she never mentioned her travelling companion again. Presumably she and Chris had fallen out at some point during their journey.

Given that Alison didn't know anything more concrete about Chris than the wild legends spread by her classmates, I decided to travel to Edinburgh to find out more about this elusive figure. On 3 October I arrived at Waverley station. It was a bright and windy afternoon, and, after having checked into my bed and breakfast in one of the grand grey townhouses located at the edge of the Meadows (you would have loved it, George), I began to look for Mo's place. Starting at the lower end of the Cowgate near the Scottish Parliament and Holyrood Palace, I walked up every single one of the winding side-streets that branched off that gloomy road, which always makes me think of pestilence and ancient bloodshed. Perhaps not entirely surprisingly, I found that Mo's place no longer existed. Quite a few new places had been opened in that area in the past five years, though, and I tried to speak to the manager of every one of them to ask whether they remembered a pub run by a Glaswegian called Mo. Finally, in an artisan bakery on Old Fishmarket Close, I got lucky. The young couple who owned it remembered Mo and his tavern. They told me it had been on Blackfriars Street, and that it was now home to an overpriced and underspiced vegan restaurant. They had never been there, nor did they know Mo personally, but his name rang a bell because three years ago, in the summer of 2011, he had been killed in a brutal knife attack, just a few yards away from his pub after he had closed it down for the night. The killer had not just stabbed him eleven times, but had also removed a piece of skin from his face with a particular tattoo on it (the woman thought it was a Celtic cross; the man remembered it as a Japanese character). The police never managed to catch the perpetrator, but rumour had it that Mo had been murdered by a jilted lover, whom he had apparently left for a younger companion just three days prior to the attack.

The only other lead I had was the bookshop on Windmill Street, which I decided to visit the next morning. I had actually come across its name before, since it was one of the few bookshops left in the country that still invited guest speakers and hosted political debates. I had slept very badly that night, kept awake both by worries about the approaching deadline (I had four weeks left) and my lack of a narrative angle, and by the noisy sexual exploits of the inhabitants of the room right next to mine.

When I entered the bookshop around 11 a.m., I felt immediately at home: it smelled of freshly brewed tea; polished hardwood floors, white walls and glossy white shelves testified to the owner's elegant taste; and the bookcases were filled from top to bottom with exactly the kind of books I loved best. I browsed for a while, and noticed with great pleasure that some of my own pre-trial works were there, too. Finally, I turned to the man behind the till, an Iranian in his late forties with turquoise eyes and very white teeth. In a mellow voice, he asked what he could do for me. I told him I was writing a book about Julia White and was looking for someone called Chris, with whom Julia seemed to have formed a bond while studying in Edinburgh a few years ago. I watched his face closely, but his features didn't betray anything.

'I don't think I can help you there,' he said. 'I'm sorry.'

I looked at him in silence for a while. Silences usually disconcert people. Often, they grow uncomfortable and start talking, and eventually give away something, however small and unintended it may be – and that's all I need. Once they open their door, even if ever so slightly, I, like a good double-glazing salesman, get my foot in. But this man simply held my gaze, not at all put off by the silence.

'Chris must have spent a lot of time in this bookshop in December 2009 and early in 2010, according to my sources,' I finally added.

'Sorry,' the man said. 'I don't remember anyone called Chris.'

'When did you start working here? Were you around at that time?'

'I own this shop. I've been around since 2005,' he said with a sweet little smile that betrayed just a hint of pride.

Fortunately, I'd done my research that morning. 'I see. You must be Tariq Ghaznavi, then. It's so nice to meet you. I love your shop. My name is Clare Hardenberg.'

'Clare Hardenberg?' He looked surprised. 'Of *The Deal* fame?'

'Yes, that's me,' I said, and now it was I who broke into a small, shy smile.

Then Tariq locked the shop door, invited me to sit, offered me tea, and asked me to tell him all about my current project. We chatted for hours. I must have drunk at least a dozen glasses of the sweet, strong black tea Tariq kept pouring from a samovar into our coloured glasses (I wasn't able to sleep that night, either). Tariq did remember Chris, but it took me a long time to convince him that Chris would at no point be in danger of prosecution as a result of my project. (I also promised him that I would deliver my first public reading after the launch of Julia's biography in his bookshop, and eventually, after I added a hundred exclusively signed copies to the deal, he began to talk.)

Tariq first met Chris in 2007. Chris was studying for a doctorate in anthropology at that time, and used to spend a lot of time hanging out in Tariq's bookshop. According to Tariq, Chris was a bright, passionate idealist and an active member of numerous NGOs. His thesis was supposed to be a study of trade and barter patterns of the Ogoni people in Nigeria, but he got sidetracked by their ongoing struggle against the exploitation of their lands by Shell Oil, a sustained campaign of resistance initiated by the then already brutally murdered Ken Saro-Wiwa. Chris grew ever more disgusted with what he learned about the Ogoni's plight. He changed his research topic to 'Biopiracy in Nigeria' and went to live with the Ogoni in the Niger Delta for six months. When he returned, he gave up his studies in order to concentrate more fully on campaigning for their rights.

Tariq didn't know much about Chris's background, but suspected he came from a rich family. It was the way he spoke, he said, and the fact that he never seemed to have to work and always appeared to have enough money to pay for his accommodation, travels and so on. I asked Tariq about the dealer and the bank robber rumours, but he just laughed.

With Tariq's support Chris organized a few anti-Shell campaigns in Edinburgh. Chris was arrested a couple of times on anti-G8 and WTO protests, and for chaining himself to a petrol station gate. He was a likeable, outgoing person, Tariq said, with an easy manner and bags of charm, and many people, especially women, felt drawn to him. He had hundreds of friends and acquaintances, and Tariq reckoned he was one of the best-connected people in the Scottish left-wing scene. Tariq had even met Julia once – Chris introduced her just before the two of them left town. He remembered thinking her very beautiful and that the couple seemed very much in love, but couldn't recall any other impressions. He received a few postcards from Chris while the two of them were abroad. After his travels, Chris didn't return to Edinburgh, but stayed in touch with Tariq. Finally, Tariq told me that Chris was currently working in a camp for illegal immigrants awaiting deportation in the South of France, and agreed to email him to ask whether he would be prepared to speak to me.

He was a lovely man, Tariq, and that evening, after he had closed his shop for the day, we went for a drink, and then he invited me to his place, where he cooked a delicious chicken and almond tagine, which we enjoyed with a bottle of strong, spicy Syrah. I didn't return to the B&B that night. You never liked that about me, my ability to enjoy such encounters entirely without guilt or false expectations. You always got grumpy and paternal when I told you about them, even long after our relationships had ended, and I liked to imagine that there was, perhaps, a part of you that was still in love with me on some level, and a little jealous. But who knows? Maybe you simply disapproved. You were never like me that way.

I left my card with Tariq the next morning, and, while I was on the train back to London, he called to say that Chris had agreed to get in touch with me. Until I went to bed that night, I kept checking my email every two minutes to see whether he had written, and I grew increasingly anxious that he might have changed his mind. Meeting Chris, I felt, was my final chance – the future of the entire project seemed to hinge on the frame of mind of Julia's former lover.

XV

Once again I slept badly that night, tossing and turning, and imagining all kinds of horror scenarios that would ensue if I were unable to deliver the manuscript on time. I got up early, and to my enormous relief found a message from Chris in my inbox. He told me to come and see him in Marseille whenever it suited me. He asked me to keep my meeting with him secret, since he had 'unresolved issues' with the UK authorities and didn't want them to find him. His email address was registered in Poland, and he didn't sign off with his real name. I booked my flight for the next day, and emailed him my mobile number and arrival time.

The very minute my plane touched down on French soil I emailed Chris again to let him know I was in town and ready to meet him whenever he was free. His email address was all I had – he had sent me neither a phone number nor an address. It took him two days to respond, during which I explored the city's famous promenades, the harbour and the winding alleyways of its labyrinthine centre, and spent many hours in a charmingly run-down brasserie at the Old Port. It was evening and I was at the brasserie reading over my notes when Chris finally contacted me, just after

I'd ordered my fourth glass of the house pastis – I had grown very anxious, fearing that my trip had been in vain, and that I wouldn't hear from Chris again. However, he suggested we meet two hours later in a shisha café in the French-African part of town, near the old market. I cursed my lack of faith, as I hate conducting interviews when I'm not sober, ordered a strong double espresso, and then tried to find a cab to take me to our meeting place. Three taxi-drivers refused me before an old Berber with a thin white beard agreed to drive me to the edge of the African quarter. Even he, however, declined to take me all the way, and, once I climbed out of the taxi, I could see why.

The area was ruin-strewn. More than half of the buildings in this apocalyptic urban wasteland were boarded up; many had broken or missing roofs and neither doors nor windows, and I could see the shadowy figures of ragged children lurking in the entrances. Rubbish lined the streets, and the potholes in the cracked tarmac were so deep they looked like bomb-craters. At first my fear concentrated on a big rat that rushed right past me, but soon my focus shifted to the groups of hooded youths with hostile eyes who loitered at the street corners. The hissed sing-song with which they greeted me was bristling with sexual aggression. I attempted to follow the vague instructions of the taxi-driver as faithfully as possible, while I hurried deeper into this maze and attracted far more attention than I should have.

Eventually, I arrived at a mosque – the café was supposed to be just around the corner from one. I walked past another large group of men, who were congregating outside their place of worship and followed me with dark eyes, and I sighed with relief when I finally spotted a café in the dusty window of which I could make out the shape of a waterpipe. The entire place was covered with thick Persian rugs and filled with smoke, and groups of men in kaftans were sitting cross-legged around low tables on which stood magnificent azure-coloured hookahs. When I entered, a tall, bearded man with sand-coloured dreadlocks tied together at his neck, who had been chatting to the proprietor behind the counter, raised his hand and came to greet me.

'Clare, glad you found it,' he said in a bright, clear voice while he firmly shook my hand. 'Come, follow me.'

He led me to a quieter corner at the back of the café, and arranged some cushions for me so that I could lean against the wall. He wore dirty jeans and a white linen shirt. His bushy beard covered most of his features, but his brow was high and clear, and something about his alert blueberry eyes drew me to him immediately. His skin was tanned and I noticed his smooth, cat-like movements; he clearly felt very at home in his body. His age was difficult to establish: he could have been anything between twenty-five and forty. He emanated a faint woodland smell, of ferns and pine trees. We looked at each other for a while without speaking.

'You should try the mint tea – it's excellent,' he said finally.

'With pleasure,' I responded, and he signalled to the waiter.

After the tea had arrived, having poured me a glass he stretched back languorously and said: 'OK, Clare, shoot. What do you want to know?'

'Right, let's get started,' I said and switched on my recording device. 'Why did Julia and you fall out?' I was nervous and flustered from the unpleasant trip to the café and dizzy from all the pastis I had drunk before our meeting; I didn't quite feel myself.

Chris raised his eyebrows, leaned forward and studied me. 'Seriously? That's a really weird first question. Why don't we start at the beginning? Or are you in a rush? There's so much basic stuff to cover before anyone can even begin to understand why Julia and I eventually fell out.'

He was right, of course. It was a silly first question. I blushed and sipped some of my mint tea. 'Fine by me,' I said eventually. 'Please start wherever you want. I'll interrupt if I have any questions, if that's OK.'

'Sure, chip in anytime, Clare. Well, it makes most sense to start with our first meeting, don't you think? We met by chance, in a bar in Edinburgh owned by a friend of mine.'

'Mo's place,' I said, keen to make up for my blundering opening and to show that I wasn't completely ignorant of their story.

Chris looked surprised. 'Yeah, that's right. How did you know that? Anyway, Julia and I hit it off immediately. We were completely on the same wavelength. It was totally intense, sparks, tension, chemistry in spades and all that: have you ever met someone you thought was your soul-mate? That's what it was: we seemed to think exactly the same way about everything we talked about that night. I mean, *everything*. I'd never met anyone before who was so super-sharp and articulate, and so hot! She *is* beautiful, don't you think? That milky-white skin, those cat-like eyes, the pert ass, the long legs. Man, I was totally blown away.

'That night we just talked and talked and never got tired, until Mo threw us out. Then we went back to my place and talked some more until the sun rose, and only then did we finally kiss. And we both knew that we were made for each other, you know? Like in a film or something. It was so clear and simple. We were together from then on, no questions asked. She was the first and only woman I ever met who was as crazy and passionate as me about all the things that really matter in this world. Women like that are bloody rare, you know.'

I smiled and nodded. Chris's enthusiasm was rather fetching. He sounded much younger than he looked.

'Julia was still at uni when we met,' he continued, 'and was going through a really radical disenchantment. I'd already gone through exactly the same thing a while ago. She very quickly became totally disillusioned with the pointless phrase-mongering, the narcissistic glory-hunting, the sickening hypocrisy of it all, the blahdiblah, the whole fucking rhetorical-bullshit-producing machinery. You know what I mean, right? But she got there much faster than me. It took me years to realize all that shit, but that woman does everything fast – really fast. I mean, she's definitely the brightest person I've ever met. She just *got* me, you know? I still miss her like crazy.'

'Really?' I asked. 'Even after what she's done?'

'Yes, well... we'll get to that. Relax, Clare. Where was I? Julia and I soon decided we had to get out of Edinburgh.

The whole arty-farty pseudo-boho posh student blah circus just started to get massively on our nerves. And we didn't just want out of Edinburgh – we wanted to get away from all of it, the whole fucking perverse system, you know? We'd come up with a project: we wanted to go on a fact-finding mission to chronicle the sufferings of the wretched of this earth. The idea was to honour the people who slave away on sun-scorched coffee fields and in toxic textile and technology factories so that we can indulge our insatiable thirst for supremo skinny latte macchiatos and the newest distressed denim and blahdiblah super-light-tablet crazes, and that kind of shit. Our plan was to compile a dossier, sort of a graphic report with lots of pictures, documenting the exploitation of so-called Third World workers. We wanted to redirect attention away from the glossy surface of our endless shopping-phantasmagorias to the dirty underbelly of Western capitalism, to the dire sites of production, you know. We wanted to send a stern reminder to all those careless consumers that their caramel frappuccinos and iPhones and neon trainers were bloodstained.'

It was strange, hearing Chris say all these things. A very similar agenda had driven me to write *Why Your Sneakers Kill*, but hearing these ideas articulated by him made me feel uneasy. It sounded so… naive. The world doesn't work that way. Grow up, I wanted to say. I longed to tell him about *The Deal* and its afterlife, but I decided to listen instead. After all, that was why I was there.

'We were of course totally aware that lots of people before us had tried something just like that,' Chris continued, as though he had guessed my thoughts. 'I mean, we knew that many of the things we were hoping to expose were already well-known and out there in the public domain, and so on. But we were hoping to discover something new, something big, something different, you know. We wanted to cause a splash, an uproar, a scandal. We wanted to create a more lasting moral outrage, something that would turn into a consumer backlash with real financial consequences for the multinational corporations that are to blame for all of this shit. You know, something like the Shell boycott, or just brand image damage? Like when it became known that Amazon were mistreating their workers, and that Starbucks and Google were dodging their taxes. Something like that, only bigger. What we wanted was for our message to go viral, you know, to make a real difference somehow.'

'And how exactly were you planning to do that?' I asked. I was aware that I sounded prim and weary, like a bitter old spoilsport, but I couldn't help it. I knew he wouldn't like the question. Chris didn't seem to be the type who dealt much in practical details.

He did indeed look displeased. Once again he raised one of his eyebrows. 'We didn't really know *how* we'd manage to get there, and exactly what form our dossier would take, but we were planning to figure it all out during the trip. The mission was explorative, right? An adventure; blue-sky thinking. We just trusted that we'd find a way somehow. That we'd discover something. And go with the flow?'

I was touched but also completely unconvinced by his naive idealism – my own story had taught me all too painfully that no factual revelation of any kind, no matter how shocking and ethically outrageous, has the capacity to shake up anything at all these days. Teenage revolutionary fantasies, I thought, oddly out of place in the age of twenty-first-century techno-capitalism. I'd worked as an investigative journalist all my life and traded in precisely the kinds of scandalous exposures the two had been envisaging, and although my work had attracted as much attention as one could realistically hope for, I am now firmly convinced that ultimately it has achieved nothing. Nothing at all. Adrian Temple was the living proof of this, of course, a mocking reminder.

To be honest, George, I was astonished to hear that Julia seemed to have believed so firmly in the power of information to generate change. I wouldn't have thought she would ever have subscribed to the classic consciousness-raising-as-political-activism idea. Or perhaps Chris merely assumed she did? Or was she just pretending? I think my face must have betrayed my doubts in spite of my best efforts, as Chris paused once again, and looked at me intently. He must have decided that my sceptical expression related to his political convictions, not the means for their implementation, since he broke into a lengthy anti-corporate diatribe during which my mind grew hazy. The peculiar atmosphere in the café intensified the dream-like state I found myself in while attempting to listen to him, dominated as it was by groups of cross-legged men murmuring in unfamiliar tongues, half-hidden in the white smoke of their shishas that hovered in the room like the kind of Dickensian fog that rises from English rivers on wet nights.

'Clare, Clare, you're not with me, I can tell. But can't you see?' Chris began. 'Shopping is the new opiate of the masses: our age fetishizes goods, not gods. All people care about is how much spending money they have in their pockets – shopping is like literally their *religion*. Our government can get away with *everything* these days: with massacring the NHS, tripling student fees, spending billions on leaking nuclear submarines, lying about wars, fiddling expenses, covering up child abuse in its own ranks – you name it, right? People don't give a fuck. But as soon as politicians touch their spending money, they riot. They *riot*, Clare. Take away the people's power to shop and they'll rise up like newborn zombies. You know I'm right. Hitting the high streets to hunt for spoils is the only thing this sorry society has left. I mean, the term "retail therapy" says it all, right?'

It was ironic that Chris was lecturing me on these points, but unfortunately the irony was entirely lost on him. I realized he really didn't have a clue who I was.

'But there's a nasty catch,' Chris continued. 'So that we can buy loads of cheap shit all the time and keep the economy growing and all the rest of it, corporations outsource the production of their goods to countries where workers are hungry, labour laws lax and taxes tiny, right? Otherwise, if they were paying fair salaries, stuff wouldn't be so ridiculously cheap. I mean, how else can people here buy school uniforms for, like, four quid or something? Who do you think stitches them together?'

Chris paused and looked at me. 'I can see you think you know all this already, and you know what? You're not alone.

But the funny thing is that although *everyone* knows the facts, nobody can even begin to imagine what this set-up *really* means for the workers who are at the producing end. They're hidden from sight like Wells's Morlocks or something. Their tragic stories don't even make it into the news. Literally nobody gives a shit about them. You know I'm right, Clare.'

Chris's lecture began to annoy me. How could he be so smug, preaching to me about these things as though I was some imbecilic gossip columnist? But Chris, unaware of my feelings, continued. He went on and on about the brutality of factory managers and the appalling working conditions in the so-called free-trade zones; young children collapsing in sweatshops after inhaling lethal doses of carcinogenic fumes during their fifteen-hour shifts; people burning to death in their thousands each year in shockingly unsafe buildings; and the ransacked lands and seared coffee fields in Mexico and Guatemala. I'm sure Chris would have gone on for ever. But at some point I couldn't stand it any longer. His sermon wasn't just patronizing, it was also far too abstract for my taste. After all, I'd travelled all the way to the South of France to hear stories about Julia, not the usual spiel from the anti-globalization handbook.

'Tell me more about the specifics, Chris,' I finally interrupted him. 'I can't picture Julia and you on your trip. Where did you sleep, what did you eat, how did you travel? What did you talk about? What did you do all day? Can you remember any concrete events and episodes?'

Again Chris fell silent and glared at me. He was annoyed by my intervention, and signalled to the waiter to fill our glasses. He didn't speak until we had a fresh pot of steaming mint tea in front of us. In the meantime, he rubbed one of his matted coils between his fingers and ignored me.

'You're bored with the politics already, just like everybody else,' he said eventually. 'You want to hear about the personal, right? Fine. Our time together is limited, after all. You need to think about your readers and all that, don't you?'

'That's right,' I said curtly.

'Well. So. Let's see what I can come up with for you... Sex? You want to hear about sex with Julia, Clare? OK then. Let's see... She had beautifully formed tits, firm and round, like small, ripe honeydew melons, with hard, peachy-pink little nipples. She had a hot tight little pussy, I can tell you that. Oh, and she had a real thing for...'

'Actually, I was hoping you could tell me about your travels, not about Julia's genitalia,' I interrupted. 'Look, Chris,' I added more gently. 'I'm trying to understand who Julia White is. What she liked and disliked, what she believed in, what she cared about, what drove her. I want to understand what kind of person she was. And what might have led her to kill twenty-four innocent people. Can we focus on that? Why don't you just tell me what travelling with her was like? Some everyday bits.'

Chris looked at me, once again for a long time. I feared he might just get up and walk away, but I held his gaze and tried not to let him see my anxiety. Eventually, he nodded.

'OK, OK. Fine. Let's see what I can come up with,' he said. He took a long sip from his mint tea, and rearranged his cushions beside me, so that he, too, could sit with his back against the wall. 'I'll try again then. We went to Indonesia first. At the beginning, everything was just, I don't know, magical. We were so excited about everything we saw, everyone we met, all the new impressions and sensations and tastes around us. We stayed in backpacker haunts and checked out all the markets, beaches and cool places. It was great. I don't think I've ever been as happy as in those days. But Julia soon grew bored with all that, and decided it was time we got started on the dossier. She doesn't really do fun, you know. It just doesn't come naturally to her. She's actually a very serious person. Too serious, really... And you didn't argue with Julia. Especially not if her mind was set on something.

'So after a couple of weeks or so we took a boat to Batam, one of Indonesia's main free-trade zones. It was super-hot and humid. Really oppressive. We were, like, appalled by the abject poverty hidden behind the glitzy inner-city facades. They seemed to exist only for the tourists. When you looked behind them, shit started to pour out everywhere. I mean literally, you know. Outside the centre, there was no infrastructure to speak of; sewage, rubbish and dead animals were left to rot in the blistering sun; the roads were mere dirt tracks. The workers from the villages on the mainland, who flock to the island in their thousands each year, live in the most pitifully fragile makeshift huts.

'The workers we encountered during our first week there were great but really scared. Most of them offered us food and drink although they barely had enough to survive on themselves, you know. Like totally humbling, those guys. But they refused to tell us anything. Eventually, after two weeks or so, a young woman called Lily, who'd heard about us and our project, came to our hotel on the outskirts of that sorry city. She was super-skinny, absolutely terrified and looked about twelve years old. I think she was actually seventeen or eighteen. Lily told us that she and her thirteen-year-old sister used to work inhumanely long shifts in one of the nearby assembly halls, where baby clothes were manufactured. A couple of months ago, her sister had been beaten so savagely by one of the guards that she died in Lily's arms three days later. Her sister's crime had been to return two minutes late from her lunch break. I mean, imagine, Clare! We couldn't believe what we were hearing. Lily wanted revenge; she wanted the guard to be punished for killing her sister. She told us everything we wanted to know. She even let us into her former workplace at night so that we could, like, take pictures and all the rest of it. She encouraged other colleagues to tell us their stories, too. That was kind of our watershed moment, you know. Suddenly, we received five to ten visitors every day at our hotel who described their plight in the most harrowing tones. Some brought a relative to translate for them, but most of them were able to express themselves very well in English.'

I nodded my head. I, too, had interviewed many South-East Asian textile workers in the past, and the horror stories they told me beggared belief.

'We stayed in Batam for four weeks, until someone warned us that the factory managers knew what we were doing and had hired hit-men to beat us up. Julia had been totally focused during that period. She took massive amounts of notes; she recorded and later transcribed every conversation, and she took literally hundreds of pictures. She was driven by a kind of cold fury, like an inner ice-storm or something.'

Again I nodded. To that feeling, too, I could relate very well.

'But you know what was kind of strange? After a couple of months or so, Julia wouldn't really let me touch her anymore. Or only super-reluctantly, like once in a blue moon. She'd never really seemed massively interested in sex – but hey, nobody's perfect, right? But we were very close – I mean, really close, properly physically close – in Edinburgh. We were totally loved up, at the beginning. We just couldn't keep our hands off each other, you know? And also at the start of our trip. But the longer we were on our mission, the more she went off it – sex, I mean. She'd work late into the night on her transcriptions, and get up super early. Whenever I put my hand on her leg or her arm or her back, or her hair, she shook it off, like a bothersome fly or something. Her lack of interest became really hurtful, because I was crazy about her. I mean, I was in love with her, totally in love, you know. And I've got needs. Like normal needs. I'm not ashamed of it. I didn't like being made to feel like some kind of annoying pest. I've never had that problem before, you know. Normally, women… well, whatever. I tried to talk to Julia about it a couple of times, but she always dismissed it. In the end, she'd always make me feel as though I was being totally unreasonable, like it was *my* fault.

'"Come *on*, Chris," she'd say and laugh and give me a peck on the cheek, or pat me on the back, or something. "We're on a mission, we have a cause, remember? I need to concentrate. This" – and she'd point to whatever it was she was working on – "is *slightly* more important right now, don't you think?"

'And that's just how it continued, really. We travelled on to Vietnam and to the Philippines, and we had really similar experiences there. At first, the workers would be too scared to open up, but eventually, one of them would break the spell and then suddenly lots of them would queue up to speak to us. It was some dark shit they told us, Clare. Julia was, like, increasingly possessed; she never stopped working and she talked about nothing else. Ever. And she just didn't let me touch her at all at some point. I don't remember exactly when – about seven or eight months into our relationship? Can you believe that? I mean, picture it: I was with this gorgeous woman, who I was head over heels in love with, and we were on this great adventure together, but she'd all of a sudden turned cold on me, like she was dead inside or something. It was strange, Clare, well weird. Back in Edinburgh, we were totally amazing together, in bed and out and everywhere. Or at least I thought we were. And then, suddenly: complete chastity on her part.

'I became restless, and a bit depressed, to be honest. I started doing other things when Julia visited factories and spoke to the workers; it all got a bit too intense for me, you know. But she continued, relentlessly – she was totally obsessed. In Vietnam I wanted to visit the ancient

Thien Mu Pagoda and the Co Chi tunnels; I wanted to wander through the old city centre of Hanoi and climb the Sa Pa rice terraces; I wanted to explore the pristine beaches of Phu Quoc and take a boat up the Mekong past the thousand islands of Ha Long Bay. You know, the kind of stuff every normal person visiting the country would want to do? But Julia refused to waste time on any of that. So I went off on my own for a few weeks. I missed her badly, but when I got back she gave the impression that she hadn't missed me at all. She didn't even really want to hear about my experiences.'

He looked sad all of a sudden. 'That must have been very difficult for you, Chris,' I said. 'What happened next?'

'Well, it just got worse, really. I mean, I felt more and more miserable and unloved. After about thirteen months in Asia, Julia decided it was time to move on to Central America, to strengthen our dossier further. She'd grown pretty fanatical by then, quite cold, somehow. For example, she really didn't like all the Western tourists we met and refused to have anything to do with them. I was totally starved of contact with people I could talk to, people who made me feel like my existence and my thoughts mattered somehow, you know? People who didn't just ignore me all day and treat me like shit. So I started to hang out more with travellers, while Julia visited dozens of "Maquilladoras" in the US-Mexican border territory. Have you heard of them?'

I nodded. I had indeed.

'They're just as gruesome as their South-East Asian counterparts,' Chris explained, in spite of my nod. 'Basically, multinational corporations send raw materials and equipment to these places, where they're, like, assembled mainly by female teenagers with nimble fingers, for a pittance, obviously, and then sent back to the country of origin. Duty-free and tariff-free, of course. I guess it's fair to say that Julia and I had become pretty estranged by then, though I'm not sure Julia even registered that I was in a bad place. I started to feel pretty resentful towards her. I'm not proud of it, Clare, but this is what happened: I had a few flings with Australian and Israeli backpackers. I can say in my defence that Julia never found out about them. And even if she had, I'm pretty sure she wouldn't even have cared. At that stage, you know, I genuinely believed that she didn't give a shit about me anymore. Really. I felt like I could jump off a cliff or get eaten by a shark or something, and she wouldn't even notice I'd disappeared. I saw her only in the evenings and at night, sometimes for a short, strained dinner, when she'd pontificate about what she'd seen and heard that day. Then she'd go back to the hotel room and work on her transcripts and I don't know what else, and I'd go out to meet friends.

'Oh yes, and I forgot to mention. I drank quite a bit back then, and also smoked dope and popped the odd pill. I mean, nothing bad or over the top, I just had to self-soothe a little somehow, you know? I was, like, really hurting. I just couldn't understand why Julia didn't love me anymore, all of a sudden. I felt like she despised me for that, too. When I came to bed in the early hours she'd often crinkle her nose in disgust, or tell me that I smelled bad and needed to get my act together.'

'But why did you stay with her?' I asked. 'It's difficult to understand from the outside… It sounds pretty awful, the state of your relationship at that point.'

He shrugged his shoulders and stared into his empty tea glass. 'I guess I was simply still in love with her,' he said, 'and was hoping that things would return to how they'd been at the beginning of our relationship, once that bloody dossier was finished. I think I probably believed that she was just genuinely busy and totally immersed in the whole project thing, and shaken by all the shit she saw on a daily basis. I mean, the kind of stuff we witnessed *can* kill your sex drive. I could see that, too. We saw some pretty dark stuff. I don't know… I guess I'm an optimist at heart? And I cared for her, I really did. She hasn't exactly had an easy life, you know? The shit about her parents and all that.'

'What about her parents?' I asked, intrigued.

'Didn't they tell you? I thought you'd met them. Julia's adopted.'

I gasped. 'Adopted?'

'Yeah. Actually they never intended to tell her, but just after she finished school, completely by chance apparently, she found her birth certificate. It said "father unknown" and the mother's name was blacked out. Obviously she was, like, totally freaked out by that. When she confronted her parents they stuttered and spluttered and got all aggravated. Eventually they admitted that after her brother was born the doctors thought that her mother couldn't have any more kids, medical complications and all that, but they desperately wanted a bigger family and so decided to adopt. I think her older brother must have been two or three at the time. Obviously Julia's little sister came as a massive surprise a few years later, showing that the doctors had been full of shit, as usual.

'Julia said that they were really horrified that she'd found out, that they never wanted her to know, that they really feared it would make her feel bad and all that. She said they swore they loved her just as much as the other two kids, and that they would never tell anyone the truth. You can imagine the scene.'

'Jesus,' I said. 'That must have been a terrible shock for her...'

Chris shrugged. 'I guess. Julia didn't really talk about it much. If it had been me, I think it would have completely destroyed my trust in them and done some pretty serious damage to my sense of identity. I mean, to find out that the people you thought of as your parents aren't and have been lying to you for eighteen years? That would fuck most people up.'

'Do you know whether she ever tried to find out who her real parents were?' I asked.

'I don't think so. She never mentioned it. But she did feel pretty alienated from her own parents, I can tell you that. She thought they were hypocrites. I mean, you can't blame her, right?'

We both sipped our mint teas for a while, before Chris continued. 'Anyway, we'd moved on to Guatemala to visit some coffee farms in the highlands, and were staying in San Pedro La Laguna, a small village at the shores of Lake

Atitlán. One afternoon, she came to look for me in one of the local backpacker hangouts. You know, like one of those hippy bars where everyone is playing billiards or cards and drinking beer or lying around stoned in hammocks. This was totally unusual. Normally, Julia wouldn't even go near places like that. I immediately knew that something bad must have happened. Julia looked even paler than normal, and seemed totally shaken. I ordered some water for her and asked her to tell me what was wrong.

It took her for ever before she could speak, but eventually she told me that she'd witnessed a horrific scene on one of the nearby coffee farms. She'd been interviewing two young women about their pay and working conditions at the edge of one of the plantations when they heard piercing screams. The three of them walked to where the sounds were coming from and saw a cluster of men, standing in a circle. Apparently some of them were wearing the usual uniforms of the plantation overseers. They were watching while a brutish-looking middle-aged man was raping a very young woman, who was crying and screaming and begging him to stop. It was clear that he'd not been the first, and wouldn't be the last, either. Julia and the women she'd been interviewing tried to break through the circle and shouted at the men to stop, but they pushed them away and told them they'd be next if they didn't get lost. Then Julia started to take pictures, which I thought was incredibly brave, you know? But one of the men grabbed her camera, threw it to the ground and stamped on it, before hitting her in the face. I felt horribly guilty that I hadn't been with her to protect her that day.

'Then she decided to run back to the village to report what she'd witnessed to the police. On her way back, she stopped two American tourists who were driving past her, and told them what had happened, and asked if they could give her a ride. But they were totally uninterested in her story. One of them shrugged his shoulders and grinned and said: "Welcome to Guatemala." Then they drove off.

'Back in San Pedro, Julia went straight to the police station. The officer she spoke to was openly hostile. Only after she threatened to involve the British Embassy did he fill out a report form, like really reluctantly and slowly, you know. But apparently the report ended up so vague and disjointed that it inspired no confidence in her at all. She said the guy didn't even bother to write down some of the key facts, and he didn't ask for her contact details, or her passport. When Julia demanded to know whether officers would be sent to the farm straight away to collect evidence and assist the victim, the officer said yes, he'd send two men out there presently. But Julia waited opposite the police station after forcing her details on the officer. She saw that nobody left the building after her for, like, two hours, and then she saw a whole crowd of officers sauntering to a nearby restaurant.

'She was absolutely furious when she told me all this – totally livid. We found out that the farm she'd visited supplied its coffee beans to Café Olé...' Chris hesitated before continuing: 'And then we decided to contact representatives of the company next, you know, so that they could request a proper investigation. From a local internet café, Julia sent a long, detailed report to numerous different Café Olé customer service email addresses, as well as to dozens of public relations officers and quality-control managers and so on. I think she must have sent it to, like, a hundred different email addresses – basically every single one she could find online. She checked for responses almost hourly over the next few days. But she didn't get a single reply. Not a single one, Clare. I mean, can you believe that? She then sent the story to various British and US media, in the hope that one of them would name and shame Café Olé into action. But again her plea was met with complete silence. She got nothing back at all. Nothing.'

Chris paused here. We both contemplated his words. After a few minutes, I asked: 'What did Julia do next?'

'Well, she stopped working on the dossier. Just like that. That was pretty radical, you know, given that she'd been doing nothing else ever since we left Edinburgh? I mean, she'd *lived* for this bloody dossier. And then she never touched it again. From one day to the next. The fact that everyone totally ignored her gruesome story – the police, the media, the company that should have taken responsibility for injustices occurring in its supply chain – that really shattered her confidence, you know? I guess she thought that if gang-rape doesn't get punished and fails to shock, what can?'

'What happened to the dossier?' I asked.

'Don't know.' Chris shrugged. 'I hadn't been working on it for quite a while, and I don't know what she did with it in the end. It was odd, the time after the rape, Clare. She'd always been, like, super-busy, you know, out interviewing and taking pictures, all day every day, and then, all of a sudden, she just sat in our room and didn't know what to do with herself. She really didn't. She didn't really do pleasure, or relaxation, you know? She always needed projects. For a couple of days, she just paced around in our tiny hotel room, like a trapped animal or something. It was pretty disconcerting to watch. She was beginning to say weird shit, and ranted and rambled a lot. Then she got ill with a virus or food poisoning, or something. I made her stay in bed and nursed her. She couldn't keep down any food for a whole week, and her body was shaking with convulsions and cramps. It's weird, but I hadn't felt as close to her since the very beginning of our trip, you know? I sat next to her on the bed for hours on end and held her hand and wiped her forehead with wet towels and listened to her feverish talk and tried to calm her down.

'When her temperature finally dropped she became all morose and hostile. She was totally at a loose end without her work. For a couple of days, we argued a lot. And then came the final argument... Since Julia's health had stabilized, and since she'd become pretty unbearable, I'd started to go out again. I'd gone out to meet some friends one evening, and when I returned to our hotel room around one in the morning she was waiting up for me. I knew something was up. She looked like she was intent on picking a fight, and she did. She could be pretty intimidating when she was in fighting mode, you know? She was sitting on the bed, her arms folded across her chest, and her green eyes were fixed on me. There was, like, no sympathy, let alone anything resembling love left. Her gaze was just ice-cold.

'"You smell of drugs and drink again," she said when I entered. "I hope it was worth it. You know what, Chris? I've had enough. You've let me down, and you've let our project down. Why weren't you with me on the day of the rape? *Why*? You could have stopped it. But instead, you were getting high, or drunk, or were fucking someone, or whatever it is you do all day now. You're full of shit, just like all the others. You just talk the let's-change-the-world talk to look cool, but in reality, you don't care. Your kind really is the worst: you're nothing but a poser. A wannabe revolutionary."

'"Oh yeah?" I said. "And what exactly is it *you*'re doing that makes you so superior to all the rest of us? Your dossier? You haven't even touched it in the last few weeks. You think pacing around in a small room and pouring scorn on normal people who talk to each other and have some fun and do all the things that make life worth living makes you a better person? You're bitter and cold, you know that?"

'"Better that than to be a junkie, or whatever it is *you* are. You think because what you consume is illegal it makes you cool and counter-cultural – but guess what: it doesn't. You're just a consumer, too. You live to consume, just like everybody else."

'"You know what? You should try it sometime. Maybe it would relax you a little, loosen you up a bit, you know? Maybe then you wouldn't be such a stuck-up, frigid bitch. I think a little pot and a drink would actually work wonders on your character, Julia."

'Julia just laughed. "There we go again. Your eternal pathetic lament. I happen to have interests that transcend the gratification of base sexual instincts. And especially yours. If you don't like it, I suggest you go and fuck some travellers."

'"You know what? I might just do that."

'It really wasn't my finest hour, Clare, but it seemed like the last straw, you know? So I grabbed my backpack and started to pack my things. Julia just kept on looking at me. She was studying me, like I was an insect on which she was about to tread or something. I got the impression she was amused rather than upset, you know? I couldn't help feeling that she'd been testing me all along, to see how far she could push me before I'd snap. But I don't know. That was probably paranoia speaking.

'"Fine," she finally said, very calmly. "Get your things and don't ever come back."'

'And that was it?' I asked, incredulous. 'You just left and never saw her again?'

'Pretty much,' Chris said. 'I packed my things right there and then and moved in with some friends. A couple of days later I was beginning to feel bad about how things had ended. I couldn't believe it was really over, and that it should have ended like *that*, after everything we'd been through together. I mean, could you, Clare? And in spite of everything that had happened I also missed her, like really badly. So I went back to the hotel to see if she wanted to talk. But she'd checked out and disappeared. I continued to travel in Guatemala, Peru and Bolivia for a few more months on my own. I followed the rough itinerary that we had drawn up together before things went wrong. I was hoping I'd run into her somewhere, and that we could talk things through. But I didn't, and it wasn't fun anymore, and so I returned to London for a while. I hated it there. Then I moved here. Someone I'd met abroad had told me about a vacancy at the refugee camp. I tried to contact Julia via email a few times. Actually, to tell you the truth, much more often than I should have, you know? But she must have blocked my address or closed down her account or something. They all bounced back.'

'How did you feel when you found out about the London attack?'

'What do you think, Clare? Pretty shitty, obviously. Numb. Surprised. Disgusted. Sad. I don't know. I'm still not quite sure what to make of it. I just remember thinking she should have done it at night, she should have done it at night, she should have done it at night, when nobody would have got hurt, over and over and over again. I mean, like an empty building, I could see why she'd do that, you know? Café Olé and all that, it kind of made sense. But with people in it, in broad daylight? Twenty-four random customers? But what more can I say? No words can patch the fucking damage Julia has caused.'

He shook his head. He looked so sunken and dejected that I put my hand on his. We sat together in silence for a while. Then he sighed and said: 'I need to leave now, Clare. It was really good talking to you. Thanks for listening.'

And then Chris got up, pressed some coins into the hand of the proprietor behind the bar, and disappeared into the mild southern night.

I returned to London the next day. I had less than four weeks before the submission deadline, and I still hadn't written a single proper chapter. I hadn't even drafted an introduction. All I had was a handful of interview transcripts. And I was still none the wiser regarding my master narrative. Chris was clearly not the great enigmatic corruptor figure who radicalized Julia, and in whose existence Timothy, Amy and Alison firmly believed. If anything, the process of corruption had probably worked the other way. It was also my strong impression that Chris's representation of Julia as a frigid, perhaps even sadistic ice-queen was primarily driven by his wounded pride. It was so obvious that he was still hurting very badly.

Chris's story certainly provided some extremely important clues: to find out that she was adopted that late on, and by pure chance, too, must have contributed substantially to Julia's sense of alienation and to the corrosion of her trust in both people and institutions. The cold, hard streak in her that some of those who knew her had observed was probably a defence mechanism, a reaction to a traumatic revelation that left her entire world in pieces. I was genuinely shocked that Rose and Timothy hadn't told me the truth – they had seemed so raw, so authentic when I met them, but quite a lot of it had clearly been play-acting. I suppose they simply wanted to keep their promise to Julia and not to act disloyally, washing their hands of their adopted child when she needed them most. I suppose they felt terribly guilty, too, convinced that their lack of honesty had contributed to Julia's radicalization. But while the revelation that Julia was adopted certainly explained some things, I didn't believe it was the key to the mystery. The majority of adopted children who find out the truth about their parents turn out just fine.

The significance of Café Olé in the saga, too, was now clear to me. But I still couldn't understand why Julia attacked the chain's *customers*, rather than, say, its CEO, or just its buildings, as Chris had suggested. I also had no doubt that witnessing the rape and her anger at not being heard and at not being able to get justice for the victim would have contributed to Julia's decision to leave legal forms of activism behind. But I strongly felt that even this extreme episode couldn't fully explain her act: many people witness gruesome scenes like that, or even worse, and don't lose faith in institutional justice. On the contrary, some people would have been spurred on in their campaign by an event like this. And most people would probably just have grown cynical and bitter, like me. Turning into a callous mass murderer, however, is on a different level altogether.

XVI

Yesterday Sarah, my silent companion with the bruise-coloured complexion, was attacked in the lunch queue. I'd arrived early, and had sat down in my usual place, waiting for her to join me. I could see it coming; in fact, I was surprised that Sarah had been spared for so long. Frail and frightened as she was, she looked like the perfect victim. That day tensions were high, and two bullies were hungry for a fight. They entered the hall together, oozing aggression, rudely pushed Sarah out of the queue and took her place. She lowered her head and joined the end of the queue once more. But one of them, Tanya, turned round and pushed Sarah again, harder this time, so that she fell on the slippery floor.

'Piss off, bitch, you're spoiling my appetite,' Tanya shouted.

Sarah tried to get up, but Tanya kicked her hard in the stomach. The hall had fallen silent, and I thought I could hear something cracking. Horrified, I jumped up to intervene, but somebody else had been even quicker and was already at the scene. It was Amelia.

'That's enough,' she said sharply. 'Drop it, ladies. Right now.'

To my amazement, Tanya obeyed her. Then Amelia lifted Sarah up, brushed her down and led her to my table.

'You take it from here. That girl needs to eat, and then she needs to see a nurse,' she said. 'I reckon they broke one of her ribs. Painful, but she's gonna be all right.' I nodded and after a while joined the queue again, to get Sarah's portion for her, while she sat slumped in her seat, holding her side. Tanya and her partner watched me with narrowed eyes, but they let me be. Whether that was because they were afraid of Amelia or me was hard to tell. I still wonder whether people here know what I did. I haven't told anyone. But word gets round in a place like this. And it was in the papers, of course. Then I started wondering whether maybe I wasn't just *like* them – the Tanyas and all the other violent women – but actually *worse* than them.

The other day, Sarah broke her silence and asked me what had brought me here, but I changed the subject. I'm not ready to talk about it. Far from it. My discussions with my lawyer, whom I'm currently meeting twice a week, are different. They are technical, factual, dry. Most of the time, it doesn't even feel as though it's my own story we are talking about, but rather some abstract intellectual problem that needs solving, to which we apply ourselves in a disinterested, rational manner.

My lawyer wants to firm up our strategy in the run-up to the trial, which will begin on 24 March (the date is now set). She strongly believes we should plead diminished responsibility owing to temporary insanity, but I refuse to go there. It's untrue, and I'm done with lying. I wasn't insane when I did it. I was perfectly compos mentis, George. Confused, distressed, despairing, physically low, emaciated, on the edge of a nervous breakdown (whatever that means), yes, absolutely – but I knew what I was doing, and why I was doing it. At least at the time I did. Now, of course, I'm no longer sure. Now I wish I could go back and undo it all, banish those haunting eyes from my memory and live again without constantly feeling wracked by guilt.

My lawyer, as you can imagine, is not happy with my attitude, and neither are Amanda and Laura – they all think I'm deliberately risking a much heavier sentence than necessary, owing to a misdirected desire for self-punishment. Maybe they're right. I do want to pay for what I've done. But above all I want to be able to embrace my sentence with dignity – I want it served clean and pure, untainted by any plea-bargaining. What's more, I really am done with all the lying and pretending; I don't have the energy for games and strategies, even legal ones (and what good have they done me in the past, in any case). I've decided to face the consequences of my actions, whatever they may be. I will speak the truth in court. Or at least whatever feels like the truth at the time. Truth has become so slippery. It continues to slide through my hands like wriggling jellyfish. This, too, is Julia's dark work.

After I returned from Marseille, my energy reserves were low. I spent five days holed up in my apartment, transcribing the interview with Chris and studying my notes, over and over again, and worrying about the deadline. I was feeling increasingly paralysed, and a numb sense of panic was beginning to take hold. I didn't change out of my pyjamas, and I slept badly. I self-medicated with whisky (as you know, smoky single malts have always been my soul-soothing substance of choice in times of crisis), but that only made me feel even more wretched in the mornings. I didn't have the strength to deal with my emails, and I ignored the repeated ringing of my mobile. I knew that you were on my case (I'd stopped sending you updates), and that you were eager to know how I was getting on. But I simply couldn't face talking to you. I began to imagine the unspeakable awfulness of the moment when I would have to confess that all my efforts had come to nothing and that I had let you down.

Poring over my notes, I realized there was one final avenue for me to explore. But I procrastinated for a few days, probably because I suspected it would end in failure. Failure was something I felt increasingly unable to cope with. But on 16 October I pulled myself together to confront Julia's last traceable acquaintances on my list: her former colleagues in the vegetable shop in Camden, where she'd worked in the months prior to the attack.

It was a dreary Wednesday morning, but, spurred on by sheer desperation, I managed to drag myself into the shower (the first time in days), put on proper clothes and took the Tube to Camden. The shop was in a particularly derelict street in a run-down corner of the borough. All the houses were in bad repair, paint peeling like dead skin from uncared-for facades and rotting woodwork. Most of the shop-fronts were boarded up. Although it was ten o'clock in the morning, there wasn't a soul to be seen on the litter-strewn street. It took me a while to find the place, since its small wooden sign announcing 'Organic Fruit & Veg' was awkwardly positioned, its faded letters barely legible.

The door was stuck and I had to push hard against it to enter. Inside, I was overwhelmed by an all-pervading sense of gloom. I felt like the narrator of Poe's 'The Fall of the House of Usher', so strongly did the dreariness of the place affect me. Everything looked grey. The wooden floorboards were old and worn. The heaps of undersized and misshapen fruit and vegetables, carelessly displayed in wooden boxes placed on a long narrow table, were covered in dried soil, looking as though they would taste of ashes. There was a dusty makeshift shelf on which grains, pulses and rice in brown paper bags with handwritten labels were stacked. An antiquated till sat on a smaller table on the left-hand side of the room, next to which there was also a pair of rusty scales. A woman sitting on a chair behind it had been scrutinizing me suspiciously while I took all of this in. A mangy German shepherd was dozing at her feet.

'Can I help you?' she said sharply. She was already bristling with hostility, although I had not even opened my mouth. In perfect keeping with the furnishings, her face, too, seemed to have a grey sheen. Her mushroom-coloured hair was scraped back tightly in a short ponytail, and exposed a prominent white forehead. Her colourless lashes and eyebrows emphasized further the peculiar flatness of her features.

'Uh, yes, I hope so,' I said. Then my words failed me. I should have rehearsed my lines before entering, and I found myself freezing under the woman's lashless stare.

'Well, how? What is it you want?' she said.

'My name's Clare Hardenberg,' I finally managed. 'I'm a writer and I'm currently working on a book about Julia White. I wondered whether I might speak with you about her. And what she did. It's my understanding that she worked here before the attack.'

When I mentioned Julia's name, something that looked like pain flickered across the woman's face, before it regained its former hostile expression.

'That's right,' she said. 'She did.'

'Would you mind if I asked you a few questions? It wouldn't take long.'

'Yes, I would mind. I've nothing to say about her.'

'I realize it must be difficult for you, but I'd be really grateful if you'd let me ask you just a few questions. You see, I'm in a predicament...'

But the woman interrupted me. 'I already talked to the police and told them all I had to say on the matter. Julia's dead for me. For all of us here. We renounce violence – all violence – against people, animals, even against plants. Julia's no longer one of us and we had nothing to do with her actions.'

'I know that, of course,' I said hastily. 'I wasn't at all trying to imply that you did. I just wanted to ask you some questions about her as a person. A lot of people are trying to come to terms with what she has done, and to understand how it all got to that point, and I'm hoping to speak to the people she knew to find out more about what might have motivated her. How would you describe your relationship with her?'

'What do you mean by that?' the woman snapped. 'We had no relationship. We were co-workers. That's all. And I already told you I'm not answering questions.'

'But you must have talked to her, must have some impression of her character, some memories…' I tried again. 'In such a small, intimate shop you would get to know a co-worker quite well, wouldn't you?'

The woman folded her arms over her chest and stared at me.

I wasn't getting anywhere with her. I needed to change tactics. 'Could you at least tell me a bit more about your shop, then? It looks… special. What's your philosophy? Where do you buy your stock? Who are your typical customers?'

'On the web.'

'Pardon?'

'That information is on the web.'

God, I wasn't on form that day, George. In the past, I would have known how to crack this woman's armour, how to chase that contemptuous frown from her forehead and get her to share her most secret thoughts with me. In just a few minutes, I would have managed to find out what she cared about most in this world and what her darkest fears were. I'd succeeded with much worse cases. But on that day I just lost it. Completely. Suddenly, all my frustration at the futility of my task and the difficulties I had encountered during this accursed project turned into anger. And it was all directed at the poor, pale creature in front of me. I'm not proud of it, George. It wasn't my finest hour. I should send her a letter someday to apologize.

In spite of my hazy state of mind, I was still able to notice her reaction to the word 'relationship' and her strangely insistent assertion that she and Julia had been no more than co-workers. Clearly there was a story there. It was obvious that the woman had been hurt by Julia, just like everybody else. She had probably thought of Julia as a friend. Yes, I became convinced that the woman in front of me was the rude, pale friend Timothy and Rose had mentioned, and with whom Julia had cohabited before the attack. They might even have been lovers. It wouldn't have surprised me at all if Julia had turned to another woman for comfort. It would fit perfectly. Upon her return from South America, disgusted not just by the injustices of the global economic system but also by men in general and with her ex-boyfriend in particular, still reeling from the terrifying rape she had witnessed, alone and alienated from her former friends and family, Julia must have been looking for companionship, some human warmth. And she found it where she least expected it – in this most joyless of sanctuaries, in the shopkeeper's bony white embrace.

'You were lovers, weren't you?' I blurted out. 'And she broke your heart. Just like everybody else's. You're not alone – Julia has a habit of using and then dropping people. What did she do to you? You can tell me; I've heard it all before.'

But the woman just continued to stare at me, cadaverously

expressionless. Her dog, in contrast, had perked up, sensing the tension between us, and it had started to growl. The woman took hold of its collar.

'I bet she stumbled in here one day,' I continued, 'beautiful and auratic and highly intelligent and articulate and all that, everything you ever dreamed of being, and you were completely smitten. Thunderstruck. You just melted away, and gave her everything she wanted. Didn't you? A job, your heart, your finest crooked carrots, even a place to stay... Yes, I bet she moved straight in with you – she didn't have anywhere to go after her parents cut off her allowance, did you know that? She must have been so desperate that even staying with someone as lacklustre and lifeless as you would have seemed acceptable. She had sunk that low, and you jumped at the chance.

'Julia has the gift of making people feel very special when she wants something from them, you know? And you, you gave her everything, expecting gratitude, friendship, love in return, but she just took and took and never gave you anything. I bet you let her stay in your apartment, in your bed, even, hoping that once she'd recovered from all her traumatic experiences abroad, she'd appreciate what a good, decent person you are, and respond accordingly.

'But it didn't work out that way, did it? Instead, Julia just used your flat and your money, and soon stopped bothering to hide the fact that she found you really irritating. And boring. She began to stay out late. Sometimes, she stayed away for days. She didn't even bother to call you to let you know; she didn't talk to you much anymore.

'And you suffered. You were in love with her, weren't you? You tried desperately to please her, but no matter what you did, it didn't work. And when you heard the news, you went straight home and burned all her notebooks and letters, so that when the police searched your flat, all they found were some old clothes and a few books. Isn't that exactly what you did?'

The dog had started to bark ever more loudly during my crude monologue, and was straining hard against its collar, ready to attack.

'Are you done with your crazy rant?' the woman eventually asked in her flat, lifeless voice. 'Then get the fuck out of here before I let the dog loose on you.'

At that moment, another woman entered the shop, and when she saw me she said: 'Oh, you're busy, honey. I'll come back later.'

But the shopkeeper, whose lashless gaze remained directed at me, said: 'No, stay. The lady was just leaving.'

And leave I did.

XVII

The date of the trial is fast approaching, and I have to see you before then; I have to speak to you and hear your thoughts, on everything, before I can face my judge and jury. I still feel so confused and bewildered; and night after night I'm visited by the apparition of that still, white face with the wide-open grey eyes. I think about the little girl all the time, George. She must be about the same age as your daughter.

After my doomed trip to Camden I once again withdrew to my apartment, like a wounded animal. On my way back from the humiliating encounter, I stopped at my local supermarket. I'd lost my appetite back in Marseille, and couldn't muster the energy to think about food, although I was vaguely aware that my fridge and cupboards were empty. But all I managed to purchase was some whisky and crackers, as well as cat food for Aisha.

In the middle of life's path, I found myself in the dark wood of my psyche, alone and fearful. I'd always managed to find fulfilment in my work, but now I felt adrift, deprived of the stable intellectual ground that I had always taken for granted, my moral certainties sorely shaken by the events of the past few weeks. I always used to know exactly what I thought and felt, who the bad and the good characters were, whom to trust and whose accounts to take with a pinch of salt. I used to have firm views and clear opinions. But I just didn't know what to think anymore. And I still don't.

Worse, the corrosion of my certainties spread like cancer. What had begun as a specific and localized crisis of faith in my work proved virulently infectious. Above all else, I felt terribly lonely – where was the partner to whom I could turn, and who would embrace me and stroke my hair and take my hand and listen to my sorrows? Where were *you*, George? You're the one who should have been with me all along, and I don't mean as an angry contractor, nor simply as a slightly concerned friend. It was you I needed – your mind, your body, your love. What had I done, throwing it all away so carelessly? And where was the daughter I never had, with whom I could have talked all of this through, who would be as worried about me as Laura was for Amanda when she went through her two divorces?

All I had was a crippling mountain of debt, a cat, a sister harbouring old resentments and a lovely but always busy niece. And my work, what good had it done? The biggest criminal I'd ever exposed was about to receive the highest honour in his field – like the rest of my life, my work had been in vain, a fiasco; I could just as well have saved the paper. I had to face the truth and stop pretending. Given my state of mind, I wouldn't be able to write this book, not in two and a half weeks, not even with a massive extension of my deadline, not ever. And what was left, now that I could no longer write? Dead paper. The taste of failure in my mouth. Ashes.

I stayed at home for five long days, unable to sleep, wrestling with dark thoughts. I stopped working on my notes. I no longer knew what to think and what to believe. I simply couldn't tell whether Julia was right or wrong, a victim or a corrupter, psychologically disturbed or politically confused, a product of our sickeningly materialist age or a brave soul staging a valid protest against its perverse values. I couldn't decide whether she was an ice-cold monster, a psychopath, or whether she had legitimate reasons for her actions. Most of the time, I sat in a darkened room in my big armchair, wearing my pyjamas and primrose-coloured dressing gown, drinking too much, trying but failing to get things clear in my head. I'd put my phone on silent; its ring-tune hurt my head.

I thought about calling my sister a few times, to talk things through with her. But I just knew what her spiel would be – psychoanalysts are so predictable. I could hear her explaining the effects on a young woman's psyche of finding out she was adopted and had been lied to for all those years by those whose responsibility it was to provide her with love and support. I could also hear her reflecting more generally on cold mothers with high expectations and weak, adoring fathers who love their daughters far too much. Like a vulture that has spotted carrion, Amanda would focus on Julia's alleged emotional and sexual coldness, which she would interpret as a perverse amplification of her mother's own detachment and affective dysfunctionality. Then she would spin theories about early infant-mother bonding problems, and argue that Julia's murderous revenge fantasies about her 'bad' mothers (the real one who abandoned her, and Rose) had not been contained, which is why they resurfaced in a murderous act many years later. But this blaming-the-mother culture has always made me deeply uneasy, George. It's a dangerous path to tread.

Julia, Amanda would say, developed typical narcissistic defence mechanisms at a very young age. In my mind I could also hear Amanda explaining in great detail the repercussions for Julia's vulnerable psyche of the traumatic moment when she witnessed her father kissing her music teacher – a double rival. She would then move on to what always constitutes the climax of any of her analyses, and it was this, the anticipation of yet another dull discourse on Oedipal triangles, that nipped in the bud my desire to call her. I'd heard that particular narrative too many times, and although I appreciate many of the often brilliant and much more nuanced insights that psychoanalysis can offer, the Oedipus complex has always struck me as a highly overrated cliché. I just couldn't face it.

On the afternoon of 22 October, numb and intoxicated, and for the first time since my return from Marseille, I managed to find the courage to open my email, and listlessly skim-read the 211 email headers that aggressively announced their unread status in bold, reproachful letters. A relatively recent one, flagged as urgent, caught my attention – 'VICTIM WANTS TO MEET YOU – RESPOND!' it read. It turned out to be from you (as were at least fifty other emails).

'Christ, Clare, WHERE ARE YOU? Can you please ANSWER MY EMAILS AND MY CALLS?' it read. 'Grace Taylor, one of the victims who survived the coffee-shop bombing, heard about the book project and contacted me. She wants to meet you. Please call her as a MATTER OF URGENCY.'

So call her I did. Grace Taylor's voice sounded like the deep murmur of a mountain stream lapping gently against moss-covered rocks. When I introduced myself she simply said, 'Yes, Clare, hello. I've been expecting your call. When would be a good time for you to come and see me?'

We agreed to meet the following day, at eleven o'clock in the morning. This would leave me enough time to make myself presentable, and to cover up some of the traces the previous weeks had left in my face. When I put my trousers on I realized I must have lost weight – I needed a belt to keep them in place. My blazer, too, felt baggier than it used to. I hadn't eaten anything much apart from crackers; everything else I'd consumed was of a liquid nature.

Grace lived in the ground-floor flat of a small white house with a cherry-coloured door in a chestnut-lined side-street in Notting Hill, just far enough from the endless stream of treasure-hunting tourists that congests Portobello market. She opened the door only seconds after I'd rung the bell.

'It's lovely to meet you, Clare,' she said and took my hand. She held it between hers for a long time, and I felt quite overwhelmed by the unexpected intimacy of this act. Grace smelled of lavender, and was perhaps in her sixties or seventies, or even eighties – it was very difficult to tell, since her face was round and kind, and very smooth, as though she hadn't known much sorrow in her life. Her pale-blue eyes, however, never properly focused on mine – whenever I sought to hold them they flickered across my face and then glided downwards, like tears.

She led me to the living room. The first thing I noticed was that it was populated with hundreds of photographs – they were everywhere, on the walls, on the mantelpiece, on the chests of drawers, on the old grand piano – this was clearly a woman who resided right at the heart of a remarkably wide-ranging network of relationships. When she sat down in a purple armchair, she appeared to me as someone cherished by this multitude of phantoms, as though she was their queen and they her loving subjects. Here was a woman with more than just a cat to accompany her into old age, someone who had chosen people rather than words.

On the coffee table between us stood an old-fashioned porcelain teapot on a candle-lit stove. Two teacups on saucers and a jug of milk and a sugar bowl were also in reach, as well as a plate with a selection of shortbread fingers. The biscuits looked self-made and smelled of honey and burned butter.

A young woman popped her head in and called, 'Is everything OK, Grandma?'

Grace smiled and waved in her direction. 'Yes, darling, we're fine. I'll be all right. Don't you worry. You can go now if you want.'

'Would you mind pouring us a cup of tea?' Grace asked when the woman had disappeared. 'And please, do have some biscuits.'

It was only then that I saw that Grace's hands were resting on a stick. Again I noticed that her gaze was strangely directionless, constantly sinking to the ground, like a limpet with weak suction sliding down a pane of glass. And then it came to me – Grace was blind.

I poured the tea and pushed the cup in her direction. The room was small but cosy – it was dominated by a grand piano with golden feet, flanked by numerous healthy-looking plants. There was a birdcage in the bay window that looked out onto the street, with two bright canaries in it. I realized then I knew nothing about Grace – I hadn't even done the most basic background check. I stuttered something about my editor and managed to produce a few generalities about my project. Grace's face was turned in my direction. Her gentle smile made me think of a benign full moon illuminating a clearing in a dark wood. At some point, she closed her eyes.

'I see,' she said. 'Now, tell me, dear. How's your research been going so far?'

'Not well,' I blurted out. I suddenly felt the strong need to share my sorrows with her, unprofessional as this might have been in this particular situation. I just started talking then, incontinently, telling Grace about my doubts and my inability to construct a coherent narrative about Julia in which I could actually believe. Grace listened intently, nodding her head as though what I told her coincided with something she had already concluded herself.

'I see. I understand your problem,' she said when I'd finished. 'But unfortunately, I won't be able to help you solve it. I didn't know Julia. I know nothing about her. Nothing apart from what's been reported in the press. But I saw her. I looked her in the eye. Julia, you see, was the last thing I saw before she took away my sight for good. That's what I wanted to talk to you about. My last vision. But I'm afraid that's all I can offer. It's not really what you've been hoping for, dear, is it?'

'You lost your sight as a result of the bombing?' I asked. Grace nodded. Christ, I thought. How they must haunt her, her last visual impressions – Julia's face, her gaze, her movements.

'Could you describe the day of the attack, Grace? What were you doing in that part of London? How did you end up in the coffee shop at that particular time?'

'With pleasure, dear. But first, let me tell you a few things about me. I'm a music teacher. Piano, mainly. I taught at various primary schools and now I give private lessons. I've always loved being a teacher. I never had any delusions of grandeur, you see? It makes life so much easier. I never saw myself as a thwarted concert pianist, or what have you. I know my strengths and weaknesses. It's a strength in itself, you see, to realize what you can and can't achieve in life. And to make your peace with it. And I like to think I'm a rather good teacher, too. I love my students. Many of them have gone on to accomplish great things. But I try not to boast about them. Don't let me get started on that, dear! I've other people I can bore with these tales.'

'Are you married, Grace?' I asked without thinking. A bad habit of mine. To associate boredom and marriage, and dusty old tales told too many times.

Grace smiled. 'I was, for thirty-nine most wonderful years. Then he died, my husband. John. Cancer, you see? I've children, though, four. And two grandchildren. And a third on the way. You just met one of them, Samantha. It was Sam I was about to meet on the day of the bombing. She was late, that day. Thank God. Had she been on time, who knows what might have happened. It's quite likely she'd be dead. There were only five survivors, you see. Yes, thank God Sam was late that day. She said she ran into an old school friend.' Grace chuckled. 'That's her story, anyway. Truth is, Sam's always late. Couldn't be on time if her life depended on it. No matter how hard she tries. Some people are like that.

'I'd seen a student that morning. Bernard. Such a talented young boy. Only twelve, but so very gifted. He'll go far, I'm sure of that. We spent the entire hour practising Chopin's "Raindrop" Prelude. Do you know it?' Grace hummed the first notes, and to my own surprise I did indeed recognize it. 'We worked on Bernard's delivery. Timing, you see, is the key. To everything. It's the secret ingredient, the difference between mere sounds and music. Once my students manage to hit all the right keys, which is just a matter of practice, really, my job starts properly. Deceleration and acceleration, hesitation, tension, teasing, climax, release... but I'm digressing. I just remembered that lesson, because when I left to catch the bus to Covent Garden that day I was struck by the sound of the raindrops pelting the cloth of my umbrella. I kept thinking, what a genius. You see, Chopin had managed to capture their voice so brilliantly.

Of course, he must have heard it often, the rain, especially here in England...

'Anyway, dear. So I took the bus. I had a few errands to run. Nothing very important. I wanted to buy some soft wool to knit a pullover for Alma, my other grandchild. Her second birthday was coming up. I also needed a new blouse. I'd been invited to a student's concert, a premiere, you see. I really rather dislike shopping. But I didn't want to end up being a terrible embarrassment to my poor student on her big evening, in my weird old gowns. So I thought I'd better plan something to look forward to at the end of the trip. And I hadn't seen Sam for a while in any case. She studies on the Strand, you see. Architecture. She wants to be an architect. Isn't that wonderful? I hope I'll live to see her first building. Or to feel it, rather. Sometimes I forget. So I proposed we meet in that area to catch up over a cuppa in the afternoon. It was Sam who suggested that particular café. I'd never been to any of the Café Olé branches before. You see, they're not really my cup of tea, chains like that. They're so... I don't know. Generic. Sterile. I like old broken things, with character. Like myself.' Again Grace chuckled.

'Of course the poor girl has never forgiven herself for suggesting it. You can imagine, dear. She still feels so guilty. After all these weeks. It breaks my heart. Not a day goes by when she doesn't bring it up. And I know she thinks of it all the time. I can tell what's happening behind that furrowed brow of hers. Sam thinks it's her fault, you see. She's hardly left my side since the bombing. She visits every day. She does the shopping and the cleaning and what have you. She even wants to move in with me. But I said no to that. Much as I love Sam's company, I won't exploit the situation. No. She needs to live her own life. Finish her studies, go to parties, have fun, fall in love, and what have you. Caring for a boring old woman like me won't do her any good. Once I've managed to convince her it wasn't her fault, I'll tell her to stop hovering over me like a worried nurse. I'll send her home. Back to her old life. I'll tell her she can visit every two weeks. But no more than that. With a heavy heart, but I'll do it. This isn't good for either of us.

'I'm learning just fine to live without eyesight. One of the advantages of being a musician, you see. I always did pay a lot of attention to sounds. They can guide you if you let them. And I've many friends. I'll be fine. You know, dear, actually I *am* fine. It's Sam who isn't. I still have quite some work cut out before I can let her go. It's not easy, banishing someone's bad thoughts from their minds. Once they're there, it's hard to expel them again. They're strong and stubborn. They suck you dry in no time if you're not careful.'

Here Grace paused. I filled up our teacups again. I tried one of the shortbread fingers. It was the first morsel of decent food I'd eaten for days, and it tasted like paradise.

'Where were we?' Grace continued. 'Ah yes, the day. Well, I found the wool I was looking for in one of the bigger department stores. That was the easy part. Then I tried on various blouses, but they all looked wrong on me. You see, clothes just don't hang right on my body. I'm not lucky that way. John always used to tease me about that. My clothes crinkle and pucker in the most curious places. So I very quickly grew frustrated. Eventually, I found something cream-coloured and silken, tent-shaped and what have you. I didn't like it much. But I bought it anyway just to end my plight.

'Then I found myself with plenty of time on my hands. I had two whole hours to fill before my meeting with Sam. I wandered around a little. I went to the lovely little street with only music shops on it. Do you know it, dear? I browsed in various shops. In one of them I played a few chords on their display pianos. But they all sounded soulless. A lot of the modern pianos do. Have you noticed? Especially the Japanese ones. Perfect from a technical point of view, but something is lacking. Something important. I can never quite put my finger on it. Then I leafed through the piles of sheet music. I bought a few pieces I thought my students would enjoy. It was still early when I went to Paternoster Square to find the Café Olé branch.

'I didn't like it much. Bad music was playing. It was very loud and distracting. But it was almost completely full. There was only one free table, right at the back. Next to the loos. I sat down. I started leafing through one of the free newspapers that was on the table. It contained nothing but gossip: a starlet whose name I didn't know had fallen over drunk on a night out and flashed her knickers. Another had gained weight. A third had been deserted by her fourth boyfriend in only one year, and so on. I wondered, who *reads* this stuff? Then I went through the music I'd bought. I thought about how to teach it. I added a few pointers in pencil for my students. Most make very similar mistakes –

it's interesting. You can almost predict it, where they will stumble or play too fast or too slow. Then I started to study the other people in the café. Discreetly, of course. People don't like feeling watched, you see. It makes them nervous.

'I've thought about them quite a lot since. You can imagine. They're almost all dead now. There was the girl behind the counter. Quick as a weasel. She had fire-engine-red hair. She was always moving and doing things. Her colleague was at the till. She had pencil-thin eyebrows and was languid, like a sleepy cat. There were three young Spanish tourists who were all talking at once. And very loudly. There was a couple in their thirties. They didn't say much and seemed sad. There was a student with a beard typing into his laptop. A woman with curly hair studying a book on Hieronymus Bosch. A young mother with a baby. She was breastfeeding it under a very colourful African shawl. There were many others. Twenty-nine in total, including myself.

'And then she entered. Julia. You see, I was watching the door by then. It was now well past the time Sam and I had agreed to meet. Julia came in at seventeen minutes past three. The first thing I noticed was how upright she walked. She held her head high. She carried a dark-blue plastic sports bag. Somehow it jarred with the rest of her look. I remember thinking how pale and pretty she was. Pure, somehow. No make-up, no frills. Just classically beautiful features. High cheekbones, a fine proud nose and snow-white skin. She scanned the room. Her eyes met mine. She ordered something. Peppermint tea, I think. She seemed calm. She took her drink to one of the places at the window. A seat had just become vacant. The student with the laptop got out just in time, bless him. Julia sat down and looked out onto the square for a few minutes. She never touched her tea.

'Then she went to the loo. With her big sports bag. When she walked past me, our eyes met again. Hers were green, quite a striking colour. I remember thinking, what an interesting face. Quite unusual. Cold, perhaps? But no, that wasn't really it. Hindsight always twists things, don't you think? It's a temptation one must resist. When she came out of the loos again she walked straight towards the exit. Neither fast nor slow. Smooth and graceful, like a panther. Very upright. I watched her. Only when her hand had pushed open the exit did I notice that she wasn't carrying her bag.

'"Your bag!" I called out. I had stood up to attract her attention. "You were carrying a bag. You must have forgotten it."

'She turned round and then she looked at me for a third and final time. She opened the door and was about to step outside. The rain had stopped. Rather unexpectedly, the sun had come out. Suddenly, she was bathed in rays of light. She looked like an angel, with her white skin sparkling. Then she blew me a kiss. It was the strangest gesture. I didn't know what to make of it. She didn't smile. Her face remained completely blank. Deadly serious. And then she disappeared from sight. And my own sight disappeared for ever shortly afterwards. How weird, I remember thinking, how weird. And then I stopped thinking.

'I woke up in hospital three days later. They'd put me into an artificial coma. They had tried to save my eyesight but failed. Apart from my eyes, though, all other injuries were minor. Bruises, cuts, contusions, damaged ribs, that sort of thing. It was a miracle of sorts. But a sad one. Sight, of all the senses... Although I really mustn't complain. Had I lost my hearing I'd be unemployed now, wouldn't I? At least I can still teach. And listen to others play. And I'm still alive. Most of the others aren't.'

We sat in silence for a while.

'Do you hate her? Julia, I mean?' I finally asked.

'Oh, of course not, dear. What would be the point of that? I don't hate anybody. Hating gets you nowhere. We should forgive others for their weaknesses. That, Clare, is really all we can do. Our only challenge in this world.'

'Why do you think she did it?'

'I've no idea. Sam read the manifesto to me. I didn't understand it. I really couldn't begin to speculate about her motives.'

'Don't you think about her, at night, and about what she took away from you and all the others? Don't you wish her dead, or blind, too, or imprisoned for life? Don't you want to know *why* she committed her atrocious act?'

Grace thought about this for a moment. Then she said: 'No. No, honestly, dear, I don't. I'm not interested. I'm interested in Sam right now. In how to get her back on track. I'm interested in tomorrow and the day after. I'm interested in the future, you see? In how to keep on living as well as we can, considering the circumstances.'

A little later, Grace showed me out. But before she closed the door, she put her warm, firm hand on my arm, leaned forward and whispered in my ear, 'Good luck, Clare. Have faith.'

Despite having found some temporary relief in Grace's calming presence, I felt even worse when I returned to my apartment. Grace's humility and generosity were humbling. I was deeply impressed by her poise and charity. I wondered whether she was religious. However, she didn't tell me anything I didn't already know. She didn't help answer any of the questions that I was burning to resolve. She told me that Julia's face was impenetrable, and her strange final gesture before blowing up the coffee shop unreadable. I was beginning to think I was doomed. Unless I could speak to Julia, unless Julia could tell me the truth about Julia, my peace of mind, I feared, would be destroyed for ever.

Talking of peace of mind, George: I, in turn, seem to have destroyed Amanda's. At least that's what she told me yesterday. During her one-hour visit (for the first time, Laura couldn't be there – she was expecting an important food critic at the Blue Nile), she broke down and let it all out. I have to confess I was waiting for something like this to happen. She has been too calm, too controlled – there was no way she could keep that up, not even her. It was the wretched defence strategy topic that triggered it – it's all my three visitors want to talk about right now.

As always, we met in the visitors' room for low-risk inmates, an inhospitable space reminiscent of an airport lounge, with bad acoustics and a row of twenty square plastic tables in it, each of which was occupied by another woman and her guests. There were five guards in the room watching us, too.

'Have you thought a bit more about it?' Amanda asked straight after we'd sat down.

'Yes. But I haven't changed my mind. I'm not going to pretend I was temporarily insane. I wasn't, and it would be unethical to claim that I was.'

My choice of words made Amanda flare up. 'Unethical? Let me tell you what's unethical: your utter selfishness – *that*'s what's unethical. Your getting on your moral high horse for the sake of some idiotic principle that'll allow you to feel self-righteous – *that*'s unethical. Your complete disregard for Laura's and my feelings – *that*'s what *I'd* call unethical. Have you any idea how bloody worried we are about you? And how much all of this has shaken Laura – and me, for that matter? Laura's so confused right now – her cherished aunt, the person she admired most in the world… Moira called yesterday. She's concerned about Laura. She's not on form, not her usual self. Apparently, she keeps dropping things in the kitchen, expensive things. Equipment, ingredients, glasses. Every day it's something. And she threw out some customers the other day who she thought were paparazzi, but actually they were just tourists… It's so *unlike* her. We want you out of here; we want the old Clare back.'

'Listen…' I began, but Amanda interrupted me.

'For fuck's sake, Clare, we're talking about a simple legal strategy, not about moral principles. Fuck the means. It's the result that matters. Everyone has to have a strategy – whatever works best, that's just how the system functions. You know that. You're self-sabotaging. There are other ways to deal with your guilt, healthier ways. Do you hear me? I'll help you with that, if you let me. It's not the right moment to play the bloody martyr. Do you even realize how much is at stake here? You could be locked up for years, even for the rest of your life. Hasn't your lawyer made that clear to you? I want you back. Outside. I need you. You and Laura are all I've got left.' Then Amanda began to sob. I tried to take her hand, but she pulled it away. The people on the neighbouring tables had stopped talking and were looking at us, and one of the guards signalled for us to keep our voices down.

'I'm aware of that,' I said as gently as possible. 'I am. I want out, too. I miss you, both of you. But I wasn't temporarily insane. I'm just not prepared to lie about it.'

Then Amanda started to shout at me. 'But of course you bloody were! How can you even *think* you weren't! That's just ridiculous. The Clare I know would never kill anyone. Never! You were completely out of your bloody mind! You'd been drinking, you had a breakdown, you were undernourished, dehydrated, hypothermic, your brain wasn't working right. You'd been under so much stress that it simply broke something in you. That *happens* – it's called a nervous bloody breakdown. You didn't know what you were doing – of course you didn't. That's what the lawyer says. And the psychiatrists. Everyone! And they're right. It's not even just a strategy. That's how it was. It's the bloody *truth*.'

'But I did, Amanda. I did,' I whispered. 'I did know what I was doing.'

'No, you didn't! You think you did, but you didn't. My sister's not a murderer! I refuse to believe it. And you better get a grip on this – I'm not going to watch you self-destruct in court, I can tell you that. I'm going to have you sectioned if you don't change your story. Do you hear me? Do you understand what I'm saying?'

And then Amanda stormed out, although our time wasn't yet up. But the word she'd used stayed behind. Murderer.

Murderer. Am I a murderer?

XVIII

Since Amanda uttered that dreaded word during her outburst in the visitors' room, I haven't been able to sleep. At all. The pills have stopped working. So I may as well use my nights to finish this job now.

After my meeting with Grace, my despair grew worse. I just about managed to transcribe our interview, but not much else besides. For days, I sat in my armchair with my blinds drawn. I forced myself to answer Amanda's calls every day, because I knew that otherwise she would have turned up at my doorstep – and she had keys to my flat. Since the announcement of the award, she had become very anxious that I might do something stupid. On 28 October, however, Amanda didn't call. And the next day, around noon, someone pounded on my door.

'Open up! I know you're in there, Clare,' a bright voice called. 'I'm not leaving until you let me in.' It was Laura.

Very slowly and reluctantly, I opened the door. I absolutely couldn't face speaking to anyone – not even Laura. But she burst in, hugged me and then took a step back to look at me.

'Jesus, what's wrong with you? You look terrible. Are you sick or something? And what's with the drinking at this time of day? It's not even twelve yet.'

She must have smelled the whisky on my breath. I mumbled something about a toothache.

'Well, then go to the dentist, and *pronto*,' Laura said. 'The days of self-medicating dental pain with spirits are long gone. This is the twenty-first century, remember?'

'Fine,' I said. 'Whatever. You're right. I'll go.'

Laura looked at me again. 'It's not even true, is it? You look really shit, you know that? Have you lost weight?'

'Look, I'm a bit stressed about my book project – important deadline coming up, and I'm behind. I just really need to work, OK?'

'Since when can you work when you're drunk? I should think that working and drinking, and drinking and thinking, are kind of mutually exclusive.' Laura wouldn't let go. She'd folded her arms and was studying me.

'I'm not drunk, Laura, I just had a drink. Small but significant difference, all right? I was just about to take a shower and make some coffee and get started when you interrupted me.'

'Well, I'm sorry I got between you and your shower. You certainly need one, I can tell you that.'

'Thanks. That's really charming. Did Amanda send you?'

'No, she didn't. In fact, she'd kill me if she knew I was here. Do you want to know why?'

I sighed. 'Why?'

'Because you forgot her birthday! It was Mum's birthday yesterday. She was completely distraught that you didn't call her. It really, really upset her, actually. I mean, your own sister. Come *on*. You only have one. How difficult can it be to remember that one family birthday?'

'Shit,' I said. 'I'm sorry. I completely forgot what day of the week it was...'

'Yes, I can see that. And what time of day it is, and so on. You definitely do seem a little disorientated.' After a pause, Laura said, more gently: 'Hey, do you want to tell me what's wrong? Is it that Temple business? You know, Mum is really worried about it.'

'No, no, sweetheart, it's not that. I'm OK, really. I promise. But thanks for asking. As I said, I'm just a bit stressed about the deadline. Don't you have to be at the Blue Nile today? What about lunch service?' I really, *really* wanted her to leave. My head was pounding, and I was embarrassed. I didn't want her to see me like this. I was in my dressing gown, and Laura was right: I desperately needed a shower.

'Moira's doing lunch today, and we've also appointed a sous-chef. Haven't I told you? It's so exciting. Business has been very good lately, and we can't really cope with the demand anymore, just the two of us. So we asked around, and a friend recommended a friend. We interviewed her last week. She's called Lizzy, and seems really nice and enthusiastic and capable and all that. Today Moira's showing her the ropes, and tomorrow I will. We thought it would be better if we took turns. Too many cooks, and so on. Talking of cooks: you know what? I think you need something to eat. You look like you haven't eaten anything decent for days. Why don't I cook something for you? I have the afternoon off, and I'd love to make us something.'

'Laura, that's very sweet of you, darling, but I really need to work. And... my tooth, remember? Chewing hurts.'

'No, sorry, not good enough. You'll eat with me. I'm not leaving. What do you fancy? I think you need protein, and iron, and vitamins. I know: I'll make us some feta-bulgur-wheat fritters and a spinach-fennel salad. With cranberry sauce and Greek yoghurt on the side. How does that sound?'

'Sweetheart, as I said. I need to work. I mean it. Really. You should go out and have some fun. Enjoy your afternoon off. Go chanterelle hunting or something. Source some baby pig trotters. I'll order in some pizza.'

'OK, so you don't like the idea of vegetarian. I can cook meat, too, you know. If you crave meat, that's fine. How about lamb? There's a really good organic butcher around the corner. I've got it: lamb shanks resting on a bed of grilled baby gems, with a mustard-horseradish sauce.'

'How can meat be resting on anything, Laura? It's dead matter. Dead things don't rest.'

'Jesus, you really are in a super-grumpy mood today, Clare. What's eating you?' Laura rolled her eyes at me. 'That's industry speak. Everyone in the sector talks like that. Haven't you noticed? All food now rests, nestles or perches on beds of something or other. Everything's sun-blushed, succulent, free-range, forested, hand-cured, heritage, line-caught, luscious and so on, and caressed by reductions, infusions, emulsions and jus. Menu descriptions are amuse-gueules, really, the first point of contact with the customer. It's kind of an art form in itself, finding the right words to describe something in a way that tantalizes the imagination.'

'But it's distasteful, that overblown gastro-rhetoric. After all, we're not talking about art, we're talking about things like sausages and mash. When did it become acceptable to talk about food as something you can "deconstruct" or "curate"? There's something seriously wrong with all this food fanaticism. It's just another bloody form of glorified, hollow consumption. Christ, people used to bury their heads in the sand, now they bury them in jewelled couscous, sprinkled with pomegranate seeds and toasted almond flakes and a hint of orange blossom essence.'

The second I finished my diatribe, I regretted it. I didn't mean to snap at Laura. I didn't mean to attack her profession. The truth is, I am immensely proud of her and all her achievements. And I love her cooking – what she does is amazing. I was just so tired, and I so desperately wanted her to leave me be.

She looked at me aghast, her eyes widening while I spoke.

'Fine. You made your point,' she said eventually. 'Sounds like you should just order in pizza after all.' Then she grabbed her bag and banged the door shut as she left.

Although I was quite drunk, I had enough presence of mind left to realize that I'd hurt her feelings. I opened the door and stepped out onto the landing. 'Laura… wait,' I called, 'listen, hon, I'm sorry, I didn't mean to…' But Laura ran down the stairs without looking back.

I left dozens of messages on her phone that day, and texted apologies, but they all remained unanswered. And so did my attempts to call Amanda. It was completely unlike Amanda to ignore my calls, and it showed just how upset she was about my birthday blunder.

I don't know, George. At that point, it simply all became too much for me. Overwhelmed not just with regret at my past choices, but also with the futility of the project, I felt that on top of it all I was making a catastrophic mess of everything else that really mattered to me. Not only was I about to lose you for good, but I had also just alienated the two other people in my life I cared for most. Something in me snapped. Suddenly, I felt the strong need to get out of my flat, out of London. I needed to leave it all behind – my files, my notes, my computer, my phone. I had to get away from everything.

Very early the next morning (it was 30 October), I knocked on my neighbour's door and asked her to take care of Aisha for a few days, threw a few random items in a bag, and got into my car. I drove to my parents' cottage in a daze, and I don't remember much about my stay there. I remember I was cold all the time, as cold as I'd never been before in my life. I remember I couldn't eat. I remember sitting in a brown dilapidated armchair by the fireplace, wrapped in my father's dressing gown and one of his scratchy woollen blankets.

I passed seven days in a stupor, dazed and apathetic, and then, early in the morning on the eighth day of my stay, I decided to return to London and face the consequences of my failure. I've already told you this part of the story. I was ready to confess, to do penance, to start afresh. I would call you first, and then I would call Amanda and Laura. I would invite them out to our favourite restaurant, and I would try my very best to make up for the missed birthday and for my horrible speech.

Back in my flat, early in the afternoon, I gathered together all my courage and switched my phone back on to call you, George. But then I noticed that a caller with an unknown number had tried to reach me several times that morning. They'd left three messages. I listened to the first. The unknown caller was a woman named Jemima Keller. She said she was Julia White's lawyer. I hastily shuffled through my notes, and found that I had indeed contacted her firm, Keller, Cain & Candle, at the very beginning of my research to request an interview with Julia. Jemima asked me to call her back immediately. I listened to the second message, in which she once again urged me to get back to her. She said she thought I'd be very interested in what she had to tell me. In her third message, she said that it was of the utmost importance that I call her back right away. And call her is precisely what I did. God, if only I hadn't. If only I'd done what I'd been meaning to do, and called you instead, George.

'It's Clare, Clare Hardenberg,' I said when she answered. 'You said you had something important to tell me?'

'Indeed,' Jemima Keller responded crisply. 'Julia White would like to see you. Tomorrow. At ten. We've already put you on her visitors' list, and the formalities are all sorted. I assume you can make it?'

'Yes, I can, definitely,' I said, trying to control my breathing. 'Where?'

Jemima told me the name of the institution and instructed me to bring ID. Before I could ask any further questions, she'd hung up.

XIX

Unsurprisingly, I couldn't sleep again that night. The next morning – it was 7 November – I got up very early, showered, washed my hair, put on my favourite silk blouse and skirt, and tried to render my drawn and tired face at least semi-presentable. I put on lipstick and perfume. I felt nervous, almost nauseous, as though someone with whom I was secretly in love had, after months of shy, persistent courtship, finally consented to grant me an interview.

HM Prison Holloway, an all-female Victorian detention centre in Islington, has had its share of famous inmates – the suffragettes, Diana Mitford and Myra Hindley had all served time in the shoebox-shaped red-brick building in which Julia was being held. Although my name was on the official visitors' list, just as Jemima had told me, the security checks to which I was submitted when I reported to the woman in charge were excruciating. I was only allowed my pen and my notebook, and had to leave everything else in a storage box – my phone, key, purse, even my tissues. But when she also demanded I surrender my recording device I protested.

'How am I supposed to conduct an interview without this?' I asked.

The guard just shrugged her shoulders. She evidently didn't care. But I just couldn't allow her to ruin this unique chance by disturbing the most important conversation of my life with frantic scribbling, nor could I trust my memory alone, so I pleaded and pleaded, until finally she threw up her hands and said: 'What*ever*. Take it in, then.'

Eventually, one of her colleagues (a portly, kind-looking Indian woman) opened a massive iron door and led me down a long corridor. We had to pass through various other locked doors until we reached our destination. The room we entered looked like a cell rather than a visitors' room – lime-green tiles covered not just the floor, but also the walls and the ceiling, from which a naked lightbulb dangled, casting everything in an unforgiving, clinical brightness. Apart from a table in the centre of the room and two chairs, the space was empty. The guard (who had not spoken a word) signalled for me to sit down on one of the chairs while she remained standing next to the door. I put my recording device and my pen and notebook on the table. Although there were a million things I wanted to ask Julia, I'd written down a few questions, just in case nerves got the better of me. My last two interviews had not exactly gone according to plan, and I wanted to be prepared if I lost my footing again. I tried to read them over while I waited, but was too nervous to concentrate. I felt sick, and also utterly exhausted and very agitated at the same time. When I switched on the recording device I noticed my hands were shaking. A couple of minutes later, another guard opened the door. And then, in came Julia, her hands handcuffed in front of her.

She was wearing khaki-coloured military trousers and a large knitted brown pullover. Her face was white and taut. She looked paler and older than in the pictures I'd seen. The two parenthetical lines on either side of her mouth had deepened. She put her cuffed hands on the table between us and sat down on the edge of her chair, carefully and very upright, without saying anything. She held her head slightly tilted backwards and slanted to the left, as though she was scrutinizing something potentially dangerous. And then she looked at me with her deep pond-green eyes. I found it difficult to hold her gaze; in fact, it profoundly disconcerted me. It was so different from what I had expected. Instead of the hard, cold stare of a ruthless sociopath, I saw in Julia's eyes something I couldn't quite name – sorrow, perhaps? Sympathy? Or something else entirely? Nobody had ever looked at me like that, and I felt myself blushing, averted my eyes and checked my recording device.

'Hello, Clare,' Julia said eventually. 'You wanted to meet me.' Her voice, too, was nothing like I'd imagined it – deep and resonant like a cello, it was also gentle and quiet. It must have been the quietness in that voice that caused me to lean slightly towards it, as though afraid I might lose it in the cavernous space.

Julia gestured with her head to the guard who had brought me there, and who was staring straight ahead at the wall behind us. 'The guard will remain in the room with us. Don't worry about her. She doesn't care what we say. She's heard it all before. Haven't you, Anita?'

We both looked at her. Anita didn't respond, and her face betrayed no emotion.

'See?' Julia said. 'Feel free to say whatever you want. Ask me anything. You must have questions for me. Fire away, Clare. We have fifty minutes.'

My heart sank. How on earth would I be able to ask Julia in such a short time all the questions that had been burning in my mind? There was so much I needed to know. I cleared my voice.

'Thank you for meeting with me,' I said, feeling very self-conscious. 'I appreciate that. As you may know, I'm writing a book about you.'

Julia smiled, and I was utterly surprised to see the transformative effect it had on her features. She was breathtakingly beautiful when she smiled, her marble-hard countenance suddenly becoming gentle, soft and kind. 'So I've been told,' she said. 'That's why I wanted to meet you. I know who you are. I hope it's going OK?'

Again I felt myself blushing. 'It's going fine,' I said, 'but I wondered whether I could ask you to clarify a few things for me. I've been talking to your family and to some friends of yours, and the picture they've painted of your character has not always been... well, it's a mixed bag. I wanted to give you an opportunity to respond to their version of events. So...' Again I cleared my throat. My voice sounded hoarse and rusty, as though I'd spent all night talking in a smoke-filled nightclub. I found myself wishing I'd brought along some water. I felt very hot. 'Amy. I spoke to your sister first.'

When I mentioned Amy's name, I saw something like sorrow in Julia's face, and she raised her cuffed hands to her forehead to push back a strand of hair that had escaped from her bun.

'Yes, I thought Amy would want to talk to you. How is she doing?' Julia had bent forward a little in her seat, eager to hear my response, her eyes wide open. She looked vulnerable.

'Not well, I'm afraid. She seemed lost, very lonely and confused. She's awfully thin – but you know that, of course. She feels that you've stopped loving her, and that you no longer care about her. She said you've been ignoring her for years, ever since you came back from your travels, and that you used to be very close in the past. She can't make sense of what's happened between the two of you. Is it true – have you abandoned her because she fell ill?'

For a split second, Julia looked genuinely shocked. I could hear her breathing in sharply. Again she tried to brush the unruly loose strand of hair from her forehead. 'Of course not,' she said eventually. 'It makes me sad to hear that Amy feels that way. I love my sister, and I always will. I had to make a very, very difficult decision. Amy's illness has been so painful for everyone in our family. We all have different opinions on how best to deal with it. I miss my sister terribly, and I wish we could be close again, but I really believe that any form of contact with me while she continues to self-destruct would make things worse.

'Above all Amy wants pity, and to be looked after. I think that by falling ill, she tried to force me to continue caring for her just as one cares for a little child. It's no coincidence that she stopped eating exactly at the moment when it was time for her to become more independent. I know she's scared and desperate, but I believe that allowing her to think that her illness behaviour *works* would destroy any chance of her ever recovering. Amy wants to continue to play the helpless victim for ever, and I just can't encourage that. It's wrong. She needs to learn to take responsibility for her life. She has to *want* to get better. When she does that, we can have a proper relationship again, but not before. She knows that. It's the same as with alcoholics and drug addicts – at a certain point, their family has to stop enabling their destructive behaviour. It's hard, it's terribly difficult, but you need to let them hit rock bottom, and only then will they find the will to recover.'

'But that's so *extreme*, Julia,' I objected. 'Don't you feel pity, don't you feel any sympathy for your sister's weakness? I take your point about the manipulative dimension of her behaviour, but can't you see beyond that? I don't think she's in control of any of it. What if she dies? What if rock bottom means death in her case?'

Again Julia looked aghast. 'Of course I pity her, and I miss her dreadfully; I can't even begin to tell you how much. But if I give her what she wants now, she'll never recover. Her self-inflicted illness will have *worked*, can't you see that? And then she'll continue to use it all her life. The only chance she has is to learn that such behaviour *doesn't* work, not with me, and not with others, either, and that if she wants me back she'll have to change.'

'But what if she can't change?'

'But she can. Of course she can. Everyone can. I believe in free will, Clare. We're all born with the ability to make rational choices – that's the ultimate prerogative of our species. All those deterministic theories about weakness, trauma, bad parenting and so on, they're one of the true banes of our times. They're always the ultimate excuse for *not* taking responsibility. Freud's done more harm to human society than any other theorist of our age. He's generated an epidemic of self-pitying narcissism, a reactionary concentration on repairing the self rather than society, of privileging the ego over the community. We live in the age of the *selfie* – that really says it all.'

I thought about that for a while, and I couldn't altogether disagree with her. 'What about Jonathan?' I said eventually. 'Your brother believes you were born evil – that's the word he used: *evil*. He thinks *you're* responsible for Amy's illness, and that you've destroyed your entire family. He thinks it's all personal, what you did, designed to make your parents and him suffer.'

Julia sighed. 'Jonathan and I never got on. He hated me from the very start. He thought of me as an intruder and felt jealous of me, and he believed I'd destroyed his special relationship with our father. He could never get over the fact that Tim loved all of us equally, not just him. Or that, at least, he tried very hard to make it look that way. But that's another story. I'm not surprised that Jonathan presented things in that way. He's not a very imaginative person. You could see that, I'm sure. As for describing me as evil…' Julia paused for a moment. 'That fits perfectly, actually. Evil is a concept that tends to be used by those who prefer not to think, not to question, not to understand more complex causes. It's the resort of the lazy.'

Again, I found myself agreeing with her. 'Jonathan seemed particularly upset about a speech you made at his wedding, which he felt was very hostile and designed to ruin his special day.'

Julia laughed. 'I can't believe he's still talking about that. I'm the first to admit that his wedding wasn't my finest hour, and I've tried to apologize to him many times. But he made that impossible because he stopped speaking to me. Yes, I suppose I wanted to tease him a little bit about his conformist life choices. I wanted it to be funny, you know? But maybe I got the tone wrong, and I can also see that his wedding wasn't the right moment to do what I did. And I should obviously also have known that he lacks any sense of humour whatsoever. I mean any! His guests got what I was trying to do, though. They were all laughing and cheering. I got standing ovations, Clare. They *loved* it. The whole party was in stitches. It was only Jonathan who didn't get it. And his wife, of course. Anyway. *Mea culpa.*'

That completely contradicted Jonathan's account of the scene. He had mentioned that all his guests were horrified and disgusted, and that Julia's speech was met with icy silence.

'And what about your parents, Julia?' I asked next. 'They're distraught. They just can't believe that their beloved, brilliant daughter has killed twenty-four people. Your father desperately wants to see you. Your mother is drinking like a fish. Their lives are ruined. They may never recover.'

Julia shifted in her seat and looked uncomfortable, and then defiant. 'You do know I'm adopted, right? Didn't Rose and Tim tell you?'

'I did know, but only because Chris told me. Your parents didn't mention it.'

She looked genuinely surprised. 'Well, that's interesting. I guess they're keeping their promise then. I didn't think they would, to be honest. It would have been so much easier for them to tell the truth. That I'm not theirs, I mean. That in my case, the most well-meaning and heart-warming nurture couldn't overcome my evil nature, or whatever comforting theories people try to embrace in situations like this.'

'How did it make you feel, learning that you were adopted?' I asked.

Julia shrugged. 'I don't know. I was obviously shocked when I found out, but in the end, it didn't really change much. They were nice about it, emphasizing how much they loved me, and promising that they'd never tell anyone, including Jonathan and Amy. That it would remain our secret. That they loved me just as much as my siblings. But I think I'd always felt very different from most people, including my family. In other ways, it also made sense to me. It explained why Tim had always been so over-indulgent and over-protective of me – I always suspected there was something suspicious about that. You know, that there was something insincere about his too-showy adoration? Deep down, he was probably trying to compensate for the fact that, despite his best intentions, he just couldn't love me as much as Jonathan and Amy. No matter how hard he tried. But I don't blame him. It must be difficult.'

Julia reflected for a while before she continued: 'You know, his excessive veneration of me actually caused a lot of tension in the family. Jonathan and Amy felt threatened by it, obviously, and so did Rose. I think she always thought of it as *wrong*, the way he was so in awe of me. Ultimately, it turned her against me. I think at some point Rose even started to see me as a rival. I often wish I wasn't what people think of as beautiful, you know? I hate it. I want people to like me for who I am, not how I look. I just don't think Tim ever really did.'

For a moment, Julia looked very sad and vulnerable. I felt a strong urge to take her hand into mine and to comfort her. 'What about your real mother? Have you ever tried to find out about her?' I asked.

Julia shrugged again. 'Why? She made her choice and she must have had her reasons.' Then her gaze hardened, and she straightened her back. 'In any case I'm sorry to hear that Tim is in a bad place. As for Rose, she always drank too much – apparently even before my arrival. So that particular problem has absolutely nothing to do with me. And anyway, I prefer not to discuss my parents. I'm obviously very sorry that I've caused them pain. They don't deserve that. Neither of them.' Then she leaned back in her chair and raised her chin. She seemed to have closed up like a clam sensing danger, and I decided to move on to my next question.

'Do you remember Alison Fisher, with whom you studied in Edinburgh before you dropped out?'

Julia reflected for a while. 'Yes, Alison. That does ring a bell. I think she and I took the same classes, before I left. What about her?'

'Oh, I met her, too, and she told me that the two of you had been close friends before you met Chris.'

'That's strange. I only vaguely remember her... Pretty, black hair? A little hyperactive? I think we might have had coffee a few times.'

'And then you met Chris, and the two of you went travelling.'

'That's right.'

'Chris mentioned you were working on a dossier together – what became of it?'

'I lost faith in it. I lost faith in the power of words. Words – they're hot air, black marks on dead paper. People consume them just as mindlessly as they consume everything else.' Then Julia paused and looked at me again, intently, her eyes burning their way right into my soul. 'What about you, Clare? Do you still believe in the power of words? After everything that's happened to you?'

This time, I held her gaze. 'I used to,' I said. 'But now I don't know anymore.' Then we both remained silent for a while.

'What triggered your change of heart?' I asked her eventually. 'Chris said you changed completely on that trip, so much so that at some point he didn't recognize you anymore, and that you suddenly turned cold on him.'

'Well, that's *his* side of the story. I was completely in

love with Chris, but he turned out to be a real bastard. He broke my heart. Did he tell you that he slept with just about every backpacker who happened to cross his path when he thought I wasn't looking? That he was high and drunk *all* the time? That he had the attention span and work ethic of a puppy dog and lost interest in our project after about a month or so, and that I did all the hard work on my own while he hung out in bars and chatted up women? And did he tell you about what I witnessed on the coffee farm, and what happened afterwards?'

'He did tell me about the coffee farm incident, yes.'

'I'm glad he did. Although even he never understood the true significance of those events. He just didn't get it. Instead, he became really unpleasant about the fact that I took the dossier work seriously and didn't constantly want to sleep with him. But you know, anyone would have lost interest in sex after seeing what I saw on that trip. And his sleeping around didn't exactly help, either, obviously. His reaction was pathetic, really. Instead of supporting me, he turned into a self-pitying whiner, interested only in getting high and getting laid. He, too, was just all words and no action. I'd completely misjudged him.'

I felt as though all the stories I'd been told were melting into air. All seemed biased, shaped by frustrated emotions, misunderstandings or outright lies. I was about to say something to that effect when I noticed Julia shuddering. All colour had drained from her face. Her lips were pressed into a tight, ashen line. She shook her head as though she was trying to banish an unwanted memory.

'What is it, Julia? Tell me what's happening to you,' I said as gently as I could.

But Julia shook her head again, straightened her back and then met my gaze. It seemed to cost her a tremendous amount of energy to do so. 'Let me ask you something now, Clare,' she said eventually. 'You're probably disappointed with what you've found out about me so far. Am I right?'

I didn't respond.

'What I mean is, there are no great revelations, no dark secrets, no terrible childhood traumas with the power to explain how a good girl like me could have done what I did. Your readers will feel cheated. No fall on the head as a small child that radically altered my personality, no horrific sexual abuse in my family, no satanic corrupter figure who twisted me around his little finger and wreaked havoc with my soul. No hard evidence that I'm simply insane or plain evil, either. Nothing particularly dramatic, nothing very much out of the ordinary. Just the combination of a unique set of circumstances, none of which are very remarkable in their own right. Isn't that correct?'

Again I didn't respond.

Julia leaned towards me. In what was almost a whisper, she continued: 'But let me ask you this: isn't this scenario perhaps even more disturbing than any mono-causal explanation you might have been able to produce? Doesn't this absence of simple answers suggest the most unsettling possibility of all – that I might be *right*, Clare? Right, sane, justified? Think about it.'

'I have thought about it. A lot. Believe me. But killing people, innocent people, can never be justified. Don't you feel any remorse for what you've done at all?'

'No,' Julia said. 'I don't. I feel sorrow for the pain I've caused, absolutely, but not remorse. What I did was necessary. It was the only way to make people realize that their own comfortable way of life is built on appalling exploitation and barbarity.'

'Do you ever think about your victims, and their families, and their friends?'

'Sometimes,' Julia said. 'But I try not to.'

'But how can't you? How can twenty-four deaths not keep you awake at night?'

'You think I sleep at night?' Julia paused for a few seconds, sighed, and then said: 'I believe that privileging the wellbeing of a few individuals over the wellbeing of the many is wrong. Sometimes it's necessary to make sacrifices for the greater good. Sometimes it's necessary to commit acts of violence so that the far greater violence to which many more people are subjected can be stopped.'

'What do you mean by that?'

Julia leaned forward once again, her eyes glowing. 'Terrorism, Clare, is above all a gesture. It's a symbolic act that registers a discontent that can't be alleviated by institutional means. It makes real change possible.'

'But I don't believe that,' I interrupted. 'Most people simply abhor the callous disregard that you've shown for the lives of your victims, and they reject out of principle any message you might have wished to communicate. They reject it because of the way you've chosen to deliver it. Your message is discredited by the blood you've spilled.'

Julia straightened her back. 'Is that what you really think? I guess it's easy to think that, it's reassuring, and I understand why many people would choose to do so. But you? You know that it's so much more complex than that. People might hate me, and I have to accept that, but it doesn't follow that they necessarily hate my ideas. In fact, I know that a lot of people out there agree with them. And the fact that my ideas have received so much press coverage is in itself an achievement in our apolitical, apathetic times.'

'But you're wrong, Julia,' I objected hotly. 'Haven't you been following the news? Your ideas are not at all what's being debated. Nobody's interested in your manifesto. Nobody's talking about the abuse of workers in the Third World. Nobody's talking about Café Olé's employment practices. You know what most people are talking about? Most people are interested in just one question: whether you're mad or evil. *That*'s what the world's talking about. Your character and your looks. And how and why you became what you are. It's the personal, not the political, that captures everyone's attention.'

Julia's eyes flashed. 'No, Clare. It's *you* who're interested in my character. Don't project your own preoccupations onto others.'

'But I'm not! Can you name any articles or TV programmes that have seriously engaged with your political demands? You can't, can you?'

'No, but for the simple reason that I gave up following the news a long time ago. As I said, I no longer believe in the power of words. Anything printed, like anything made for consumption, achieves nothing. It's part of the problem, not the solution. You of all people should know that. The life span of a news story is shorter than that of a mayfly – do you remember when 276 girls were kidnapped by Islamist fanatics in Nigeria, and how two days later the media stopped reporting on it? And do you know what happened next? Of course you don't.

'The media always home in on the sensationalist psychodrama – that's how they hook their audience. But that doesn't mean that what I said earlier isn't true. What goes on in people's minds is not necessarily directly reflected in the media circus. Altered states of mind are not measurable in such simplistic terms.'

'But that's kettle-logic. How do you know change is taking place if you deny it can be measured or even observed?'

'How do you know it *isn't* happening? Your claim is just as speculative as mine. And at least mine is born out of hope. It would be naive to expect the gradual destruction of false ideology to translate directly into riots and revolutions, or into more sophisticated debates on television. It just doesn't work that way.'

'Then how *does* it work? How on earth can you justify murdering twenty-four people for something you can't even prove is actually taking place?'

Julia raised her voice for the first time. 'Let me put it this way: how can anyone justify *not* doing anything, when thousands of people die each year as a direct result of our exploitation of vulnerable workers in poorer countries? I don't follow your logic. You think twenty-four Western lives are worth more than, say, the lives of the 1,130 Bangladeshi textile workers who died last year when their derelict building collapsed? Or the 114 young women and children who perished in the most recent sweatshop blaze in Vietnam? Do the maths – add all the other threshold states into the mix. How many deaths a year are we talking about? Ten thousand? Twenty? If those deaths were the result of warfare, or ethnic cleansing, the UN would take military action.'

'You're right, the numbers are shocking,' I said. 'But you can't just measure deaths against one another like that. That's ridiculous! It's not a tit-for-tat thing. Every death is a tragedy. Adding to the number of unnecessary deaths, as you've done, is utterly wrong!' I was growing ever more agitated. I felt that a rhetorical sling was tightening around my neck, but I couldn't see how to get out of it.

'Is it? But what if those few deaths contributed to the demise of forms of exploitation that would lead to many thousands of deaths in the future? What really troubles people in the West is that those few deaths in a café in London are visible, while it's so easy to turn your back on the thousands of deaths elsewhere.'

'But they were innocent people, your victims! They were just drinking *coffee*, for Christ's sake. That's hardly a reason to blow them to pieces.'

'There's no such thing as innocence. Everyone in the West is complicit in some way. There *are* no blameless victims. But there are different levels of culpability. Each and every one of us can make a difference. We can bring down multinational corporations simply by boycotting their products. We can withhold and redistribute our money in any way we see fit. It's our money, much more than our vote, that matters. It's that simple, Clare. And no one who buys products whose producers have blood on their hands is innocent. No one.'

'That's so extreme; it's inhumane! You can't seriously think that. Surely the answer is not to just kill everyone who happens to be sipping a big-chain coffee or wearing a sweatshop-produced T-shirt. You'd have to kill almost everyone!'

'Yes, more actions like mine will be needed before true change takes place. But I think there's hope. I think people like you and me can do something that really makes a difference.'

'But the change you're talking about, Julia, it comes at far too high a price. I happened to speak to one of your victims – a wonderful person, a charitable person, a person full of love and kindness. You know what you did to her? You blinded her. You took away her sight. And she isn't at all the kind of thoughtless, throw-away consumer you had in mind when you went on your killing spree. Ironically, she hates shopping, and she'd never even set foot in a Café Olé branch before in her life. It was pure chance that she was there. How do you feel about that?'

'I think I know who you mean. An elderly lady? I remember her. We made eye contact when I was leaving the café. She struck me as out of place. I wish she hadn't been there. I really wish she hadn't. I'm glad to hear she's alive. But I stand by what I did. Sometimes painful sacrifices are necessary for the greater good.'

'And how can you be so sure that you, of all people, know what the greater good is? Isn't it terribly presumptuous, to pass judgement on which lives are worth living and which ones can be sacrificed? You're not God!'

'All I did was choose a venue. I didn't choose the individuals who happened to be there. They made a choice to be there, and all choices have consequences.'

'And why Café Olé, of all places? Because of what you'd witnessed in Guatemala?' Again I noticed her stiffening. She shifted in her seat, but remained stubbornly silent. 'Surely there are much more evil corporations you could have singled out, and more symbolically relevant ones,' I continued. 'Why not banks, why not hedge funds, why not pharmaceutical companies, why not a cheap clothing chain? And surely there are customers of more dubious products you could have targeted. What about diamonds, weapons, pornography, sex? But *coffee*, Julia? *Lattes* and *cappuccinos*?'

'You're right. The number of justified targets is infinite. But I had to start somewhere. It didn't matter where.'

I didn't know how to respond. I felt as though all the blood had drained from my brain. I could no longer think clearly. I could no longer speak.

Eventually, Julia broke our silence. 'You've asked me a lot of questions, Clare. Now let me ask *you* a few. You surprise me. You're an investigative journalist. What are you hoping your writing will achieve?'

I could find no words with which to answer her.

'Let me answer for you,' Julia said. 'You assume a two-step process: that sharing shocking facts with the public leads to moral outrage, and that those responsible for them will be punished. Your underlying assumption is always that moral outrage leads to change: legal action, boycotts, fines, and so on. In other words, you believe that everything you write helps to bring about justice, in one form or another. Isn't that right?'

Again I didn't respond.

'You know I'm right. And deep down, you also know that this assumption is naive, and that its premise doesn't hold. Any attempt to educate by reasoning is futile. The public imagination can only be seized by *unreason* – in our cynical age, only a shocking, seemingly gratuitous act of violence can awaken people to political issues.'

Then Julia embarked on a long monologue on the history and psychology of terrorism. First, she reflected on the practices of nineteenth-century Russian anarchists, and marvelled at how they assassinated only the highest-ranking representatives of forces they perceived as evil – tsars, police chiefs and military men. She went on to praise the cleanliness of classical tyrannicide, and commended the German Red Army Faction for striking blows only at the very heart of the system and nowhere else. Yet unfortunately, she claimed, these methods have become impracticable in our times, as political evil no longer has a clearly distinguishable face, affairs of state being now inextricably enmeshed with highly abstract economic structures, all of which have reached a level of complexity that doesn't allow for the kind of clean, neat blows that still made a difference in the past. If you chop off one of the heads of that many-headed hydra that tyrannizes our age, two more will grow in its place.

I'd been listening to her in a daze. My blood was rushing and my mind was racing. But at that point in her speech, I jolted as if stung, and thought, no, that isn't true – evil *does* have a face. At least in my world it does.

Julia continued, and her precise, clipped words cut through the heavy air like the strikes of a sickle. 'Think about it. What good has your writing ever done? Sure, it won you a few prizes and paid your mortgage, but apart from that?' Then she bent forward again, her face almost touching mine. 'Clare,' she whispered, 'I feel your pain. I understand your dilemma. Trust me, I *know* how you feel. But there's another way.'

For what felt like a long time, neither of us spoke. Then I gently folded her cuffed hands into mine.

'What really happened to you in Guatemala, Julia?' I asked. 'Please. Just tell me.'

She pressed my hands. Then, completely without warning, tears started to stream down her face. I continued to stroke her fingers, whispering soothing words, the kind I would have spoken to my own child in times of trouble. Eventually, Julia began to talk.

'That day, in Guatemala, on the coffee field, when I witnessed the rape... I never told anyone. Nobody, Clare. They didn't just destroy my camera. The woman I had interviewed and I... when we ran towards where the screams were coming from… they pounced on us. Like wild, frenzied animals. There was nothing we could do. We screamed our hearts out, I kicked and struggled and bit, but they held me down, my legs, my arms, my hair. There were so many of them. They took turns. It seemed to last for ever. Then finally they left us lying there in the mud, with our insides ripped to pieces and our bodies covered in bruises. And the shame and the pain. But suddenly we were surrounded by women, farm workers, colleagues of the other two. They carried us to a nearby shelter, they cleaned us up and clad us in fresh clothes. They made us drink tequila, lots of it, to forget and to wash away the dirt on the inside, they said. I sat with them, drinking, and then they started to sing. Strange, soothing songs. Eventually, I felt strong enough to walk back to the village. I tried to report the incident, but nobody was interested. The police just took the piss. They didn't even take down my details.'

'But why didn't you tell Chris, Julia? Why didn't you go to the embassy?'

Julia rubbed her hands over her face. 'I didn't want to be a victim. It wasn't supposed to be about me, none of it. I didn't want to destroy everything I had worked so hard for. It wasn't supposed to be yet another "Westerner getting harmed abroad" story. It was supposed to be the other way round.'

'But how could you just go on, as though nothing had happened? You must have been hurt, traumatized, you can't just shake something like that off…'

'Well, I did. That's exactly what I did.'

But I'm sure you didn't, I thought. That's just not possible. Nobody can do that.

Julia was watching me intently. 'I mean it,' she said. 'It didn't affect me in the way you think it did. I wish I hadn't even told you. I don't know what came over me.'

'But...' I started, but Julia interrupted me.

'Don't do it, Clare. Don't reduce me to a pathetic victim figure. I can see what you're thinking now: post-traumatic stress disorder, borderline personality, disassociation, shame, guilt, translated into hate – you think you've got me pinned down, don't you?'

I didn't respond.

'But you know what – you don't. The rape doesn't explain anything. As I said, I put it behind me. It's too simple, the assumption that one traumatic event can explain it all. Please don't make it all about this.'

'Time's up,' the guard said. We stood up awkwardly. Another guard entered and led Julia out of the room. Before they left, she turned around and looked at me one last time – a long, green, impermeable look that made me shudder, and that still haunts me.

My guard accompanied me through the long corridor to the visitors' check-in area where my belongings were being held. We walked in silence. I tried hard to control my breathing, hoping that I would make it out into the open air without fainting or throwing up. But just after we passed through the final door, before returning to her duties in some other part of the building, the guard looked at me, put her hand on my shoulder, and said:

'Don't you listen to a word that woman says. Don't you do that, now. She's a snake. That's what she is.'

Then she shook her head, clicked her tongue and locked the heavy iron door from the inside.

I just about managed to drag myself outside, and then I was violently sick on the pavement.

X X

It's time now for the final chapter in my own confession, too, George, time to tackle the most difficult part of my story. I fear going there. But I must finish this, and soon – I want to see you. I want so desperately to see you. Apart from sharing some basic facts with my lawyer, I haven't yet told anyone about the hours that followed my meeting with Julia. Not even Amanda. I don't think she'd want to hear this – she's scared of what I might disclose, scared that it will for ever change her perception of me.

I still find it difficult to revisit the scene, to connect with and understand the person I became, for those fatal few hours. But it wasn't insanity, temporary or otherwise. On that point I remain adamant. And I won't let anyone present it as such. Two days ago, I signed a paper confirming that I understand I'm acting against legal counsel and that I'm prepared to live with the consequences. Laura and Amanda (who acts as though her outburst never happened) don't yet know. Bless them; I know they only want what they think is best for me. But I can't do them that favour: what else do I have left now but the afterlife of my act, in all its stark, paradoxical and ugly imperfection? I don't want to see it twisted, or instrumentalized, or misrepresented in any way.

My meeting with Julia on that fateful November day last year had put a seal on a period at the end of which, having invested everything (and I mean *everything*) in my writing, I was forced to acknowledge that all my hopes had come to nothing. I was confronted with the consequences of my choices: I had failed in everything I'd ever cared for.

On leaving Holloway prison I felt sick, numb and utterly exhausted. I'd stopped thinking. I'd ceased agonizing over all of the questions that had been torturing me. In a daze, I took the Tube back home. I poured myself a drink. And another. And another. And possibly another. Then I went into my bedroom, and opened a box in which I keep my most treasured family heirlooms. Jewellery, mainly. But also my grandmother's revolver.

It was ancient. My grandmother had carried it with her, ready for use, in her threadbare coat pocket when, with my mother in tow, she had wandered through the icy German forests towards safety. I've no doubt that she would have used it had the need arisen. It looked like a museum piece – heavy steel with a mother-of-pearl handle, a curiously shaped artefact from a bygone era. I opened the cylinder and found there was a bullet in each one of the six chambers.

I still can't really explain my thinking during those fateful hours, George. All I can say with any accuracy is that it wasn't really thinking, but a confused, emotionally warped gut-reaction. I was under Julia's spell – I both admired and despised her. She had planted an idea in my head, an idea that seemed to be the only way out, the solution to all my problems. I wanted desperately to save my life's work. To restore meaning to my existence. So that not everything would have been in vain.

Although at some point I'd stopped following the reports on the award ceremony that was to take place that very evening at the Institute of Directors, I had memorized the details disclosed in earlier articles on the subject. Doors would open for invited guests at seven; the guests of honour would arrive at seven thirty; proceedings would start at eight sharp.

It was early afternoon when I left my flat. I walked from Gilbert Place to Oxford Street; I traversed Oxford Circus and walked down Upper Regent Street; I crossed Piccadilly Circus, continued down Lower Regent Street and Waterloo Place until I reached the Mall. I stopped a few times to have a drink on the way. I remember contemplating the hordes of shoppers that now congest the arteries of our city in such astounding numbers, drawn like sleepwalkers to some unspecified promise of salvation that they never find, no matter how much they purchase. I remember thinking: Julia, you're right.

On Regent Street I saw what looked from afar like a political demonstration, a large crowd clustering in front of the Apple flagship store, which occupies a beautiful building that, a long time ago, used to be a place of worship. But when I came closer I saw that they were bearded hipsters, clutching cups of flat whites in one hand, and artfully discoloured retro rucksacks in the other, queuing to purchase some newly released gadget. It struck me as such an apt symbol of our times. Fornication with objects, and the raw pink pain of holes that can't ever be filled that way. We're living in the end times, George, the sad times. Why is it that everyone seems to have given up on anything that transcends the satisfaction of hollow consumer fantasies? What's wrong with this twee, backwards-looking new generation of retro-fetishists? I felt a sharp pang of nostalgia for the messy, hot-headed age of isms in which I grew up, and sorrow for the disappearance of our polarized political landscape which had turned into one big, corporate-sponsored blur. Again I thought: Julia, you're right.

I'd arrived far too early at the Institute, earlier even than the security guards who started patrolling the area an hour later. I positioned myself close to the entrance, next to a set of pillars supporting a portico, and to the red carpet that reached out of the grand neoclassical building like a limp scarlet tongue. I remained stoically at my post. I must have looked a little deranged, since people kept their distance from me. A security guard enquired about my business at some point when he and his colleagues started to cordon off the red carpet area. I showed him my old journalist's pass, which appeared to satisfy him.

I stood amidst a slowly growing crowd consisting mainly of photographers, onlookers, and, who knows, perhaps even the odd Adrian Temple fan, for more than three hours. I stood there silently and still. My hand was in my pocket, clutching my grandmother's revolver. I can't remember what went through my mind. I recall only one thing: although it was bitingly cold on that Sunday early in November, I'd stopped shivering.

I watched while a stream of minor celebrities began to file past. I watched the head of the Bank of England and his wife flashing big white transatlantic smiles at onlookers. I watched as various high-profile CEOs, many of them knighted, walked by. Finally, I heard some journalists announce his name. A black limousine had stopped on the opposite side of the street. I saw the chauffeur stepping out and opening the door. And then I saw *him*. He was wearing a blue cashmere coat and a Bordeaux-coloured scarf. His floppy brown hair was brushed casually to one side. I saw his haughty smile that exposed the tight row of small bright teeth that had been haunting me for so long. And then he was already on the carpet, strutting towards the entrance.

I dived under the cord that had been put in place to keep the onlookers at bay. All of a sudden, the buzzing of the voices around me stopped. And then we were standing face to face, Temple and I. We looked each other in the eye. His were the colour of a frozen lake, strangely similar to mine. He recognized me immediately. A cruel smile flickered across his face.

'Clare,' he said. 'How charming. Have you come to congratulate me?'

I still had both of my hands in my pockets. I clutched my weapon. The security guards watching the entrance were about to move towards me, but Adrian Temple lifted his hand.

'It's fine. We're old acquaintances,' he said. 'Clare's a big fan of mine.'

'Not exactly,' I said. My voice sounded like that of a stranger. In the silence that surrounded us, its echo reverberated eerily.

Temple was about to walk past me when I cocked my weapon. Then I lifted the hand holding the revolver from my pocket and put it on his forehead. I could see his eyes widening in surprise. And George: it felt *good*, seeing his fear. It felt *good*, knowing that the arrogant grin would be wiped from this face for eternity. That nothing could ever bring it back. It felt *good*, George, that finally someone was making this man pay, and it felt *good* that the someone was me. And then I fired. He didn't fall over, he didn't even tilt backwards; he sank. Slowly, like a battleship holed beneath the waterline. Quite naturally, he sank to his knees, his eyes wide open. He raised his arms, as though trying to surrender. And then he collapsed on his side, his eyes still wide open. His head came to rest on the carpet, where the blood gushing from the small hole in his head formed a sticky puddle that surrounded him like a dark liquid halo.

Seconds later, I was the one on my knees, having raised my hands and dropped my gun. My job was done. And then the crowd around us awoke from its stupor, and the onlookers started to scream. I was jerked up brutally by one of the guards, who pinned my arms behind my back. A flurry of camera flashes further contributed to my sense of unreality, the feeling that I was trapped in some kind of cliché-ridden film.

But then I saw them. They must, unnoticed by me, have climbed out of the limousine after him, probably to avoid the cameras. And one of them sank to the ground, too. Adrian Temple's wife, clad in white fur and candy-coloured satin, broke into a shrill, piercing wail, and shook her husband, over and over again, as though he had merely fainted and could be roused back into consciousness. His daughter, in contrast, remained eerily silent. She was perhaps five years old. Her sand-coloured hair was braided into two long plaits decorated with pink ribbons, and from her right hand dangled a white teddy bear. She'd been running towards where her father lay, and then she suddenly stopped, just two feet away from me and the guard who was clutching my arms. She remained perfectly, unnaturally still. She just stood there, frozen, her grey eyes wandering from her father to her mother and back again. And then she turned to look at me. She looked and looked. Separated from all the frantic clamour around us, she and I occupied a different space, in which an eerie underwater stillness reigned. It's *her* gaze, George, those large, grey eyes in that tiny white face, and the plaits that stopped bouncing, that I see before me every night. It was when our eyes met that I knew I wasn't like Julia.

Then I heard the sirens, and then I was pushed into a police car and was removed from the scene.

POSTSCRIPT

After completing the manuscript, I sent it straight to George. For two days, I waited anxiously for his response. Finally, he called.

'Ach, Clare…' was all he said, and then his voice broke and we both started to cry. We wailed like children, listening to each other wringing our hands and sobbing our hearts out. We didn't manage to speak during that call, but there were others, many others, afterwards. The wait for his first visit was torturous. But when the day finally came, and when I saw the familiar outline of his tall impatient figure behind the frosted window pane of the door to the visitors' room at 4.30 sharp, I understood how desperately I'd been yearning for the company of this man. I realized how much I'd needed to pass my hand through his bristly hair, how badly I'd wanted to rub my face against his stubbly cheeks, and how I'd craved for him to embrace me and finally to be able to find peace on his heaving chest. The guards had to pull us apart. When they reprimanded us, sternly reminding us of the no-touching rule, we giggled like teenagers who'd been caught making out in the bedroom.

During my trial – my second one – George stood by me once again. This time, however, Lailah didn't come along. The two of them are getting divorced.

But it will be a while before we will know if we can be properly together. Nine years, seven months and four days, to be precise. Unless I'm released early. Which is unlikely.

George's, Amanda's and Laura's visits are what keep me going. Laura impresses me so. The future, if it's shaped by the likes of her, scares me less now. To Laura, too, I showed my manuscript, but I haven't yet mustered the courage to give it to Amanda. No doubt she'll read my confession when it's published. I hope she can forgive me.

Just a few days ago, Laura and I talked about it. I argued that there is never just one truth, there are always truths. All we have are stories, I said, nothing but conflicting narratives. Each has its truth, and each has its blind spots. But Laura wasn't in the least impressed by my analysis. 'Isn't that just a poor excuse for those who are too timid to state it?' she asked. She dismissed my view as cowardly relativism, and added: 'You know what? I find it all so obvious – Julia's just a very, very fucked-up person with no capacity to empathize. A psychopathic manipulator.'

After a pause, she added: 'She played you, too, Clare, you know that, don't you? She read your soul like an open book – you know that her kind has the capacity to discover your deepest fears and greatest desires? She smelled your wounds like a shark, and she knew exactly what to say to make you do what you did. I bet she doesn't even believe in her own sick theories. Not for a second. I'm not even sure her rape story is true. I mean, how can you tell? You know what? I really think she said all those things just to push you over the edge. Just because she could.'

But Laura's wrong. It's not that simple. She's still so young.

My serpentine seducer, with a mind of winter. Still I puzzle over the meaning of it all.

Sutton Valence, Maidstone, May 2015

ACKNOWLEDGEMENTS

I am indebted to Agnès Cardinal, Andreas Essl and Hubert van den Berg for reading early drafts of the novel and for their astute feedback, and to Sarah Savitt and Sam Copeland, my tutors at the Faber Academy, for their excellent advice, which helped me to shape and develop the novel, as well as the other students on Faber's 'Edit Your Novel' course, whose passion and determination was inspiring.

Thanks are also due to Francesco Capello, Jeremy Carrette, Laurence Goldstein, Katja Haustein, Deborah Holmes, Ben Hutchinson, Heide Kunzelmann, Gordon Lynch, Patricia Novillo-Corvalán, Lucy O'Meara, Natalia Sobrevilla Perrea, Axel Stähler, Núria Triana Toribio and Mikkel Zangenberg for being amazing colleagues, and to Katharina Paschkowski, my parents, Ernst and Eva Schaffner, and Verena Trusch for moral support.

I would also like to express my gratitude to my fantastic agent, Caroline Wood, for her brilliant judgement, her support and her belief in the project, and to Amy Waite at the Felicity Bryan Literary Agency, as well as to my editors Sam Redman and Clare Drysdale at Allen & Unwin, whose perceptive comments, suggestions and enthusiasm were extremely precious.

Finally, this book would never have been written were it not for Shane Weller, love of my life, who believed in me from the start, and whose encouragement, fine judgement, sharp ideas, unremitting proof-reading skills and love made all of this possible in the first place.

ABOUT THE AUTHOR

Anna Schaffner is a Reader in Comparative Literature at the University of Kent. She has recently completed a Faber Academy writing course and *The Truth About Julia* is her first novel.